The Ration Book Baby

ELLIE CURZON

The Ration Book Baby

Bookouture

Published by Bookouture in 2023

An imprint of Storyfire Ltd.
Carmelite House
50 Victoria Embankment
London EC4Y 0DZ

www.bookouture.com

ISBN: 978-1-83790-529-4
eBook ISBN: 978-1-83790-526-3

Sir Archibald McIndoe's pioneering treatment of badly burned aircrew at the Queen Victoria Hospital in East Grinstead made medical history. The patients who benefited from his expertise formed the Guinea Pig Club, and supported one another for the rest of their lives. This book is dedicated to McIndoe's team and the men whose lives they saved.

PROLOGUE
AUGUST 1940

Annie was sitting at the kitchen table with her mother. It was late and they should've been in bed, but they both knew they wouldn't get much sleep, not with Annie's father out on his blackout patrol through the narrow streets of Bramble Heath. The airbase on the edge of the village had seemingly become a prime target in the last few weeks, and nightly battles raged in the sky overhead as enemy planes tried to get close enough to destroy the hangars and runways of that once humble little airfield. One stray beam of light from a window, and the bombers would find their target and help the Nazi invasion on its way.

The silence was cut as an aircraft throbbed overhead. Annie held her breath, tense.

'One of ours?' she whispered, as if the pilot might overhear. Norma, her mother, drew in a deep breath and listened intently, as though that alone would be enough to identify the aircraft. Living so close to the base, though, perhaps it was.

'One of the boys from the airfield coming home,' she decided. 'That must be everybody, God bless them.'

Annie breathed out, relieved. 'Thank goodness.' Safe for tonight, at least.

The room became silent again, and Annie looked at her watch. Another half an hour and her father would've finished his rounds, then she and her mother would listen out for his step. She turned the flimsy page of the newspaper in front of her, but she didn't take in the reports. Her concentration was a thing of the past these days.

And then she heard a knock at the door.

She leapt up from her chair. 'I'll get it. It's probably for me.' It usually was.

'No rest for the district nurse,' Norma said with a smile, reaching out to extinguish the lamp before Annie could reach the front door to answer the knock.

It must be urgent if they've turned up in the blackout, Annie reasoned, steeling herself for what she might be about to encounter.

She opened the front door, but there was no one there.

If it's Jamie and one of his pranks, I'll...

But just then, she heard a whimper. She looked down and noticed that on the doorstep, in the thin light cast by the pale moon, there was a hatbox.

A hatbox?

She knelt down, and heard the whimper again. Her heart hammered in her chest.

Could it be?

She levered off the lid, her hands trembling, and there inside the box, swaddled warmly, was a baby. A tiny newborn baby, which puckered up its lips before wailing.

Annie picked up the crying infant, holding it as she glanced around in the darkness. There was no one in the small front garden and, with the baby in her arms, she hurried to the end of the path and through the gate. She stared up and down the lane.

'Stop! Come back, please!' she called. 'I can help you!' She strained her ears over the sound of the crying, hoping to hear a footstep, anything that would tell her that whoever had abandoned the child was still there.

But there was nothing, save for the baby's cries.

ONE

Had the baby been born in secret?

Annie couldn't get her head around this. She had experienced a lot of strange things in her time, but this was a new one. What a strange thing to happen in Bramble Heath, of all places.

'Let's get you inside, and then we can find out who you are.' She turned and headed back to the house. She wondered what on earth her mother would think. At the door she called out, 'Mum? We have a visitor. A rather noisy one!'

'Is that a baby I can hear?' Norma said. She appeared in the gloom of the hallway as the sound of another aircraft could be heard overhead. 'Get yourself back inside, Annie, come on.'

Annie pushed the hatbox over the threshold with her toe as she jiggled the baby. She closed the door behind her, her thoughts whirling, hurried and disconnected. 'Poor little thing. I had to go out to check in case they were still there. Whoever it was who brought it here. Its mother, or... I need to check the baby over. That's what I'll do. Such a tiny little thing. Must be newborn, or as good as. And just there, on the step – in a hatbox.'

Norma swept the heavy curtain back across the front door

and stooped to gather up the box as Annie carried the baby to the kitchen. 'Whoever it was, they must've been desperate,' she said.

The baby's cries had grown quieter and the squirming infant seemed more settled in Annie's arms now it was out of the cool air of late summer and safe in the warm kitchen. Norma set the hatbox down on the table and turned the lamp on again. Its soft glow illuminated the familiar room, casting a gentle light as she drew closer and peered into the swaddled blanket at the child.

'That's a *very* young one,' she whispered.

'Very.' Annie glanced at the baby, concerned for both mother and child. 'I don't think it's a coincidence that this little one's been left here. Must be someone local who knows I'm the nurse. But I didn't have any mums about to reach their time...'

She looked up at her mother and wondered if she was thinking the same thing. She must be. In the decades that Norma had served as the district midwife, she had seen her fair share of secret babies. She met Annie's gaze and murmured, 'The poor girl. I wish she'd waited, but... Let's look this little one over, then we'll think about what comes next.'

Annie passed the baby to her mother before fetching her medical bag from the corner, her hands trembling. The baby was quieter now, resting its head against Norma's shoulder. Perhaps it realised it was in experienced hands.

Annie spread a towel on the kitchen table, smoothing it out. 'Now let's have a look at you,' she told the baby. Norma laid the infant down on the towel with a gentle, soothing coo. She carefully unwrapped the knitted blanket, and a jolt of sympathy went through Annie as she watched. Someone had sat with needles and wool and made this simple blanket from nothing. Likely the desperate mother who had believed she had no choice but to abandon her child. Her heart ached for the unknown woman, out there in the darkness, hoping that her newborn was safe.

Under the blanket, the baby was wearing a simple cotton nightdress with a small scrap of lace around the neck. It looked hand-made, but the lace told Annie that whoever had sewn it cared enough for the child to make it something pretty to wear. Annie and Norma wriggled the baby out of the nightdress and the nappy underneath.

'A little girl,' Annie sighed. Someone had done their best – the girl's mother, perhaps – as the cord had been tied with a thick piece of cotton, and Annie tidied it up. 'I wonder what condition her mother is in,' she said. 'Someone in the village must know. I'm worried, Mum.'

'You're a bonny little thing,' Norma cooed to the baby. 'And whoever your poor mummy is, she's made sure you're all looked after.' She glanced at Annie. 'She's not more than a couple of hours old, but she looks a good size and weight. Maybe your dad'll have heard something when he gets in.'

'He won't be long now,' Annie said hopefully, as she dressed the baby again. 'I'm sure it won't be long until we find her mum, if she wants to be found, but we better find some bits and bobs for the baby.'

She glanced at the hatbox with its silver and purple stripes. The shop's name was emblazoned across the lid in looping letters. *Miss Clara's Millinery, East Grinstead.*

'Miss Clara?' She touched her fingertip to the baby's face. 'Is that what we should call you until we find your mummy?'

As if in reply, the baby grabbed Annie's finger in a surprisingly strong grip.

'Miss Clara!' Norma announced, clasping her own hands together for a moment before she reached into the hatbox and drew out a small white shape. 'A pretty name for a pretty little girl. And look, your mummy sent a toy for you too!'

'A bird,' Annie said, her breath catching. *If only I'd been quicker. If only I'd run to the door and seen the hatbox right away and not thought it was one of Jamie's pranks. I might've been in time to see Clara's mum. I could've helped her.* 'A little hand-made bird. Isn't that lovely, Clara?'

'A stork for Miss Clara, like the stork who brought you here!' Norma cooed as she passed the humble toy to Annie. 'Something for you to love.'

Clara dragged Annie's finger to her mouth and sucked. She was clearly hungry.

'We've got a little milk left, haven't we?' Annie asked, relieved that they could at least feed the child.

Norma nodded. 'We have.' She gave Annie a tender smile and crossed the kitchen.

With her free hand, Annie waggled the stork at Clara. She was aware that newborns couldn't see a great deal, but she was sure that Clara was watching the stork move. Her heart filled with pity. She saw plenty of babies in her work, day after day, but she'd never had one abandoned on her doorstep before, with the knowledge that there was nobody else to care for her. Someone was desperate enough to abandon their daughter, and trusted Annie to look after her. Annie was nervous of the responsibility placed on her, but she wouldn't let Clara's mother down.

'We'll look after you, don't you worry, and soon you'll see your mum again,' she promised.

She could hear her mum rattling pots and pans, no doubt looking for something she could use to hold Clara's milk, but the little girl didn't seem too worried by the noise. Instead, she continued to watch the little rag stork. It was a simple toy, but there was something almost heartbreaking in its pretty hand-sewn innocence, and the bright eyes that the needle had created. Even its beak, made out of a remnant of orange cotton that had been stuffed and sewn to the soft white body of the bird, seemed to be smiling. Annie noticed something on the wing: a small but beautiful poppy, vivid red with a ring of tiny white petals around its black centre.

She was so engaged with Clara that she didn't notice the footsteps in the hall until her father, Henry, was almost in the kitchen.

'Annie? Norma? I've brought Wing Command...' He paused, evidently taking in the unexpected scene before him. 'Well, I was about to say I'd brought a visitor, but it looks like we've already got one. Whose baby is this?' There was something affectionate, even amused in his tone, though.

Annie turned and saw a tall, square-jawed man in RAF uniform following her father into the kitchen. It was Wing Commander William Chambers, who she knew from her visits to Heath Place, where the RAF officers were billeted. His face was spattered with blood.

'It's really just a scratch,' he assured her apologetically, in response to her startled look. 'And it would seem your hands are already rather full.'

'No, no, not at all. I'd never send one of you boys away without at least a plaster,' Annie said, adding, as if it explained the sudden appearance of a baby, 'This is Clara.'

'She's very sorry she's not decent.' Norma was parcelling Clara back up in the outsized nappy she'd arrived in. She glanced towards the men with a smile as William tucked his cap beneath one arm. 'But she didn't know we were going to have guests.'

'I bumped into the wing commander on my way back,' Henry explained as he took off his police helmet. 'He said he didn't want anyone to make a fuss, but I insisted he came home with me so's you could give him the once-over, Annie.'

'Of course,' Annie said. It seemed a ridiculous question to ask, but she said, 'Were you flying tonight, Wing Commander?'

'This night and every night for the moment, it seems,' he replied, as casual as if he was discussing a Saturday-afternoon trip to the seaside. 'You do look to be rather busy, Miss Russell, without a few paltry pilot's scratches to patch up. You should see the other fellow, though!'

'More like *fellows*!' Henry chuckled. 'Do you know, he took down *two* planes this evening?'

'Goodness me!' Annie exclaimed. 'And really, it's no trouble at all. We don't want to see those cuts getting sore, do we? And my mother is an old hand when it comes to babies. We can manage.'

'The second was a real blighter,' William said eagerly. 'He came screaming downhill, all guns blazing. Put a hole in the canopy... you know how the splinters find every which way to get in!'

And it's so matter-of-fact these days, Annie reflected. Young men with minor burns, broken bones and acrylic splinters from the shattered canopies were just another part of her regular rounds nowadays.

Norma swaddled Clara in her blanket and scooped the little girl up into her arms, just as she had with countless babies over the years. But there was something in her eyes, looking down at this one. She cuddled her close and turned to Annie.

'Dad and I can take her through and give her some supper. I've found one of the old bottles from my round and mixed up a spot of milk and warm water. That'll do until morning.' She gave Henry a prompting nod. 'Come on, Constable, let's leave Nurse Russell to her work.'

'A brandy, Wing Commander?' Henry asked William, miming taking a drink.

'I never say no to an offer like that,' William beamed. 'Thank you, Constable Russell!'

'Any time. It's an honour to have an ace in this very house!' And with that, Henry followed Norma out of the room.

'Take a seat, Wing Commander.' Annie nodded to the wooden chair by the unlit stove, then reached into her bag.

From an abandoned baby to an injured pilot, all in one evening. She knew very well how hard the pilots were working, and what gruelling, exhausting work it was at that. She couldn't imagine what it was like to wake up every morning knowing you were lucky to be alive.

And William was perhaps luckier than most.

Here he was, more or less still in one piece despite his exploits. A month ago, he'd been the first of the Bramble Heath boys to take out five enemy planes in one sortie, achieving a strange sort of fame for his exploits in a world where topping league tables of downed enemy aircraft offered a celebrity all of its own. Wing Commander Chambers topped the league at Bramble Heath, whether among the British pilots or their Polish comrades, and he was never short of admiring glances or drinks on the house when he ventured into the village.

For now, though, he was just one of Annie's patients, regardless of his celebrity status, and as he settled into the seat he looked as exhausted as any of the men under his command. For a moment he closed his eyes and drew in a steady deep breath. Then he let out the breath and blinked, his expression betraying just how tired he truly was. Only for a moment, though.

'They're throwing everything at us,' he said, 'but we'll knock every ball Jerry bowls for six.'

'I'm sure you will.' Annie heard the effort it took him to make his words sound anything like light. She leaned over him, examining the cut on his neck. It didn't look like any splinters of acrylic were in there, but she took care as she dabbed it with a piece of damp cotton wool. As she did, her thoughts went back to Clara's mother. Had she given birth alone? Did she need Annie to examine her too? Annie would've done – and not judged her for leaving her baby on the doorstep – but she had no idea where the poor girl was. Right now, she could only help this brave man who was sitting in her kitchen. 'Tell me if it's sore – don't try to be brave.'

William cast her an amused glance and teased, 'I've had worse cuts shaving!'

'I take it you're not normally flying a plane at the same time, though!' Annie replied with a chuckle. Now that the wound was clean, she turned to the iodine. As she unscrewed the bottle, its sharp smell spilled out.

The kitchen door opened and Henry came in carrying a brandy balloon. It was one of his most precious objects, a retirement present. He'd joked that he'd have to give it back when he rejoined the force once war broke out. Barely a fingerful of brandy glowed in the bottom of it. Annie suspected that her father didn't have much left.

'Here we go, ace!' he beamed, and held out the glass. William took it and raised it in a toast.

'To the family Russell. Keeping the village safe and the Spitfire boys patched up. What would we do without you?'

Henry grinned. 'But what would we do without *you*? Boys like you are keeping the whole country safe.' He was so proud of the fact that the village where he'd been born and bred had become home to an airbase and the brave pilots who flew from it.

'You should've seen the Polish lads tonight,' William said, keen as a puppy. 'A few of them made ace up there, I'd say. It was a heck of a thing; sent the Luftwaffe limping home with its tail between its legs to give Adolf the bad news!'

Henry leaned against the mantelpiece, chuckling. 'That's what we like to hear! Those poor lads have every reason to give the Luftwaffe a spanking. A nice bit of revenge for what they've done to Poland.'

'He's underestimated them,' William agreed. 'As far as Jerry's concerned, the drawbridge is well and truly up!'

While William was distracted, Annie held up the bottle of

iodine. Wincing, Henry took his cue and went back to the sitting room.

Annie dabbed on the iodine. Much like tearing off a plaster, the element of surprise helped. 'There you are, Wing Commander!'

William started in the chair. 'Didn't feel a thing,' he told her with a chuckle, then dropped his voice to a theatrical whisper to add, 'I lied.'

'Even the bravest fighter aces aren't immune to the sting of iodine,' Annie said. 'I'll give you a plaster, and I'll come by and check on you in a day or two when I'm on my rounds. It's not enough of an injury to prevent you from flying, but you might consider taking a little break, perhaps, if they can spare you tomorrow. Just to give it time to heal.'

She knew it was unlikely he'd agree, but she had to suggest it anyway.

'I shall take it under advisement, Miss Russell,' William promised. 'But if we're scrambled, I might just happen to forget your wise words.'

'I shall pretend to be surprised... although I'm not,' Annie said as she dressed the wound with a small bandage. 'Is that all right? Not too tight? You can still move your head? I wouldn't want you to go up in a plane and feel like you're in some sort of straitjacket.'

Even if he did, he'd still fly anyway. She'd had quite a time convincing one of the pilots up at Heath Place that he really shouldn't fly with his arm in a plaster cast.

'Good as new.' He took a sip of brandy, savouring the taste for a moment. 'I don't mean to pry, Miss Russell, but the baby's mother... is she quite all right? Only, with the child being here, I wondered... well, I just wondered.'

Annie sighed as she dropped into the chair opposite. She was glad he'd asked, even though she couldn't answer. 'I have no idea who the mother is. There was a knock at the door, and when I opened it there was no one there. At least, I didn't think so at first, until I realised that the hatbox at my feet contained a baby.' A thought occurred to her. 'Hang on – on your way up to the house, did you see anybody in the lane?'

He shook his head apologetically. 'Not a bean,' he admitted. 'I've only been back on solid ground for about half an hour, just enough time to count the boys home. We've taken a few knocks tonight, so the docs over at Brambles had more on their plates than a bit of a flesh wound. One of the lads suggested you might be the girl to see if I needed a stitch or two, and I met your pa on the way over. I didn't see another soul, I'm afraid.'

Annie suppressed her shiver of fear at the thought of the casualties at the airbase. 'I wonder... there's a lot more girls in the village these days, and it's entirely possible that Clara's mother is a Land Girl on one of the farms. Whoever she is, I really ought to check her over, just like I do with all the new mums in the village. I'll be honest with you, Wing Commander, it worries me.'

As if there weren't already plenty of other things to worry about.

'It's a sorry business, especially when she's likely in need of help,' William murmured. He took another sip of his brandy, thoughtful for a second or two. 'And with an airbase on the edge of the village, one can't help but wonder... I'll keep an ear to the ground.'

'Thank you, Wing Commander, if you wouldn't mind finding out if any of your boys have been carousing with the local ladies, it'd be a help.' That would've been most of them, though, wouldn't it?

'It's a dashed pretty name, though how did you know she was called Clara?' he asked.

'I have no idea what her name is, not really,' Annie confessed. 'But she arrived in a Miss Clara of East Grinstead hatbox, and I couldn't keep referring to her as *the baby*.'

'Miss Clara,' William repeated, the name just a little plummy when he spoke. Suddenly she sounded like a debutante from a genteel suburb of the Home Counties. 'I'll make enquiries, Miss Russell. You'll be the first to know if I hear anything.'

'Thank you so much.' Annie wondered if it maybe helped him to have something to think about other than the daily horrors that awaited him in the skies. 'But do try to get some rest. That's your first priority.'

'Yes, ma'am!' He shot her a mischievous salute, then held out the brandy glass to her. 'You look like you need a snifter of this yourself.'

Annie took the glass and had a tiny sip. The brandy burned its way down her throat and she did feel a little steadier. She passed it back to William. 'It's such a funny feeling, to know that someone trusts me and my family enough to leave their baby here.'

He smiled gently. 'What will happen if you aren't able to find her parents?'

'The authorities will come and she'll be fostered, perhaps, or put in a children's home,' Annie explained. 'Maybe she'll be adopted. I have no idea if that's what her mother wants, if she even realises that's what will happen.'

William answered with a nod, the gesture striking Annie as curiously tight, though that was no doubt due to the dressing on his neck. He drained what was left in the glass and reached over to place it on the table.

'It's a sorry start to a life.' He rose to his feet and replaced his cap on his head with just a hint of a tilt. There was always something rakish about the Spitfire pilots, Annie had long since decided. It seemed to go with the job. 'But I think her mother made a good choice when she knocked at your door. I'll leave you to your young house guest, Miss Russell. Thank you for being as gentle as iodine allows.'

'That's what I'm here for,' Annie replied. 'I'll show you out. Take care, won't you?'

As if that'll make any difference to what happens in the air.

'I'll certainly try,' he promised with a polite bow of his head. 'And make sure you get some rest too. We're all a little run ragged tonight.'

'I'll try my best, although I don't hold out much hope with a baby in the house!' Annie smiled.

She led the way to the door. As they passed the front room, she looked in to see her parents sitting with Clara, Henry looking on as Norma fed her in the soft light of the lamp.

She closed the door behind the wing commander with a gentle click before drawing the heavy curtain, mindful of the blackout. Keeping all their lights hidden meant the little village of Bramble Heath was disguised from the forces of the Luftwaffe as they made their assaults on England, one after the other, each more terrifying than the last. It had been a matter of a few short months ago when Winston Churchill had warned the nation that the Battle of Britain was about to begin, and now everyone knew it was raging. In the skies above, the planes clashed night after night, hour after hour, and in church on Sunday the roll call of those lost in the fight grew longer. But still the young men from Bramble Heath took to the air, never knowing if they would feel solid ground beneath their feet again.

And maybe one of those young men was now a father. It was up to Annie and Wing Commander Chambers to find out.

TWO

A ration book? There'll be a name on it, an address!

How had they missed it? The hatbox had sat on a chair in the kitchen all night while Annie had lain awake until the small hours wondering who on earth had left Clara on the doorstep. A customer of Miss Clara's of East Grinstead? But that could be anyone – the town was only a bus ride away, after all. She had turned the unhappy mystery over and over in her head as she ate breakfast, and it wasn't until she had snapped shut the clasps on her medical bag that she had decided to take one last look at the box before beginning her rounds. And that was when she had seen it, poking out from under the piece of flannel cloth that had been placed at the bottom.

The corner of a piece of beige card.

Her heart leapt. She hastily whipped away the cloth and grabbed the ration book, then ran into the front room, where her mother and father were enjoying playing at being grandparents. Norma was sitting in the rocking chair, Clara in her arms. The mellow wood of the chair was worn smooth from several generations of Russell mothers nursing their infants. The radio was on, a cheerful, bright, morale-boosting tune playing as Henry knelt on the hearthrug in front of Norma, waving the stork at Clara.

'Mum! Dad!' Annie exclaimed, breathless with excitement. 'Look, it's a ration book!'

'Excellent! Is the mystery solved?' enquired Henry. He turned to Clara to say kindly, 'We'll soon have you back with your mum.'

Norma snuggled Clara close and sat up a little taller, the better to see what her daughter was holding. 'See, she *did* want us to know where to find her,' she said with characteristic optimism.

'Exactly! It was right there at the bottom of the hatbox, waiting for us to find it.' Annie beamed, all the worries that had kept her awake last night melting away. The mystery baby was a mystery no longer. 'It says...'

She stared at the ration book, and her excitement vanished in a moment. Utterly deflated, she realised that someone had made sure it was untraceable. The name, the address, the registration and serial numbers, all had been determinedly scribbled out. The one clue that could've helped was a dead end.

She sighed, full of disappointment. 'I... I can't read it. It's been crossed out. Look.' She held it out to Norma, and Henry craned his neck to see it too.

'Oh, love.' He got to his feet. 'You know I have to telephone this in, Annie. It's procedure when a foundling arrives on a copper's patch. Usually the social workers will find a foster carer or pop 'em into a children's home, but I'm sure I can convince them otherwise, don't you worry.'

Annie knew her father could keep the authorities at bay for a little while at least. 'I'm sure it won't be long before we find Clara's mum. This is Bramble Heath – everyone knows everyone else.'

'It's an adult's ration book,' he observed. 'You think she'd have the…' He rocked back on his heels. 'If Clara was a secret, her mum'd never have had a green one, would she?'

Annie nodded. Her father was right. They'd only had ration books for a few months, and they were still getting used to them. Buff-coloured for adults, green for pregnant women, babies and small children, and blue for older children.

'Oh heck, she doesn't have a ration book at all now,' she said.

Norma shook her head. 'Poor lamb,' she murmured. She looked at Henry, then turned her gaze back to Annie. 'Dad and I have had a talk, and, if you've no objections, we think it'd be for the best if Miss Clara stayed with us just until her mum's ready to take her back. There can't be many houses as have a midwife, a nurse and a constable happy to look after a little one, especially these days.'

Annie nodded keenly. 'I agree, she's in the best place here. And after all, her mum thought so, didn't she? She trusted us with Clara. And when she's ready, she'll come back for her.' She stroked Clara's pudgy cheek and smiled affectionately as the baby grabbed her finger. 'I'm off to work now, poppet. I'll ask around and I'm sure I'll find your mum. You be a good girl.'

'She's no trouble at all.' Norma smiled. 'Sometimes new mums don't know where to turn. They don't mean any harm, but they panic. I saw it often enough before I retired, and that's what's happened here. She just needs to know she's got people who want to help her.'

Annie sighed. There had to be some way to find Clara's mum. The ration book might not give them a name or address, but surely it could still provide clues. And there were other leads. The hatbox, perhaps? Could Annie ask the milliner if she had any pregnant customers? Even Clara's clothes could offer a hint, if they could be traced back to a shop. And the village was full of people she could ask. She wasn't giving up hope any time soon.

THREE

Annie headed out to the shed where she kept her motorbike, put her bag in the pannier and set off.

She couldn't help but wonder if she might meet Clara's mother on her rounds. It wasn't impossible that a mum who'd given birth in secret might try to disguise any issues as general 'women's problems'. And there were lots of girls in the village who could've had a baby. Apart from the Land Girls, there was Sally, and the other girls who flew in and out of the airbase with the Air Transport Auxiliary. The more Annie thought about it, the more candidates she could think of. All of them were single women who would need to keep a baby secret.

As she mulled everything over, she tried to enjoy the bright, sunny weather, though she couldn't help reminding herself that the cloudless skies only provided the enemy with good conditions for their daytime raids.

Oh, bother. Why should we let the enemy spoil a beautiful summer's day?

Her first call was at Mr Gosling's farm, where several Land Girls were staying. A couple of days before, one of the girls had slipped on a steep, muddy slope and turned her ankle badly.

Annie got off the motorbike in the lane and pushed it the last little way to the farmhouse, not wanting to spook the animals. Mrs Gosling was on the step, casting food to the chickens pecking their way around the yard as two of the Land Girls hunted around for eggs.

'Found one!' one of the girls declared as she produced an egg from an overturned crate. 'I dunno how the chicken managed to get in there, but she did somehow!'

'Morning,' Annie said. She kicked down the stand on her bike and retrieved her medical bag. 'How's the patient this morning?'

'Limping!' came Nicola's answering shout from the open kitchen window. 'But still making myself useful!'

Mrs Gosling stepped aside. 'They're such good girls, you know.'

As Annie went into the large, cosy farmhouse kitchen, the cogs in her mind immediately turned. Was Mrs Gosling aware of a Land Girl baby? If so, she clearly wasn't going to judge and call Clara's mother a *bad girl*.

But she pushed her suspicions aside at once when she saw Nicola sitting at the kitchen table, her foot resting on a chair as she kneaded dough.

'Nicola, I *did* recommend lots of rest,' she chided with amusement. 'Are you sure you're happy to keep working?'

'You're joking?' Nicola asked in her cheery Geordie brogue. 'I'm not made to sit down. I'm missing being out there in the fresh air, digging up them tatties! The sooner this ankle's looking less like an egg, the better.'

'Once you're out there again, just be more careful,' Annie said with a wink. 'How's the swelling? Do you mind if I take a look?'

'Help yourself.' Nicola smiled, nodding towards her bare foot. 'How's life treating you and yours?'

'Not too bad,' Annie said, crouching down to look at the

swollen ankle. Nicola's foot was bruised all over, green in parts, dark purple in others, with an angry-looking red heading for her toes. 'That's one heck of a bruise you've got there, Nicola. But it's a good sign that you're healing. It just takes time. Keep it raised and keep off it, and you'll be back to digging tatties in no time. Actually... you know, a funny thing happened yesterday evening...'

At least she could cross Nicola off the list of potential mums – she couldn't very well have limped to Annie's house with a baby, and, in any case, Annie hadn't spotted any signs of pregnancy when she'd come to the farm a couple of days earlier. Besides, she got on with Nicola, and hoped the girl would've told her if she'd got herself into trouble and needed help.

But what about the others?

'Oh aye?' Nicola asked, merrily kneading the dough with her knuckles, the table rocking with her efforts. 'If it involved a pilot and a blackout, I don't know if I want to hear!'

Annie laughed, but then thought to herself: I wouldn't be at all surprised if it did.

'A surprise parcel arrived on my doorstep last night. A hatbox. And can you guess what was in it?' She couldn't detect any signs that Nicola was hiding anything. Thinking of Clara being cared for by Norma and Henry while her mother could be in a desperate state somewhere, she just came out with it. 'A baby.'

'A baby?' Nicola asked with disbelief, and, unless she was an actress of some considerable talent, Annie was sure that her shock was genuine. 'You're pulling my leg? My good one, mind!'

'Yes! A newborn baby, a little girl,' Annie told her. She'd finished examining Nicola's ankle and took a seat at the table. 'I need to find her mum, in case she needs my help. I don't suppose... If you'd heard anything, you'd let me know?'

Nicola nodded and stilled her hands atop the dough. 'Aye, I would,' she said. 'We all look out for each other, and I've heard nothing. It's not the sort of thing you could hide working on the land like we do either.'

Annie bit her lip. Nicola was quite right. How could a pregnant woman be out driving tractors and lugging bales of hay around, and all the other things the Land Girls did, without anyone noticing? Besides, they all lived on top of each other. Nicola stayed at the farm, but other girls who worked for the Goslings boarded at a hostel. It'd be impossible to hide a pregnancy.

'I'll have a word with the others,' Annie said. 'It's rather delicate. I don't want to scare the mum off. If you *do* get a sense that there's a girl with a secret, will you make sure she understands that I only want to help? I don't judge. I don't want her to be frightened to come forward.'

'You can count on us, pet.' Nicola patted Annie's hand, leaving a dusting of flour on her skin. 'We won't make a song and dance about it.'

'Thank you,' Annie said. 'I'll come back again this time tomorrow, if it's convenient. And I don't suppose you'd have a tiny splash of milk going spare? For Clara – that's the baby.'

Nicola smiled. 'Help yourself from the larder. We might live in the middle of nowhere with more cows than people, but at least that means plenty of milk to go round.' She waggled her bare toes. 'I'd do the honours, but this nurse I know says I'm not allowed to leave my chair!'

Annie chuckled. 'That's quite right. I don't want you hopping around. I'll come back later to collect the milk. It'll end up churned to butter if I take it out on my bike!'

The sleek black farm cat coiled around her legs for a moment, until finally releasing her. Annie said goodbye to Nicola, then she was off again.

FOUR

The next stop on Annie's rounds was the hamlet on the edge of Bramble Heath that had become home to a group of Polish refugees. The old farm labourers' cottages, which had sat empty for some time, had been tidied up and turned into warm, welcoming homes. Some of the Polish pilots who flew out of Bramble Heath airbase lived there with their families, who had managed to escape Hitler's bloody onslaught on their country. Annie was proud that her village had given them a home.

Although not everyone was.

As she rounded the bend, she spotted a group of boys in the middle of the road.

That blasted little Jamie and his gang.

'All right, Nurse?' Jamie called, spinning on his heel with a swagger that no fifteen-year-old boy should have but plenty probably did. 'They won't let you in here... they only trust their own witch doctors! There's an old bird with a pointy black hat says she can cure anything!' He turned to spit onto the ground. 'Or I think that's what she said. Hard to tell when they all talk piccalilli or whatever the lingo is!'

Annie swerved her bike to a stop. She gripped the handlebars. 'They speak Polish, Jamie. As you well know. Haven't you got anything better to do than lurk around here with your chums?'

The other boys scuffed their feet on the dusty lane. One of them kicked a stone, which ricocheted against the garden wall of one of the cottages. A moment later the cottage door opened and Ewa appeared in the doorway, her arms folded tight across her chest.

'I told you already!' she snapped, her tone fierce and her jaw set. 'You get away from here. You're not welcome!'

Jamie gave a scoff of laughter and looked to his gang, who followed their leader's prompt and joined in with his sneer.

'No, love,' he replied. '*You're* not welcome. But you're here anyway, aren't you? Taking your share of our food, using up our rations... looking after your own. *You* get away from here.'

'James Farthing, wash your mouth out!' Annie told him, sounding like her father when he gave local kids a dressing-down. 'I'll tell your mother what you've been up to, you...'

The throb of aeroplane engines drowned her out. She looked up to see a clutch of Spitfires passing overhead. Jamie looked up too, shielding his eyes against the sun as the planes flew beneath the clouds. Annie saw the red and white chequerboard of their Polish markings at roughly the same moment as Jamie, but, as a surge of pride and concern flowed through her, the teenager spat a wad of phlegm onto the ground.

'I'll tell you something,' he sneered. 'They'll make sure their lot all come home. It's just the British lads they don't like to look out for. Ain't that right, boys?'

His gang all nodded. 'Yeah!' they said.

'If it weren't for them...' Joe, the farrier's son, wrinkled his nose as if he'd noticed a bad smell. 'Well, Jamie knows what I mean, right?'

Annie went cold. Jamie's brother, Neil. Annie had been friends with him, went to school with him. She was best friends with Betty, Jamie and Neil's sister. She had cried into her pillow when she'd heard Neil had been killed. But she'd never blamed the Polish airmen he'd been flying with for what had happened. There was only one person to blame, and he was in Berlin and wore a ridiculous little moustache.

'Don't,' she said, her voice quavering with emotion.

'We all know what you mean!' Ewa's anger was growing, which wouldn't help the situation at all. Jamie would only relish knowing the reaction he was able to elicit from the innocent Polish residents of Bramble Heath. It was the last thing his late brother would have wanted. 'What good does this do anyone? Go home!'

'I *am* home!' Joe winked at Jamie. 'But *you* ain't.'

'That's enough,' Annie said. 'Do you want me to send for my father? You're obstructing the highway, for one thing. He'll give you all a thick ear if you're not careful.'

Jamie curled his lip, but Annie wasn't about to let him intimidate her, and she already knew that Ewa certainly wouldn't back down. For a moment he glared at the Polish woman, then he turned to his gang and said, 'C'mon, lads. Stinks of foreign grub round here anyway.'

The only thing that stinks around here is your attitude.

But Annie wasn't about to say that aloud and make matters worse. She watched the boys ambling away, kicking stones and spitting as they went.

She smiled over at Ewa. '*Cześć!*' she greeted her. 'I'm sorry about those boys, Ewa.'

Ewa shrugged one shoulder, her arms still crossed as tightly as ever. There was no possibility that she might be the mother who had abandoned her child; she was rail thin, drawn and pale. Besides, whenever the hamlet needed a translator she filled that role, and Annie had seen no evidence of any pregnancy at all on her visits.

'Perhaps, if he is lucky, he will grow up one day,' she

replied. 'Or perhaps he will always be this way. He isn't welcome here; he upsets people just to entertain himself.'

'I know, he's a horrible lad,' Annie said, wheeling her bike along. 'I'll speak to his mother again when I pop by later this morning. How is everyone, by the way?'

She always asked this question, but now it took on an extra layer of meaning. What if Clara's mother was from the Polish community?

'Surviving,' Ewa said. Although she was often the spokesperson for the Polish women who lived in the little hamlet, she had never been the warmest of the residents. Annie could hardly blame her for that, of course. After all, she had fled her home to come here with her husband's squadron only to find a gang of children – because they *were* still children, however they behaved – who were determined to make everyone's existence thoroughly miserable. Life had not been easy for Ewa Glinka, and she had hardened herself to it.

'Ewa, you do know – and I hope everyone else around here knows too – that you can come to me if you need anything?' Annie said gently, hoping it might help Ewa to open up if she knew anything. 'Healthwise, or anything else for that matter.'

'We know.' But Annie knew that they often didn't. Instead, this little community that had been through so much often preferred to keep its own counsel, and the likes of Jamie certainly didn't help. For a long moment Ewa matched Annie's gaze, then she finally gave a nod. 'Mrs Kubal's little boy has a very nasty cold and I think she would like to see you. We've been treating the cold, but she is worried for him.'

'Of course I'll see him,' Annie said. She was a district nurse, health visitor and midwife all rolled into one, after all. And a cold, she knew, could turn into something much worse if they weren't careful. 'And Mrs Duglosz, she had that cut on her arm? I can look at her bandage while I'm here.'

Mrs Duglosz was an older lady who had followed her son to

England and now had to witness the bad behaviour of someone else's child. Jamie didn't speak for all of Bramble Heath, though, and the Polish newcomers had largely been given a warm welcome regardless of whether they were here seeking sanctuary or part of 319 Squadron.

Ewa gave a curt nod. 'You want me to translate, yes?'

Annie nodded back, slightly more enthusiastically. 'If you wouldn't mind, Ewa. It's ever so kind of you to help. Could I leave this old girl in your front garden again?'

This time Ewa's reply was a shrug of one shoulder. Then she stepped out of the door and pulled it shut, folding her arms again as she watched Annie wheel the motorbike along the path, careful to avoid the flowers growing there.

I'll ask Ewa about Clara now, so it won't look like a big deal.

'A funny thing happened to me last night,' Annie said as casually as she could, as she kicked down the stand on the bike. Ewa said nothing, but simply kept that watchful gaze fixed on her a little longer.

A second or so passed before she finally asked, 'What?'

'I don't know what you say in Poland, but in England, when children ask, we say that babies are found under the gooseberry bush.' Annie tried her best to sound light and conversational. 'But this one appeared on my doorstep!'

'I don't understand,' Ewa admitted, frowning. 'You delivered a baby last night?'

'It's not unusual for me to deliver a baby, but *this* baby was delivered to me,' Annie said. She peeled off her leather gloves. 'Someone knocked on my door, and when I opened it there was a hatbox on the doorstep, and inside it... a newborn baby. My parents are looking after her, but I really do need to find her mum. She might need to be checked over. I can help her.'

Ewa nodded and stepped out of her garden onto the narrow pavement. She shrugged that one shoulder again and asked, 'The little one is healthy, I hope?'

'Oh, ever so.' Annie looked at her carefully. It was impossible to know if Ewa was being her usual curt self, or if she was hiding something. 'But I do hope her mum's all right. You see, a little thing now might not seem too troubling, but it needs to be seen to before it becomes a serious problem.'

'You are asking me to ask our community.' It was a statement, not a question, and Ewa's manner was as brusque as ever. She gave a very brief nod, then added, 'I hope you will ask the English women too, yes? There are more of them than us, after all.'

Annie swallowed.

Oh heck. I hope she doesn't think I'm like Jamie.

'I... Well, yes, Ewa, if you wouldn't mind asking around,' she said. 'Like I say, I'm just concerned for her welfare. And I certainly am asking the English girls too. I've already spoken to some of the Land Girls. You know what they're like,' she chuckled. 'A romp in the hay with a handsome pilot, and a baby'll soon come along! I'm not about to scold anyone for that sort of thing. I'm not the vicar.'

The answer was another nod, then Ewa set off at a clip.

'I shall ask.' She glanced over her shoulder at Annie. 'Mrs Kubal is waiting.'

FIVE

On her travels that morning, Annie had seen patients from a few weeks old to nearly ninety, dotted all over the village. But she hadn't seen any women with problems that could indicate they'd just been through a secret birth. Maybe Clara's mother had got through it without any issues, but it still troubled her. She hated to think of how frightened the woman could be, and how wretched she might feel at giving up her baby.

She rode along the high street, with its bakery, greengrocer's and butcher's, and pulled up outside the post office. The little hanging baskets outside were still a riot of colour, even though the last weeks of summer were drawing in fast, and the bright sunlight gleamed on windows that had been polished to a shine despite the tape that was criss-crossed on each little pane. At that moment, it was almost as if the war had missed Bramble Heath, until the bell over the door tinkled and a young man strolled out wearing the familiar blue uniform of the Polish Air Force.

Annie recognised Pilot Officer Mateusz Glinka at once, his smile as broad and cheerful as his wife's shrug had been guarded and disinterested, even though his eyes were heavy with exhaustion.

'Good afternoon, Miss Russell,' he beamed, lifting his cap to her. 'A beautiful day to be on the ground!'

'Isn't it just?' Annie said with a nod. 'You enjoy a good rest, won't you?' The poor man looked ready to drop. All the pilots did. Hitler wasn't giving them a moment's rest.

'When I get one, I'll be sure to.' He held the door for her and stepped to the side with a polite nod.

'Thank you,' Annie said, as she exchanged the heat of the summer's day for the cool interior of the post office. Every spare inch of wall carried posters advertising war bonds, and sage advice to *Always carry your gas mask!* and *Don't be a squander bug!* Aside from a few movie magazines and the *Radio Times*, the stands mostly carried knitting periodicals. Their cover stars, both male and female, were sporting khaki tank tops. A rack of children's toys stood in the middle of the room, most of the pegs empty as supplies ran low.

Annie waved to Betty and her mother behind the counter. She'd caught them at a rare quiet time, and went straight up to talk to them.

'Hello there, dear!' Mrs Farthing greeted as she fanned herself with a receipt book. 'Lovely day, isn't it? What can we do for you, or are you just here for a chat?' She gave Annie a wink.

'Did Mateusz tell you the news?' Betty asked with a grin. 'Woolly got his fifth last night, so Bramble Heath has another ace! You wouldn't have guessed it'd be little Woolly, would you?'

Annie chuckled. Woolly was a gentle, unassuming man with a soft Devonshire accent. 'Well done him!'

'We should have some sort of party to celebrate!' Mrs Farthing said. She paused her fanning for a moment, then said,

'Actually, I suppose that'd better wait until all this business has died down a bit.'

Annie nodded. 'Yes, otherwise the pilots won't be able to come to their own party!' She lowered her voice confidentially. 'But I need to tell you what's happened. You'll never believe it.'

As she told them about the discovery of Clara the night before, Betty and Mrs Farthing stared at her in increasing amazement. They promised they'd ask around discreetly and, if they heard anything, Annie would be the first to know.

'And another thing...' Annie decided to speak quickly. Reporting to Jamie's family made her uncomfortable, but it had to be done. 'I was down the hamlet earlier, and so were Jamie and his gang. They're bothering the Polish again.'

Betty rolled her eyes and let out a seething breath. '*Again*. Honestly, Mum, what're we going to do?'

Mrs Farthing visibly sagged. 'I don't know, dear. If your father was still alive, he'd tan Jamie's hide, though I wonder if that sort of thing hasn't made Jamie worse. And he's taken our Neil's passing very badly. He was sad to begin with, but now he's just angry.'

Annie felt so sorry for the two women. Mrs Farthing had lost her husband, then her older son. And now the only son she had left was going about the village terrorising a community that had already suffered enough. Annie didn't want to say so, but he was becoming as unpopular as his father had been.

'We all miss Neil,' Betty sighed. 'Jamie thought the world of him. It'd break Neil's heart to hear what he's getting up to, but I can't get any sense into that thick head.'

'I suppose all you can do is keep trying,' Annie said. 'And if Dad or I catch him down there, we'll send him packing, don't you worry!'

The door flew back with a bang and there stood Jamie himself, his gang flanking him on the road outside. He didn't look angry this time, though, but full of excitement.

'Woolly's coming along the street!' he exclaimed. 'Everybody's turning out to cheer. C'mon! Another bloody ace for us Brits!'

'Jamie!' Betty admonished, but she was already heading around the counter. 'Don't swear like that!'

Mrs Farthing followed her, plucking Union Jack sandcastle flags from the rack of toys.

'One each!' she said proudly, handing them out to Betty and Annie, and then to Jamie and his friends.

Out they all went into the street, where the sun beat down from a cloudless blue sky. Mr Knapp the greengrocer and his daughter came out onto their step, and the Parker sisters, who ran the bakery, appeared outside their shop, waving. The little teashop emptied itself into the street, with customers in sundresses and waitresses in black dresses and neat white aprons. The vicar pulled up to a dusty halt on his bicycle outside the butcher's and joined Mr and Mrs Stokes. The plumber arrived too, still carrying his tool bag, and waved his pipe wrench as if it was a flag. Even the drinkers from the George and Dragon pub left their watery pints and stood outside cheering. Mrs Pearson parked her pram and lifted out her twins, one on each hip, to see what was going on. Older women put down their baskets and wafted their embroidered hankies. A group of evacuees who'd been helping with the harvest rested their wheelbarrows and cheered too. And Henry arrived on the scene as well, joining in with the celebrations even as he kept an eye on the excited crowd.

It seemed as if the whole village was there.

'Is that him? Is that him?' some giggling girls asked, pointing along the street just as the men outside the pub began a chorus of 'For He's a Jolly Good Fellow'.

Around the corner came an unassuming figure on a rickety bicycle, his bright blue scarf flying out behind him. If not for his uniform, he might've been mistaken for a butcher's boy or one of the lads who used to come every year to help harvest the crops, but today he was a hero. With his unruly blond hair and ruddy cheeks, he might not be the dashing sort, but that didn't matter to Bramble Heath or the people he had defended so valiantly. He was their newest ace, and that meant the red carpet had to be rolled out for him.

He squeezed the brakes on his bicycle, and it came to a shuddering halt in the middle of the cheering crowd. His face grew redder than ever as Jamie and his pals whooped and hollered, stamping their feet and punching their fists against the air.

'I only came for liquorice,' was Woolly's bashful exclamation. Then he gave a nod of thanks, his cheeks scarlet by now. 'Wait until I tell the folks back home about you lot!'

'You can have all the liquorice you want!' Mrs Farthing chuckled.

'Hip-hip-hooray!' the plumber shouted, and everyone joined in. The men from the pub rushed forward, and for a moment Woolly was lost in a scrum, before reappearing carried aloft on the shoulders of men who'd spent years in the fields hefting bales of hay and sacks of potatoes. He was cheering along with them, calling out thanks and assuring everyone that it was really nothing, just a chap doing his duty. But the duty he and his comrades undertook was far from nothing. Everyone knew it, even if Woolly was too modest to admit it.

SIX

After the excitement had subsided and the street had emptied again, Annie got back onto her motorbike and headed for Heath Place. A welcome breeze cut through the warm air as she made her way along the lanes, and finally up the grand, sweeping drive that led to the requisitioned house. It had quickly gained a military air; the fountain in front of the three-storey Palladian building had been turned off, and jeeps were parked up on the carriage circle. Tape criss-crossed the windows, and a sentry booth had been set up by the foot of the stairs.

Annie was a familiar face though, and, on showing her card, she was allowed into the inner sanctum. The entrance hall, with its high ceiling and marble floor, was cool compared to the heat of the day outside.

A man in RAF uniform marched past with a buff card-board file under his arm, and a nurse hurried by the other way, a syringe rattling in the metal kidney dish she was carrying. Then, strangely for Heath Place, a man in civvies swept along the corridor. He was immaculately dressed in a dark suit, holding a fedora in one hand. His eyes were steely, and Annie felt his gaze sweep over her, assessing her. Not the lascivious look that some men gave whenever they saw a nurse's uniform, but the quick glance of a man who didn't trust anyone.

The man from the Ministry, I suppose.

She wondered what was going on. But then with the war raging, and the Nazis' constant raids, everyone was on edge. Everyone had their secrets. There had been a time when Heath Place had been a family home, but that had all changed. Annie had never encountered men from ministries before the war. They had just never crossed the path of a district nurse. But peacetime was only a memory now.

She looked back at him, wondering what his secrets could be. He narrowed his eyes and gave her the barest hint of a nod.

And with that, he was gone.

'Good afternoon, Nurse Russell!' Annie recognised the familiar Welsh tones of Dr Parry a moment before she saw him. 'Come to visit the lads, eh? You'll be a welcome respite from this grizzled old soul, I'm sure.'

'Yes, here I am,' Annie replied with a nod. 'Wing Commander Chambers needed patching up yesterday. He came by my house. How's he doing today?' Even though she dealt with all the men who needed bandages checked, and wounds, bruises and breaks assessed, it was William who leapt to her mind first.

Dr Parry tutted and gave an exaggerated roll of his eyes behind the thick lenses of his spectacles.

'Nothing but a scratch,' he said, the words laden with irony. 'You know how those chaps are. Immortal and invincible, or so they think. Mark you, I don't see how anyone could go up in one of those kites if they *didn't* think that!'

Annie chuckled. 'It takes nerves of steel! Anyway, I'll be off on my rounds, and if you need me you know where I'll be.'

'Forgive me if I say I hope I *won't* need you,' Parry admitted with a smile. 'Because if Heath Place needs the likes of us, it means our boys are having a time of it. Enjoy your rounds, Miss Russell!'

Annie headed off through the echoing corridors towards the ballroom, which now served as a makeshift ward. She went from bed to bed, smiling for the recuperating men as she checked them over. But she was haunted by an image that she couldn't shake, of a young woman lying alone and afraid and in need of help.

A group of men had clustered in their pyjamas in the garden, smoking in the sunlight. But there was nothing restful about the scene. At the slightest sound, they turned sharply, looking up at the blue sky. They were on edge, their nerves pulled taut and fraying.

As Annie drew nearer, she spotted the uniformed William among them. She stepped out through the open double doors and waved hello.

'Hello, all,' she said. 'I hope you've been telling Wing Commander Chambers that he's to follow my orders and rest up until his wound's healed?'

'Not very likely!' remarked one pilot, who was tamping down his pipe with his bandaged hands.

'I am resting, Nurse!' William laughed. 'Honest, guv!'

'Hmm...' Annie stroked her chin, teasing him. 'I'm not sure I believe you! How's that cut today?'

He touched his fingers to the dressing that was just visible above the bright blue cravat he wore with his uniform. 'I'd forgotten all about it, Miss Russell. Nothing but a paper cut!' He put down the teacup he'd been holding. 'Do you have a couple of moments for a chat?'

One or two of the men greeted that innocent question with a knowing cough and a nudge.

'Of course,' Annie replied, ignoring them. *Clara. He's found something out about her, hasn't he?* 'Perhaps we could stretch our legs on the path just down there.' She pointed down to the gravel path that wound its way between box hedges, shrubs and rose bushes.

William tucked his cap under one arm, extending the other in a courtly gesture while saying, 'After you, Miss Russell.'

The scent of the summer flowers grew stronger as she descended the stone steps. At the bottom, she turned and waited for William. 'A lovely spot, isn't it? When old Mr Carter-Gooding built his airfield practically in the back garden, it was almost as if he knew his house would make a nice billet for you chaps!'

'It's a lot nicer than the last digs I was in,' William admitted. 'We were right on the edge of a chicken farm in Lincolnshire. I suspect a prison cell would've been more comfortable... freezing in the winter, roasting in the summer and chicken feathers all year round.'

Annie chuckled. 'You poor thing. At least you had well-stuffed pillows! Now...' She glanced up to where the other pilots were sitting, then lowered her voice. 'You wanted to tell me something?'

'I've asked around,' William said in a confidential tone. 'So far, nobody's had anything to say other than what a sorry show it is, but it's difficult not to wonder if the baby's father is one of our lot. It happens, as I'm sure you know... I didn't mean *you'd* know.' He cleared his throat, composing himself after the apparent faux pas. 'But as a nurse. And the daughter of a midwife.'

'You can be frank with me, Wing Commander,' Annie told him. 'I do know where babies come from. And of course, the girls love a man in uniform, and the chaps... well, what's wrong with being bowled over by a pretty face when times are grim?'

'That's very understanding of you,' he replied. 'But if one of our boys got a girl in trouble, it's not on to abandon her, is it? I can't imagine a mother gives up her little one unless she's no other choice. But personnel change here all the time, so... I don't know, Miss Russell. I hope that if he is here, he'll come forward. How is Clara today?'

Annie mulled over his words for a moment. With all the losses suffered as planes were shot down from the sky or blown up on the airfields, it was possible that Clara's father hadn't meant to abandon her. If he knew about his child at all.

She swallowed the thought. 'She's very well. Mum and Dad dote on her, you know. Dad's got to report today that she's been left with us, and that we've decided to look after her until the authorities decide to step in. Once they do, I'm afraid Clara's mother won't be able to change her mind. But it won't take *that* long to find her, will it?'

'I'm sure it won't. She must be missing her baby.' William smiled. 'Clara's a lucky little girl to have you. Her mother did a very desperate thing, but she chose the right people. I'm certain everyone in the village would tell the sainted authorities that; everyone here at Brambles certainly would.'

'I can't imagine how the poor woman must be feeling.' Annie sighed desolately. 'We'll have to see what happens with the authorities. They can sometimes swing into action with great enthusiasm, you know, and Clara could be gone in five minutes. Let's be honest, even with this dratted war going on, there'll be people who'd love to adopt a baby. But we can't let that happen without her mum's say-so, can we?'

He shook his head. 'No, we can't. Anything we can do over here, you need but ask, and I'll keep an ear to the ground.'

'You do that.' Annie nodded, glad that William had taken such an interest in the baby. 'And keep *yourself* on the ground, too. For another day or two at least. I don't want you rushing to get back into a cockpit – you could make that cut a lot worse, you know.'

'When we've won, I'll be happy to stay on the ground,' he said breezily. 'Until then, I'm afraid I'll still be flying the kite!'

She rolled her eyes. 'Now, now, Wing Commander, you

can't—'

The siren blared so loudly, so suddenly, that she took a startled step backwards and stumbled on the gravel. She reached out, grabbing William's sleeve. She knew exactly what the siren meant. She looked up at him and saw a muscle tense in his jaw.

'Not today,' she pleaded, hating the thought of him going into the air while he was still injured. 'You can't.'

'Oh, I owe them a little scratch in return,' he said, closing his hand over Annie's where it rested on his sleeve. 'Go down to the shelter; don't try to get back to the village.'

A daytime raid. They really were upping the ante.

'Your cut could get infected, you could be very ill...' she said, desperate to stop him. Her heart was racing as she heard aeroplane engines approaching. The ground under her feet seemed to vibrate.

'But it won't, because you're such a smashing nurse, Miss Russell.' He gently lifted her hand from his arm. Shouts came from the house, where the billeted pilots were scrambling towards the neighbouring airfield. William was already backing away in the direction of the orchard, where a short path would carry him to the runways and hangars. 'Now get along to the shelter, and I'll see you in the pub when we're home.'

Annie looked around, spotting the arrow that pointed to the shelter. She knew she had no choice.

'Wing Commander!' she called.

'William!' he shouted good-naturedly as he turned to run. 'Now go!'

'Take care, William!' Annie replied.

She couldn't bear to watch as his long legs carried him through the gardens to the airfield. Instead she hurried over to help the patients down to the shelter. The last thing she saw before they closed the door was Woolly bumping over the pathways of Heath Place on his bicycle as he raced towards the waiting planes.

SEVEN

The shelter at Heath Place had been built in the old ice house. It was cold, but at least the thick walls would protect them. After a while, the ground shook and dust fell from the ceiling – a bomb had dropped. Annie gripped her hands, trying to hide her fear. She was safe here, but what about her mum and dad? What about Clara? They'd have to run to the shelter in the garden. Would Clara be scared? Poor little thing. Her short life had already been eventful.

The recuperating RAF men seemed rather bored of it, though, if they reacted at all. The men who weren't reading papers were enjoying a spirited game of cards, and the air was soon wreathed with the smoke from their pipes and Woodbines. Several men offered Annie a cigarette, but she didn't accept.

'What this place needs is a tea urn,' she suggested.

'Not with the kind of tea we get in this place! Isn't that right, Cora?' said Flight Lieutenant Bridge as he laid down a card on an upturned bucket. The young nurse at Annie's side shivered and looked up at the ceiling as she hugged herself. Cora hadn't been here long, but Annie could imagine it was a world away from the Lancashire countryside where she'd come from. The war had changed so much.

'I wouldn't have thought they'd be as frightening in the daytime as they are at night,' she admitted in a shaky voice. 'But it's worse somehow. You don't expect to see something like that coming out of the blue sky.'

Dr Parry gave her a fatherly smile. 'It'll be over soon enough. We're safe here until it is.'

'More chance we'll die of frostbite in this place than anything else!' joked a flying officer known as Squiffy. He'd earned that nickname sometime before he'd ended up wearing a bandage over his injured eye. He gallantly untied his white scarf and offered it to Cora. She took it, her cheeks showing a little flush as she tied it around her neck in a jaunty bow.

'How do I look?' she asked mischievously.

'Fabulous!' Annie assured her. 'You look like a film star!'

Squiffy chuckled. 'A warm film star, certainly.'

The ground shook again, more dust falling from the ceiling.

The men fell silent. Bridge tutted. 'Rather close, that one. Nearly sent my cards flying!'

The others laughed. Annie giggled nervously too.

Maybe if I can laugh, I won't be so scared.

Cora glanced up again, then bit her lip. For a moment Annie thought the nurse might be about to cry, but then she glanced at the rest of the crowd in the shelter and drew in a deep breath. 'Is it right somebody left a baby with you, Miss Russell? William told us about it.'

So the news was already spreading, which might be a good thing. Perhaps one or other of the parents would come forward now, if they were able.

'Yes, a newborn, a little girl. She was left on the doorstep, I have no idea who by. We've called her Clara.' An idea occurred to Annie. Clara's cord had been carefully tied. Could a nurse have done it? She hadn't thought about that last night. 'I don't suppose you've heard anything at the nurses' home?'

'Mother of the bally year, eh?' brayed one of the patients around his cigarette. On the plaster cast that covered his arm, someone had inked a little caricature of a toff in a top hat flying a Hurricane, and Annie could already see why. 'Dropping the kid off during an air raid, what?'

Cora shot him a disapproving look before turning back to Annie with a shake of her head.

'No,' she admitted. 'But that's a big secret to keep in a little village. I'll keep my ears open.'

The pilot with the broken arm examined his cards, then weighed in with his opinion.

'Own up, me boyos! Which one of you saucy lot has been teaching the Land Girls things he shouldn't?' The men laughed along with the joke and Annie looked at each in turn, wondering if the father was among them. He couldn't be, surely? No man would sit chuckling about his baby if she had been abandoned on a doorstep.

'I should jolly well hope that any of you who are having fun with the girls know how to do so in a responsible manner,' she said crossly. Surely the men didn't need a lecture, but she thought of Clara and the words spilled out. 'Because if you don't, this is just the sort of thing that ends up happening. You wouldn't want that for your own flesh and blood, would you?'

'Hear, hear,' Squiffy said. 'Can't have gents not behaving like gents. Gives the RAF a bad name. Gives *chaps* a bad name.'

Even the pilot who had led the joking looked chastened, and bowed his head in contrition as he said, 'Of course, I should know better. My ma would box my ears if she heard me; she'd break my good arm!'

The others laughed at that, and Annie smiled as the tension in the room dissipated. The men returned to their cards and their newspapers, while Annie and Cora swapped tales of their villages before the war. Annie shared stories about the locals in Bramble Heath, and Cora told her about life back home. Talking about normal things kept their fear at bay, but it couldn't banish it completely.

Not until the siren blared the all-clear.

'Back to work!' Dr Parry clapped his hands as though nothing untoward had taken place. But then it wasn't so untoward these days, was it? This was just something that happened. 'Let's go and make sure everything's still standing.'

Most of the men were able to walk, and Annie, Cora and the other nurses helped the ones who couldn't.

Annie squinted in the sunshine. The world outside seemed just the same, but the men glanced hesitantly over in the direction of the airbase, and she knew what they were thinking.

Have all the chaps come home?

Where the two bombs had landed, she couldn't tell, but both had seemed too close for comfort. She could hear raised voices from the airfield and the sound of propellers still turning, but over them she could make out something else. It was a voice, raised in urgency.

'Doctor! Doctor!'

'Can you boys manage to get back to the ward?' Annie asked, her heart racing. Was it the ground crew or one of the pilots who'd been hurt? 'I rather think we're needed.'

The other nurses shepherded the men away, leaving Annie and Dr Parry to meet William as he ran through the orchard. He still wore his flight gear, but he hadn't been slowed by the heavy boots or life jacket, and Annie knew instinctively that something awful must have happened. It wasn't the first time, sadly.

'It's Jarek!' He skidded to a halt on the grass in front of them, panting the words out breathlessly. 'He's taken shrapnel in the neck. There's blood everywhere – we've got to help him!'

With that, he turned and took off back towards the airfield, leaving Annie and the doctor to follow.

As Annie ran across the lawn, not bothering to follow the carefully laid-out paths, she thought of Squiffy's white scarf. In her mind, it was stained with blooms of red. She told herself that a neck wound was survivable. After all, there was William, a bandage still on *his* neck.

But this sounds so much worse.

They raced through the archway in the old brick wall that led into the orchard. The trees were heavy with ripening fruit, and Annie tried not to trip on the fallen pears and apples in the long grass. Finally they emerged from the other side, onto the airfield.

She saw at once that there was a bomb crater not far from the edge of the orchard that had bitten a chunk out of the landing strip. But her attention shifted almost immediately to a haphazardly parked plane, its propeller still turning, and a figure lying pale-faced on the grass nearby. Someone had pillowed their flight jacket under his head. Jarek's hand was at his neck, blood running between his fingers. And there was red everywhere – pooled on the ground, smeared over the paint-work of the plane and spattered on the canopy.

Pilots still in their flight gear were gathered around him, and Annie and Parry pushed through them. As Parry dropped to his knees, Jarek's hand slipped from the wound to the grass at his side. Blood pumped from the ragged hole in his throat and his breath came low and short, the sound a guttural, gurgling rasp.

From a few feet away, Mateusz called to his friend in Polish, his voice racked with concern. Annie didn't understand what he said, but she could guess. He was telling Jarek to hold on, assuring him that everything would be fine. But she already knew that it wouldn't be.

EIGHT

He's lost far too much blood.

Annie did her best to help Parry, cutting bandages and squares of cotton wadding to size, loosening Jarek's clothes so the doctor could work more easily. The young man looked grey, his eyes rolling up in their sockets.

'Talk to him, Mateusz. Talk to him about home. It'll help him,' Annie said gently.

Mateusz sank to his knees beside his friend and took Jarek's hand, seemingly oblivious to the blood that bathed it. William stood behind Mateusz, his palm resting on the Polish pilot's shoulder in a silent gesture of support as he began to speak gently to the dying man.

Jarek blinked, struggling to focus on Mateusz, and for a moment, no more, he seemed to do so. He whispered something that Annie didn't catch and wouldn't have understood if she had. Then he closed his eyes, the shallow, desperate rise and fall of his chest slowing until it was still.

Annie swallowed. The sun caught something shiny around Jarek's neck, and there, with his bloodied dog tags, she spotted a medal of St Christopher.

'God bless, Jarek,' she whispered. It wasn't fair. It wasn't fair that he'd survived the invasion of his homeland only to die here, his blood soaking into foreign soil.

Mateusz's head sagged and he closed his eyes. Annie saw his hand tighten on Jarek's at precisely the moment William's tightened on Mateusz's shoulder. The airfield suddenly seemed very quiet, the sort of silence that hung heavy and might never be broken, as Parry bowed his head respectfully and closed his eyes.

At last Mateusz murmured something to his fallen friend in a gentle voice. Then he laid Jarek's hand upon his chest and rose to his feet. He looked around at the assembled faces through eyes clouded with unshed tears, then gave them a polite nod and trudged away towards the hangars.

No one spoke for a long moment.

Annie glanced from one ashen face to another. 'Wing Commander, anyone need patching up? Any of your fellows need anything?'

And not physically, she wanted to add.

She looked along the runway and counted the planes. Were they all back?

'Patching up...' William repeated, a little dazed. He finally looked away from Jarek and settled his gaze on Annie. He looked as wretched as she was sure she did, and her heart went out to him. 'I don't... No, we're just waiting for... No, no patching up, thank you.'

'Would you mind sending stretcher bearers across?' Parry asked Annie, his tone respectful. 'I'll stay here with the young gentleman.'

'Of course,' Annie said, and began to make her way back to the house. She took her handkerchief from her pocket and shivered as she dabbed her eyes. The sunshine didn't seem real somehow, its warmth not quite penetrating the chill that enveloped her.

I'm a nurse, I've seen people die before.

But most of them were elderly or had been ill for some time. Their deaths took place in cosy bedrooms, surrounded by loved ones. They weren't sudden and violent like Jarek's.

'Miss Russell?' She heard the sound of footsteps hurrying over the grass, then William was at her side. He had finally cast off his cumbersome life vest, and his hands were clasped behind his back, but he looked anything but casual. He looked as though every muscle in him was tightly knotted. 'I couldn't let you walk back alone after... It wouldn't be right.'

'Thank you,' Annie said gently. It meant a lot to her that he had thought to accompany her. 'It's not easy, is it, seeing someone snatched away like that? Poor Jarek.'

'He was a fearless young man,' William replied. 'And a dashed good pilot. Always ready with an unrepeatable story in the mess. He's a great loss to us all. We all know it *could* happen, but I don't think any of us really believe it will.'

'I'm so sorry we couldn't save him.' Annie brushed her hand against William's arm. 'I wish I could save *all* of them.' There was a brief silence before she continued. 'How's that bandage? I know I said you shouldn't fly, but did it get in the way?'

Not that you'd admit as much if it had.

He brushed his fingertips to his cravat as if he'd forgotten the bandage beneath it, then shook his head.

'Not at all. You did a splendid patch-up job, Miss Russell.'

Annie smiled. 'I'm very glad to hear it, Wi—'

'Wing Commander!' a man shouted. Annie turned, looking back through the archway as a pilot ran pell-mell towards them through the orchard. 'Wing Commander, it's Woolly!'

There was something taut and urgent in his tone that she didn't like at all.

'Excuse me, Miss Russell.' William glanced towards Annie, but he must have known that whatever the news was, she would hear it sooner or later. 'What is it, Harry?'

'He... he didn't make it.' The pilot stopped a few yards away. His face was lined and grimy, as if he'd had a heck of a time himself. 'He was in formation, two of the chaps were hit, and he was trying to escort them to safety, and... those cowards, those ruddy cowards... they took him out.'

The world seemed to stop for a heartbeat, and Annie saw Woolly again, laughing and ruddy-cheeked as he was lifted onto the shoulders of the men in the village. It seemed ridiculous that just a couple of hours ago he had been pedalling his rickety bike to the post office to buy a bag of liquorice, and now he was gone. All those stories of life in his Devon home, of the silly escapades and rolling fields that he couldn't wait to return to, silenced. Was that what it meant to be a hero?

'And the chaps who were hit?' she asked. 'Did they...?'

'They came home,' Harry said, his voice quiet. He managed a tiny smile. 'They came home because of Woolly.'

Annie rushed her hand to her mouth. 'Good old Woolly,' she said, her voice suddenly thick with tears. 'Bless him. What a brave, selfless man. He was a marvellous pilot, and to have been hit shepherding the others home when he could've just flown back to safety instead... What a sacrifice he's made for those boys. For all of us. The village was so proud of him this morning, and they'll be just as proud of him now. And always.'

She looked up at the summer sky. Clouds were bubbling up, tall clouds that could turn to thunder.

'Thank you, Harry,' William said in a low voice. He drew himself up a little taller before he added, 'I'll come straight back to the airfield when I've spoken to Group Captain Conway. Would you mind awfully heading into sickbay and sending the stretcher bearers out? I think Miss Russell should get off home to the little one.'

Harry nodded. 'Of course.'

'Are you sure you don't need me?' Annie asked. She felt the

pull of home, wanting to make certain they were all safe. But what if there were cuts to bathe and bandages to fasten here?

William waited until Harry was hurrying across the grass. Only then did he rest his hand on Annie's arm and say, 'The medics in sickbay should be able to manage, though I doubt they'll be quite so gentle.' He drew in a shaky breath. 'I'm sorry you were here when...' He swallowed and whispered, 'They were two of the best men I knew.'

'I'm honoured to have been here, to have tried to...' She shook her head. 'I wish all this beastly business wasn't happening. It's not fair. None of it. But we do our best, don't we? That's what's important. And Jarek and Woolly, they were doing their best too.'

'That's all we can do,' William replied in a whisper. 'And we'll honour those lads. This is a family, whether we fly for Poland or Britain. We've all lost two brothers today.'

NINE

Annie made her way home through a village that was cautiously emerging from its cellars, understairs cupboards and kitchen tables. Over garden hedges, Bramble Heath locals spoke to their neighbours, evidently relieved that they had made it.

But Woolly and Jarek hadn't.

Annie found it hard to dispel her gloom, even on seeing that the rest of the village was unscathed. As she arrived home and wheeled her motorbike to the garage, she noticed something in the front garden that hadn't been there when she'd left.

A pram. With a pink bow tied around the handle.

The sight of such a gift, such a thoughtful, kind gift in the face of so much tragedy, made her sniff back a tear. The world wasn't a hopeless and dark place. There was still love left.

Word wouldn't have reached the villagers yet about the two men who had died keeping them safe, but soon it would. Soon heads would bow, flowers would be placed in the church doorway and there would be another memorial service to mark their names. There had been too many memorial services these past few months. It had to end soon, surely?

But Clara didn't know any of this, and nor would she for a long time. She had been born into a world where bombs were falling and lives were cut short all too easily, but that simple second-hand pram was a symbol of the good that existed still. And she would know only good if Annie had anything to do with it.

Annie put away her motorbike, then went indoors. She heard her parents in the front room, and found them tucking Clara into a wicker crib. Three teddy bears, a pile of tiny knitted clothes and some equally tiny shoes were lined up on the sofa.

'News has got around the village, then?' she said. It was a wonderful sight and, despite what she'd seen not an hour earlier, she was beginning to smile. 'All these clothes and toys, and even a pram!'

'And Clara's already worked a miracle!' Norma picked up a little bear and snuggled it into the crib beside the baby. 'Mrs Glinka came by before the raid and left this teddy for her, and you'll never guess... Clara got a smile from her!'

Annie chuckled at that. 'A smile from Mrs Glinka? Well done, little Clara.'

Clara raised her tiny hands, as if she was cheering.

'The girls came by from Gosling's farm,' Henry said, shaking a rattle, which must've been another donation from the village. 'They brought milk and eggs. And they said to tell you that Nicola is sitting down peeling spuds.'

Annie smiled. 'I'm glad to hear it!'

'We were ever so worried when the sirens blared and you were out on your rounds.' Norma crossed the room and gave Annie a brief hug. 'A bomb came down on the edge of Parker's farm. No harm done, though, God be praised. Where were you, love?'

'I was worried about you three as well.' Annie swallowed. 'I was up at Heath Place, in the bunker there.' She tried to master the quiver in her voice, but it overwhelmed her. 'Oh, Mum, Dad, I've got something awful to tell you.'

Henry stopped shaking the rattle, and Norma met Annie's gaze, reading the sadness there before she said, 'Have we lost one of the boys?'

Annie nodded, her eyes closed. 'Not just one. Woolly. And Jarek.'

There was silence for a moment.

'Woolly and Jarek...' Henry said quietly. Norma lifted a trembling hand to her mouth and gave a small gasp of horror. It was almost too much to take in, surrounded by all these trappings of childhood innocence.

'And to think of the reception Woolly got just going to buy liquorice,' Henry remarked, as if he was talking to himself. 'He had a hero's welcome, didn't he? He had *that* at least... Annie, you're very pale.'

'Jarek died beside the runway,' Annie whispered. Even though she'd changed out of her bloodied uniform and washed as best she could at Heath Place before coming home, she could still see the blood. 'I tried to save him, Dr Parry too, but we couldn't.'

Norma put her arms around her and drew her close, just as she had when Annie was a little girl and was woken by a nightmare. Annie felt like that little girl again now, but what had happened wasn't a nightmare. Two mothers had lost their sons.

'Woolly died saving two other men,' she told them, her voice trembling. 'The enemy picked him off. And Jarek... poor Mateusz saw him die. He watched his friend die.'

'Oh, love, I'm so sorry,' Henry said. 'It's an awful business. But you know, your mum and me, we're so proud of you.'

Norma drew back, taking Annie's hands in hers as she peered at her.

'And Clara's ever so glad to see you. She's such a well-behaved little thing, not like you!' She released one of Annie's hands and chucked her cheek. 'You used to give us the Hallelujah Chorus when you wanted some attention! But you've always been the best daughter anyone could wish for.'

Annie did her best to smile. 'You know me. I like to make my presence known.'

'And we've got some good news.' Henry smiled at Clara. 'I know it won't bring the boys back, but it's happy news nonetheless. I was on the blower to Social Services earlier, and they're letting us look after Clara for the time being. No one'll be descending tomorrow to whisk her away to some orphanage or the like.'

Annie sighed with relief. That was something. Clara would stay where her mother had wanted her to be. 'That *is* good news.'

'They're coming round tomorrow just to see how she is, and I promised them we'd find Clara's mum soon,' Henry said. 'It'll take a fortnight, perhaps. A month at most. She must belong to someone in the village, and it's not a big place. Won't take long to track her down, I'm sure of it.'

TEN

The next day, Annie was packing her bag for her morning rounds when a curt rap sounded on the door. Henry was in front of the hall mirror, brushing imaginary lint off his uniform in preparation to go on shift.

'I'll get it!' he called, and Annie stepped into the hallway to see who was there. Her heart bumped in her chest as a thought rushed into her mind.

Clara's mum? Could it be her, come to take her baby home now she's seen how much the village cares? All those toys and clothes, and the pram too. People do care. I hope she knows. I hope it makes her brave.

Henry opened the door. 'Morning,' he said. He was suddenly standing as straight as a poker, and Annie realised that the two women standing on their doorstep were the social workers.

'Good morning, Mr – sorry, *Constable* Russell,' the older of the pair said, looking Henry up and down rather sternly, then peering over his shoulder into the hallway. 'I'm Mrs Southgate, and this is my colleague, Miss Cook. We're here about the child.'

'Come in,' Henry said, stepping aside.

'We just need to make sure that Baby's accommodation is adequate,' Mrs Southgate said without a smile, drawing off her cotton gloves.

Miss Cook gave a bob of her head, then tucked back some strands of hair that had escaped her bun. She wiped her feet methodically on the mat before finally stepping inside.

'What a lovely village this is,' she said. Her voice was so quiet it was almost a whisper, but her smile was warm, at least.

'Very,' Mrs Southgate said as Henry showed them into the front room. 'But I'm not too happy about the proximity of the airfield.'

Annie's stomach lurched, but she was determined to do her best to present a cheerful front.

'Unfortunately, we can't really move it, I'm afraid,' she said with an ironic grin.

'We may have an airfield close by, but we have a nurse and a retired midwife under the same roof too,' said Norma as she set the teapot with its brightly crocheted cosy on the table. She greeted the women with a welcoming smile. 'Would you like a cup of tea, ladies? It's a fair journey from East Grinstead.'

'That's very kind of you,' Mrs Southgate said, scanning the room. Surely she couldn't find anything to object to? The house was as neat as a pin. 'I see you have baby things. Have you enough?'

'The village has rallied round,' Annie told her, keen for her to realise that they could care for Clara. 'We've got everything we need.'

'And we've still got Annie's bits and bobs.' Norma was already filling the cups with freshly brewed steaming tea as the women settled side by side on the sofa. 'I only retired a couple of years ago, so I've some things left from my rounds as well. Our concern is for the baby's mum, though. She left her own ration book for little Clara.'

Miss Cook's stern expression crumpled into a sympathetic frown, and she shook her head. She looked as though she might be about to say something, but instead she cast a brief glance at her colleague and remained silent.

'We'll arrange for a ration book for Baby as soon as possible.' Mrs Southgate wrote something down in her notebook. 'Miss Cook?'

'A ration book for Clara,' Miss Cook murmured, speedily making a note in shorthand with a stubby pencil that she plucked from within her bun. 'I did make enquiries at Miss Clara's hat shop, but they weren't able to shed any light. It's a shame.'

Annie sighed inwardly. She'd thought of asking there too, but just hadn't had time. She doubted a hat shop would keep a list of all their customers when it was perfectly easy for anyone to walk in off the street, buy a hat and leave with it in a box. When she visited her patients, she almost always saw hatboxes from one milliner's or another on top of the wardrobe. They were ten-a-penny.

And yet maybe Miss Clara's shop *could* yield a clue. Annie just had to think of the right question.

Henry nodded at the social worker, evidently impressed by her sleuthing. 'You should've joined the force. You've got the makings of a detective there, Miss Cook!'

Miss Cook positively bristled with pride, her cheeks flushing as she murmured her thanks.

'And here is Baby,' Mrs Southgate said, rising from the sofa to peer at Clara, sleeping soundly in her crib. Her sternness waned. 'She looks to be a healthy little thing, doesn't she?'

Norma nodded. 'She's in the pink. Whoever delivered her knew what they were doing, they took proper care.' She glanced towards Henry and Annie, then went on. 'And they chose our doorstep because they knew she'd be looked after here. There're so many little ones losing their homes and families all over

Europe... We can keep young Clara safe and sound until her mum's ready to come forward.'

Mrs Southgate wrote something in her notebook, then looked up at Norma. 'I admire your confidence. I do hope Baby's – sorry, *Clara's* mother will indeed come forward. But the child can't stay here indefinitely, you must realise that. You would have to be properly assessed as foster parents, or adoptive parents. And there's a lot of people who would love nothing more than to adopt a baby.'

Annie's heart sank. 'But you must give us time, Mrs Southgate. You must give Clara's mum time. I believe she wants us to look after her baby, but I have no idea if she knows that we can't keep Clara here for ever. But we can't send her off to be adopted, or fostered somewhere else, or, God forbid, put in a home. Because then it'll be too late for her mum.'

'Oh, we know that you've a duty to do,' Norma added graciously. 'It's a difficult job you ladies have, and you do a grand one. That's why we know you'll have Clara's very best interests at heart.' As she settled her gaze on Mrs Southgate, there was a knock at the front door. 'Would you mind seeing who that is, Henry?'

Henry was tense. He hadn't sat down and now he took the opportunity to leave the room almost at a run. Annie hoped the social workers hadn't noticed, but she suspected they would. And yet surely they were used to people being on edge around them.

'Ah, Wing Commander!' Henry's voice easily reached them in the front room. 'Do come in, or are you only passing?'

'Official visit,' Annie heard William say. He sounded more cheerful today, or at least was making an effort to. 'I've been sent by the Brambles lot bearing gifts.'

'Have you indeed? Come in, come in. We already have visitors, but I'm sure they won't mind,' Henry said as he led William in. 'These two ladies have come from the social. Wing

Commander – Mrs Southgate and Miss Cook. And ladies, this is Wing Commander Chambers of the RAF.'

Mrs Southgate nodded. 'Good morning, Wing Commander.'

'Good morning,' Miss Cook parroted in her little whisper, bobbing her head politely,

'Good morning, ladies,' William smiled, greeting them with a nod as he tucked his cap beneath his arm. A canvas rucksack hung over his shoulder and a blue cravat with white spots hid the bandage on his neck. 'Mrs Russell, Miss Russell, and Miss Clara, of course. I hope I'm not interrupting?'

'Not at all,' Annie said. She was glad to see him, even if she had hoped the knock at the door was Clara's mother. 'They just want to see that Clara's quite all right here. Which of course she is,' she turned to the two social workers, 'because as you can see, even the chaps at the airfield are making a fuss of her.'

'That's why I'm here.' He slung the canvas bag off his shoulder and held it out to Annie. 'We had a bit of a whip-round for Clara and for you, to thank you for yesterday. Just a few little things, tokens from the Brambles bunch.'

Annie took the bag and looked inside. One by one she took items from the bag and put them on the table, things for Clara, and things for Clara's temporary family. There was a small box of chocolates with *The Russells* written on the label, a rag doll, a hand-carved aeroplane, and some baby supplies in a stripy paper bag Annie recognised from the chemist in the next village – a bib, a dummy, a rusk on a ribbon, and a Bakelite teething ring.

'How lovely, and how thoughtful!' She beamed, holding each item up so that her parents – and the social workers – could see them. One day, maybe, she could tell Clara's mother how much people had cared for her baby. 'You will tell the chaps how grateful we are for all these things, won't you?'

'Of course.' William smiled. 'It was a good project for us.

Everyone needed to take their minds off yesterday, especially Mateusz.'

'That poor man,' Annie said gently. 'How's he doing? Oh, I'm sorry, Mrs Southgate, Miss Cook. Mateusz is one of the airmen. His friend didn't make it back yesterday.'

Mrs Southgate glanced at Miss Cook. 'The airfield *is* a concern, as I said.'

'A concern?' William repeated, frowning. 'With respect, ma'am, we're at war and we're fighting for the safety of Great Britain. I don't think there are many places in the south-east that won't hear air raid sirens these days.'

'But the airfield is a target, is it not, Wing Commander?' Mrs Southgate asked him. 'And that puts anyone living in its vicinity at risk.'

'But we don't live at the airfield,' Henry said. 'And we've got a good solid shelter. It's safe as houses in there.'

'It's not my place,' William said, 'but Bramble Heath is a wonderful village. Everyone's welcome here, it really is a family. If Miss Clara's mother *is* here, she must be struggling or she wouldn't have given up her little girl. Knowing that Clara is safe with the people she chose... well, it's going to help her too, isn't it? And Lord knows, the one thing the world needs at the moment is compassion.'

Compassion.

William was right. Annie gave him a grin.

Thank you! she mouthed to him.

Mrs Southgate gave a tight *ahem,* then addressed Norma. 'We're happy for you to care for Clara at present, but please understand that in the meantime we'll be considering where to place her next, in case her mother doesn't come forward.'

Miss Cook made a shorthand note, but there was no containing her smile. She clearly believed that the decision was the right one, even if she wasn't about to say so. William met Annie's gaze and offered her a supportive smile, but there was a tightness to it, an apprehension at Mrs Southgate's mention of placing Clara elsewhere.

'There are some wonderful people desperate to give a home to a child,' he said. 'But Clara has a mother not so far away. And she couldn't ask for kinder guardians than the Russells, Mrs Southgate.'

Mrs Southgate nodded. 'Thank you for offering your opinion, Wing Commander. But the situation is temporary. And of course it very much depends on what happens in terms of the war. We might've evacuated children from the cities into the countryside, but if it comes to it, we might end up evacuating children from the south.'

Invasion.

Annie shivered. 'God forbid it comes to that.' She tried to sound brave in the face of her mounting terror.

'It won't.' William's voice was firm and there was no humour in his tone. Annie could well believe him, because she'd seen the dedication with which the men jumped to answer the scramble. They knew what they were risking, but they didn't so much as pause.

'I sincerely hope you're right,' Mrs Southgate said. 'Thank you for all the hard work you chaps are putting in. It's appreciated more than anyone can adequately say, although I think Mr Churchill put it *very* well.'

'He always does,' chuckled Miss Cook.

ELEVEN

Yesterday Bramble Heath had lost two airmen, but there were still others who'd been injured while flying and needed care. On top of that, there were the men who'd been injured in the days and weeks before, who Annie would have to see anyway. It would take up her whole morning, but she didn't mind – her civilian regulars knew she was busy.

She decided to walk to Heath Place with William. She needed some fresh air after meeting the social workers, and she could save a bit of petrol. Besides, why not enjoy the last of the summer?

'It's not too far if you know the shortcuts,' she told him as they headed out of the garden gate and into the lane. 'You just have to be nimble when faced with all the stiles!'

'I rather like village life,' William told her. 'Not too many meadows where I grew up in Richmond, but I think this suits me better. I've spent most of the morning wandering about the fields, thinking about life, I suppose. About the lads.'

'I'm glad you've grown to enjoy living here, even if you're being kept rather busy by...' Annie gestured to the sky. 'The countryside is a balm to the soul, isn't it? I took Clara out for a walk yesterday evening. I still felt rather sad, but there's something about being in nature that grounds you, I always think.'

William nodded in agreement as he hopped neatly over the rickety stile that had looked ready to give up the ghost for as long as Annie could remember. Yet it never seemed to need replacing. It kept on standing and she kept on climbing over it, just as she had since she was a little girl. Just as Clara would one day, if fate was kind.

'Miss Russell.' William smiled, holding out his hand to help her.

Annie beamed at him as she took his hand and climbed over. A group of Jersey cows chewed their cud some distance away under the spreading branches of an old oak tree, and a kestrel hovered on the air currents above.

'I think he's spied a juicy field mouse, don't you?' Annie said, pointing up to the bird.

'No ration book for him.' William tutted. 'Poor old mouse.'

Annie chuckled. She led the way along the path across the field, worn into a track by centuries of feet.

'What did you used to do in Richmond?' she asked. 'Before you took to flying?'

'I was training to be an architect,' he replied. 'Following in Pa's footsteps, I suppose, and every now and then I went up for a bit of a spin in a kite, just for fun.' He gave a resigned shrug. 'And it *was* fun, but it's all a bit more serious these days, isn't it?'

Kites. It's so funny how the pilots call their planes kites, as if they were toys.

'An architect? I've never met an architect before. Or an architect-in-training either, for that matter.' Annie was impressed. And if he was flying for fun before the war, she supposed he came from a fairly well-off background. 'But yes, I suppose you can't really fly along the coast and admire the Needles or the Seven Sisters from the air nowadays.'

'Not quite!' William chuckled. 'The funny thing is, I met

my girl through flying and now she spends all her time trying to convince me not to. Can't blame her, I suppose...'

'That's... well, painfully ironic, isn't it?' Annie remarked. 'Does she fly too? Gosh, I don't suppose she's one of those brave ladies who does Spitfire test flights, and delivers them to the airbases? I'd *love* to do that!' She pictured William's girl looking chipper and beautiful in a flight jacket.

His laugh was rather knowing as he assured her, 'Georgie is definitely *not* one of those ladies. She couldn't risk her nails!'

Annie hooted with laughter. 'Oh dear, I mustn't laugh about your girlfriend. But that *is* funny. I suppose she's keen for you to get back to your blueprints?'

'I do a bit of strategic stuff along with the flying. I've got that sort of brain,' William said lightly. 'Georgie's father's in the Air Ministry and she was on the blower this morning telling me all about this marvellous desk job he could squeeze me into. So yes, she's keen for me to be behind a blotter.'

'In London?' Annie asked him. 'Well, that might be safer than being in the air, I suppose.' She nodded. 'And just as you've adjusted to village life, too!'

They reached another stile and clambered over. The next field contained sheep, which were dotted around cropping at the grass.

William shook his head firmly. 'There's no chance of that! I'm sticking with the lads to the bitter end, whenever that is. I wouldn't give up this command for all the money in the world; it's where I belong. Woolly didn't run from it. Jarek neither. And nor will I.'

Annie smiled at him. 'You're an extremely brave man, do you know that? And loyal, too. There's a lot of chaps who'd've packed their bags and jumped on the first train to London at the merest scent of a desk job. But not you, Wing Commander Chambers. I admire that.'

'I'm not sure *brave* is the word Georgie would use,' William admitted. There was something in the way he said it that seemed to carry more weight than humour, but it was hardly surprising. The war was putting pressure on everybody.

'Speaking as a woman myself, I'm sure she's just worried for you because she clearly...' *Loves you.* Annie found she couldn't say it. 'She clearly thinks the world of you, and she doesn't want you to get hurt.' *Or worse.* She couldn't say that either. William didn't need reminding.

He spun on his heel and looked around the field, then settled his gaze on Annie. For a moment he said nothing, then he blinked and nodded.

'I'm not the sort to run away.'

'I know you're not.' Annie brushed his arm affectionately. But as soon as she'd done it, she felt awkward, so she teased him. 'Besides, you even stood up to that Mrs Southgate!'

He gave a theatrical shudder. 'Wasn't she a one?' At the next stile, he offered his hand to Annie once more. 'Clara has everything she needs here. There's no sense in sending her away.'

She took his hand and climbed over. 'She really does. I'm so glad you think so too. You know...'

At the sound of aeroplane engines, she shielded her eyes from the sun and peered up at the sky. 'One of your chums out for a pootle, William? We'll have to give them a wave!'

But William's brow was furrowed, and he murmured, 'That's not one of ours. It's a 109...'

As he spoke, a fighter came hurtling out of the clouds above them, flames and a thick plume of black smoke shrouding the tail. The engine was screaming, the propeller lurching as it struggled to turn, and that was all Annie saw before William seized her shoulders and flung her down onto the ground.

Not one of ours.

One of the enemy, then, dropping from the sky. Her eyes closed tightly, she pressed herself against the earth, hoping against hope that she and William would be safe. She felt his arms around him, his body cocooning and protecting her.

All at once, the quiet summer's day was torn apart. The ground shook with the impact, and Annie smelt burning fuel and heard screeching metal.

And a scream. A human scream?

'The pilot!' she said, trying to turn her head to speak to William. 'We need to get him out of the plane!'

'Stay here,' William warned urgently. Then he scrambled to his feet and dashed towards the wreck.

Annie pushed herself up, coughing as thick black smoke rolled across the fallow field. She spotted William's figure approaching the plane, but she couldn't see well enough through the haze to make out the pilot. She got to her feet, her medical bag in her hand.

'William, can you see him? We... we have to get him out!' She couldn't think of what else to do. They needed a fire engine to put out the flames, but there was nothing in the field except the two of them.

The hinged canopy of the Messerschmitt had been blown open by the force of the crash, and, as the smoke began to clear, Annie saw to her horror that the aircraft had snapped in half. The severed tail was smoking in the grass, while the fuselage had carved out a crater in the muddy field.

William was already at the stricken plane, and he hauled himself up onto the wing, where bullet holes had strafed the metal, and looked down into the cockpit.

'Don't come over, Annie,' was all he said. It was enough.

Annie's medical bag dropped from her hand. She felt hollowed out. The pilot was dead. Another young man gone, another son, brother, friend, husband, father perhaps, lost. He was the enemy, but he was a human being too. Someone who had woken up that morning, not knowing it would be his last.

'Is there *anything* I can do?' she asked.

William didn't answer at first, but bowed his head for a moment. Then he climbed down from the wing and made his way back towards her.

'I sent telegrams last night to Woolly's people in Devon, and Jarek's where they've settled up north,' he said. 'Somebody in Germany will be getting something very similar, I expect.' He blinked rapidly, excusing himself with a quiet 'Just the smoke...'

Annie approached him and took his hand. Did she detect a tremble? It wasn't the smoke, she knew that. Because William cared. Because he'd been training to build things, to create things. Not destroy them. 'I expect it was quick, William. He didn't suffer. Who knows if he even wanted to be in that plane...'

And with that, she put her arms around Wing Commander Chambers, and he sank against her, resting his head on her shoulder, and whispered, 'Poor bloody blighter.'

TWELVE

Black cloth hung in the windows of Bramble Heath's shops and houses. Not just blackout curtains, but the outward sign of a village in mourning. The street that, just a week ago, had rung with cheering and applause for 'ace in a day' Woolly was silent, apart from the sound of mournful wood pigeons in the trees around the churchyard. The shops had closed out of respect.

The St George's flag on the top of the church tower hung at half-mast, and Reverend Ellis stood under the lychgate with the exiled Father Piotrowski, their heads bowed as they spoke quietly together.

Annie and her father went down to the village in their uniforms, black bands around their arms. They didn't say a word to each other. A solemn air hung over the village like a pall.

Three deaths in two days. Three young men from three different countries, all strangers to Bramble Heath.

Annie blinked in surprise as a figure appeared in the churchyard, approaching the gate where the two men of the cloth stood.

It's Woolly!

But then she realised it was an older version of him, and she knew that it must be Woolly's father, come to take his son home to be buried. William walked alongside him, his cap tucked beneath his elbow. At the sight of Annie, he gave a gentle nod of acknowledgement.

Annie raised her hand to him before joining the throng of mourners who were filing silently into the church. It seemed as if everyone from the Polish community was there, along with men who had been spared from Heath Place, most of them bandaged up. A great many people from Bramble Heath were there too. Annie smiled gently at Betty and her mother arm-in-arm in the crowd. The earth had not yet settled on Neil's grave, and she knew that this day would be painful for them. But perhaps by meeting Woolly's father, they could find some sort of support.

Each member of the Polish community, whether a uniformed member of 319 Squadron or one of the civilians who lived in the hamlet, wore a black ribbon pinned to their breast. Mateusz was already inside the church, accompanied by a couple who Annie knew from their stricken expressions must be Jarek's parents. How heartbreaking that these refugees who had found a safe haven in England were now mourning the boy they had tried to protect. Standing straight beside the couple, Mateusz looked every inch the squadron leader he prided himself on being, but his reddened eyes were those of a man who had lost a treasured friend.

Ewa was not beside her husband, but was seated on the end of one of the pews. Her gaze flicked watchfully around the church and her hands were clasped tight in her lap, the knuckles white as marble. She looked as though she hadn't slept in days. Annie paused beside her and rested a hand on her shoulder for a moment. She had already given the community her condolences, but it seemed that Ewa was suffering more than most. Her gaze darted towards the two coffins at the front of the church: Jarek, and the unknown German pilot. Enemies in life, side by side in death.

'I'm so sorry, Ewa,' she whispered.

'This is a disgrace,' Ewa hissed bitterly. 'A *thing* like that side-by-side with Jarek. He should not be here.'

Annie squeezed her shoulder. 'He was a man too, Ewa. We have to hope that any of ours shot down over Germany are treated with respect.'

She had heard the same argument made about prisoners of war, but it was inevitable that Ewa, who had seen the German invasion of her homeland and the cruelties meted out, would find it hard to accept.

'*Respect?*' The word was a furious barked whisper that caught the attention of more than a few of the congregation. 'What respect have they shown us? When we fled Warszawa, the likes of that *thing* fired on us. It should have been buried where it fell and never spoken of again.'

It. Ewa wouldn't even talk about the pilot as if he was a human being. But then hadn't she been treated as less than human too?

'I can appreciate that this is very hard for you, Ewa. I'm so sorry,' Annie said again. 'You've been through more than I can ever imagine.'

'It's all right,' said Natalia, who sat at Ewa's side. She looked tired and drawn too, but that was hardly surprising, since she spent her days as a radar operator on the airbase. She gave Annie a kind smile and closed her hand over Ewa's, speaking softly to her in Polish. As she did, Jarek's father stepped up to the coffin of the fallen German pilot and bowed his head. He crossed himself, then laid his hand on the plain wooden lid for a few seconds before returning to his wife in the pew.

Annie went to sit beside Betty and her mother in the pew in front of Ewa. Jamie's absence was all too obvious, but she didn't want to ask where he was. As much as she suspected he was off somewhere causing trouble, she wondered too if perhaps he had stayed at home, reflecting on the brother he had lost.

'How are you two?' she asked them.

'Oh, you know. Remembering,' Betty sighed. She gave a little smile and added, 'Looking forward to tea with your mum and Clara this afternoon. We've been knitting up a storm.'

'It must be very difficult, but I'm glad you could make it,' Annie said. 'I think... well, I think it'll help Jarek's family that we're all here. And thanks so much for the knitting – Clara's going to be the best-dressed baby in the county.'

Annie wasn't any further forward with finding Clara's mother. She'd wanted to ring the hat shop herself, but would it lead anywhere? Then there was the ration book. Any information on it had been obliterated, so how could it help? Her father had knocked on doors around the village, but no one knew anything. Yet Annie couldn't shake the feeling that Clara's mother was in Bramble Heath somewhere. Did she peer around the curtain when Annie passed on her rounds? Did she ever come up to the house and watch in secret?

Or was she relieved, because she couldn't look after the baby herself and was sure that Annie and her parents were the best people to care for her?

There was a thud behind Annie, and she turned to see Zofia bending forward to pick something up off the floor. Annie knew both Zofia and Natalia in passing from the hamlet, but neither had needed a visit from the district nurse yet. It was the older residents who needed her more.

'Don't worry, I'm always dropping my hymn book!' Annie assured her.

Zofia looked up at her through the veil on her dark-coloured hat, her large blue eyes misting with tears. She shrugged. 'I am so clumsy.'

Annie nodded, then turned back to face the front of the church. William and Woolly's father made their way along the aisle to take a seat alongside Mateusz and, as the doors closed, the congregation fell silent as one.

The service was carried out jointly by Reverend Ellis and Father Piotrowski. It felt rather unusual to begin with, but as Annie glanced around the church the medieval knight on his tomb caught her attention. This had been a Catholic church for many years before the Anglicans had laid claim to it. And Reverend Ellis reminded the congregation that in difficult times, it was important to remember what people had in common with each other rather than dwelling on the differences.

Afterwards, the coffins were carried out into the church-yard, Jarek by his fellow pilots from 319 Squadron and the unknown man by the British pilots. The village watched in respectful silence among the headstones and yew trees as the two men were laid to rest under Bramble Heath's soil.

THIRTEEN

After the funeral, Annie was glad to return home. She cooed delightedly with her mother over each of the little garments that Betty and her mother had knitted for Clara. They were evidently lightning-fast knitters, and had produced an array of delicate bootees, bonnets and cardigans. Not everything in the world was awful; Clara was a welcome light in the darkness.

Clara seemed to enjoy meeting her public and was passed from Betty to her mum without so much as a whimper. As Betty rocked the baby, Annie wondered if she and her friend would ever be mothers. Not that she herself had great ambitions that way – her calling had always been to nursing. She'd never even had a serious boyfriend, at least not the sort who seemed about to nip off to the jeweller's to buy an engagement ring.

But Betty was beautiful and always turned heads. *And* she was stepping out with Jakub, one of the Polish ground crew. Not that Jamie was particularly impressed. But Betty wasn't going to take relationship advice from her fifteen-year-old brother.

Once their visitors had gone, Annie decided to make the most of the long summer evening, and took Clara out in her pram again. As much as she knew that babies needed fresh air, she wondered if Clara's mother was watching as she wheeled the pram through Bramble Heath. She hoped so.

Clara was asleep by the time Annie arrived at the mill cottage, where the old wheel still turned and ducks were busy diving in the weeds. She watched for a little while, her thoughts returning to events earlier in the day. Then she carried on, the pram bouncing over the uneven lane towards the middle of the quiet village, Clara still snoozing.

A uniformed figure sat on the bench overlooking the village green, his hands knitted in his lap and his head bowed. He was utterly unmoving, still as a statue, but Annie recognised him as she drew closer. He was lost in thought, his gaze fixed on the bright flowers that grew along the edge of the green, clustered beneath the signpost that had been turned round more than once, all its directions now useless should the Wehrmacht ever attempt to make use of them. But they wouldn't, Annie was sure, not with men like Woolly and Jarek, Mateusz and William chasing them down.

She approached, pausing beside the bench. She didn't want to impose on William's solitude.

'Space for one more, with a pram?' she asked. 'Although feel free to tell me to buzz off if you'd prefer.'

He blinked up at her and, seeing who it was, smiled.

'Plenty of space for friends,' he said. 'Unless you'd like company for your stroll?'

'I wouldn't mind at all,' Annie said. 'And I'm sure Clara wouldn't either. She's wearing a new outfit, by the way, knitted for her by Betty and her mother. Look at her little pointy bonnet – she looks like a baby pixie!'

'She's very bonny, but she's missing something important!' William had exchanged his formal tie, which he had worn to church, for a cravat in bright blue. As he stood, he unknotted it, and Annie saw that the wound she had dressed just a week or so ago was already on its way to healing. He held out the cravat. 'It's not much of a gift, but from one child who didn't know his ma to another.'

As Annie took the cravat and tied it around the pram handle, she looked up at him sympathetically. 'Oh, William, I'm terribly sorry to hear that.'

She'd heard him talk about his father being an architect, and supposed that his mother must've died when he was only very small. Perhaps that explained why he had stood his ground when Mrs Southgate had been so determined that Clara's stay in Bramble Heath would only be temporary.

'It's quite all right,' he told her with a smile. 'I couldn't have asked for a better family than the one that chose me. I hope Clara *does* find her mother, but I've a feeling she won't want for people who love her. Not in a place like this.'

'The family that...' *He was adopted.* 'Oh, I see. I'm glad you grew up with a wonderful family, William. And yes, you're quite right, we all look out for each other in Bramble Heath. As you saw today at the church. Clara has a whole village taking care of her.'

'I don't really think about Ma and Pa not being my parents, because they are in every sense. I was extraordinarily lucky that they chose me to be their son.' They strolled on, birdsong the only sound that accompanied them. 'I was left on the doorstep of the children's home when I was only a few days old. I hope my mother and father were all right afterwards; such a desperate thing to do.'

Annie blinked at him in surprise. 'Goodness, just like Clara! But... but they never came back?' She held tighter to the handle of the pram, fighting inwardly between her hope that Clara's parents would come forward and the growing worry that they never would.

'They never came back,' he confirmed. 'But Clara's mother

chose your home, not an orphanage. That's why I have a sense that she *will* come back.'

'I do hope so,' Annie said. 'But I'm no closer to finding her. Everyone in the village knows about Clara and, let's be honest, they all know each other's business. But no one has heard of a baby being born. I don't know... perhaps she's a local girl who's living in East Grinstead? But then wouldn't using a hatbox that says East Grinstead on it be a bit silly if she wanted to be unknown?'

'She's likely not thinking very clearly,' William pointed out, frowning at the distant sound of raised voices. 'I hope she's being looked after half as well as Clara is. I know some people will judge, but... well, no mother gives up her child lightly.'

'There's that natural pull to protect your children,' Annie said. Then a thought occurred to her. 'I hope you don't think I'm prying, but did you ever try to find your parents?'

William shook his head. 'Where would I start?' he asked. 'All I had was a blanket and a sorry little basket to lie in.' That struck Annie as sad. Sad for the baby he had once been and for the parents who would never know what a fine young man their child had grown into. 'I was very lucky to be adopted by my people, and I hope my other mum and dad made something of life. But I know I'll never meet them.'

'I'm so sorry,' Annie replied. 'I wish I knew where to start finding Clara's parents, but there's nothing to go on apart from a ration book with all the information scribbled out. Though I've been wondering if Clara's mum left the pram. I don't know why I think that. Maybe it was the pink bow on it, and the fact that it was left outside the house, just like Clara was.'

That would make sense, leaving the pram outside because she didn't want to come and knock on the door. What if...

Annie's train of thought was derailed as the voices got louder, and she saw figures running into the churchyard. She recognised the lads who made up Jamie's gang and her heart sank. Whooping and hollering as they were, they obviously weren't visiting to pay their respects, and that meant that they had no business there at all.

'Oh, bother. Dad's at home, getting ready for his blackout watch!' she sighed. 'It's Jamie and his friends. They're always causing trouble. I think we'd better go and see what they're up to. They can't behave like that, especially not on a day like today.'

They quickened their pace towards the churchyard, where it sounded as though the lads were having quite the party. Annie could hear laughter and the sound of stamping feet, then Jamie's voice proclaiming, 'Roll on Guy Fawkes night! We've got our very own Kraut Guy right here... Just need to dig the bastard up and we're in business!'

Annie and William passed through the gate and onto the path that led towards the church. 'Jamie Farthing! You're a disgrace!' Annie called. 'What the dickens do you think you and your little pals are doing? This is a churchyard. People are buried here.'

Clara woke up and whimpered. Annie bounced the pram, hoping the baby wouldn't cry. She had never seen anything so disrespectful as the boys tramping on the unknown airman's grave, kicking at the fresh mound of earth and howling with laughter. At the sight of Annie and William, they at least had the grace to stop, but Jamie set his hands on his hips.

'My brother's in this churchyard,' he said. 'He doesn't want any Kraut next door to him.'

'Your brother was a brave man. And an honourable one.' William's voice was clipped, his jaw tight. 'He'd be ashamed of the lot of you. Now get off home, and you can expect that your parents will hear all about this!'

Jamie stared at him for a few seconds, then spat onto the mound of earth.

'We can wait,' he snarled. 'C'mon, lads, let's leave these lovebirds and their bastard to have a canoodle.'

To Annie's surprise, William started forward and seized Jamie by the collar with such force that the teenager's feet briefly left the ground.

'Go home,' he told the young man firmly. 'Before I forget you're nothing but a brat of a boy.'

The other lads, so puffed up and proud before, shrank back.

'Sorry, sir,' Joe said. 'We was only having a lark, honest.'

'A churchyard isn't the place for it, though, is it?' Annie said. Clara was fidgeting under her blanket, her lips puckering. *Please don't cry, Clara.*

William released Jamie and the boys scrambled for the gate, but William's attention was already on Clara. He scooped her out of the pram and gathered her to him, gently shushing her as she snuggled down.

'Come on, miss,' he said. 'Let's have a nice walk somewhere other than the churchyard. I remember my nieces and nephews when they were tiny like you. They're all a lot bigger and louder these days.' He settled his gaze on Annie. 'Miss Russell, shall we?'

'Of course.' Annie smiled at the sight of him holding Clara as if he was an expert. 'There are so many lovely places to show you.'

And with that, they left the churchyard, leaving its inhabitants to their peaceful slumbers under the darkening sky.

FOURTEEN

I can ask at the butcher's shop.

The idea had come to Annie in the middle of the night. Goodness knows what she'd been dreaming about, but she'd woken with a start and sat bolt upright in bed.

Everyone had needed to register with their local shops in order to buy rationed food. And that meant that Ernie, Bramble Heath's butcher, might have noticed that someone wasn't using their ration book at his shop any more. Each book was carefully stamped each time a purchase was made, and, with food so scarce, it would be difficult to get by without one. But *someone* was, and it worried Annie to think that Clara's mother was going hungry.

First thing the next morning, she headed to the high street clutching the ration book. The blue sign above the shop proudly declared *Ernest Hewson Esq., Quality Butcher* in gold lettering. The same words were painted on the bicycle that stood outside, its basket already well stocked with wrapped parcels. Stephen, the butcher's boy, added one more as he came out of the shop. He greeted Annie with a nod, then climbed aboard the bicycle and pedalled away, off to deliver the provisions to the elderly residents of Bramble Heath.

Ernie's window, which before the war had been full of his wares, was now empty apart from government-issued posters about food, and the ceramic bull that had always stood there.

The bell jingled as Annie went in, the sawdust on the tiles soft underfoot. 'Hello there, Ernie. How's things?'

Ernie turned from the block, where he was slicing a large joint of ham, and greeted her by lifting his straw boater from his bald head. He replied in the jolly voice that Annie had known all her life. 'Dandy as they ever were, Miss Russell! And yourself?'

'Oh, not too bad,' she said. She didn't want to add that she was worrying about a woman she might never meet. 'I was wondering if you could help me, actually. It's about Clara, the baby we've taken in. Or rather, her mother.'

'That poor little lass,' he said, shaking his head. 'I'm not sure what help I'll be, but you can try me.'

Annie swallowed as she slid the ration book over the marble counter. 'I found this with Clara, hidden at the bottom of the hatbox. It must've been put there so that she wouldn't go without, even though it's an adult's book. I rather think it could be her mother's.'

A sorry-looking thing it was, with all its details scrubbed out. But Ernie had needed to learn how to work with ration books. Maybe he'd see something in it that Annie couldn't. He picked it up in his stubby fingers and opened it, his eyes travelling over the contents that the Russells had already scrutinised. After a moment, though, he shook his head. 'They all look one and the same, don't they?'

Annie bit her lip, holding back her disappointment as best she could. 'Yes... yes, I suppose they do.' But there was still that list of customers. 'Ernie, seeing as you're the only butcher in

Bramble Heath, everyone in the village and the hamlet is registered with you, I would imagine?'

He nodded proudly. 'They are,' he declared. 'And everybody gets a fair share.'

Everyone in the village. That has to include Clara's mother.

With rising hope, she asked, 'Has anyone not been bringing their book in lately?' She pointed to the ration book. 'Because of course, they couldn't, seeing as they've left it with me.'

This time Ernie furrowed his brow as he considered the question, but he was already shaking his head again. Annie's heart sank as she watched him, seemingly one of the few people who might hold at least a clue to the identity of Clara's mother.

'The only one I can think of is Mrs Glinka,' he said thoughtfully. 'She comes in for my customers in the hamlet, you see, and a few weeks ago she lost her book. It's a devil of a job getting a replacement and I don't think she's managed it yet.'

Oh, heavens. Ewa.

'Lost her book?' Annie glanced at the defaced ration book. Could she make out Ewa's name on it? But no, the details were too thoroughly obliterated. 'And she's definitely the only person in the village who has?'

'People are careful with them,' he said. 'I was surprised, because she's not the sort of lady I'd expect to be careless. She thinks she lost it on a trip to town; must've fallen out of her handbag. Ladies and their handbags!'

'Oh, yes, I know exactly what you mean,' Annie replied with a smile. 'And to be honest, if she was carrying all those ration books, it's not surprising she managed to mislay one of them. Well, thank you for your time, Ernie. I really appreciate it.'

'I do give her what I can,' he admitted. That didn't surprise Annie either. Ernie was a kind fellow. 'But there's not a lot left, and if other folk found out... well, I'd have a queue at my door asking for extra!'

'Don't worry, Ernie, I won't say anything.' Annie tapped the side of her nose. She wasn't about to land him in trouble. 'You take care now. And if you think of anything else, will you let me know?'

He nodded. 'I'll talk to the other shopkeepers too,' he promised. 'If they've got anything to add, I'll be sure to let you know.'

'That's very kind of you,' Annie replied as she picked up the ration book. The tight-knit community of Bramble Heath always helped each other when they could, just as Ewa was helping the community in the hamlet. 'Goodbye, Ernie, and thank you!'

She left the shop with a spring in her step. Ewa's lost ration book was, she felt sure, right there in her hand. The only problem was, how would she get the woman to open up and tell her who Clara's mother was?

FIFTEEN

SEPTEMBER 1940

Henry turned up the radio, and Annie and Norma leaned in to listen. It reminded Annie of that horrible day, which in truth they had all suspected would come, when Chamberlain had announced to the country that Britain was at war with Germany.

She drew her cardigan around her as the plummy-voiced BBC newsreader delivered the dreadful update.

The Germans had attacked London.

At first Annie was confused, thinking that the enemy had invaded by sailing up the Thames in U-boats. But as her rational mind took over from her panic, she realised it was something quite different, but just as terrible.

Bombs had fallen, hitting civilians. Homes, whole streets were gone and lives had been snatched away. The docks were ablaze too. The announcer urged everyone to remain calm, to listen out for air raid sirens and to follow directions to public shelters from ARP wardens and police if there was no shelter at home. The RAF were doing a splendid job, the nation was told, and had prevented the attack from being worse than it could have been.

Annie shivered, thinking of William and the other men at Heath Place, who doubtless had been scrambled in order to ward off the enemy planes. But it sounded like there must've been so many, wave after wave of bombers and their fighter escorts.

'Heaven help us,' she whispered.

There was a sharp knock at the front door. Norma put aside her knitting and hurried through the gathering shadows in the hallway to greet their visitor. A few moments later, her footsteps could be heard returning to the sitting room.

'Annie,' she said, 'Mr Bishop's had a bit of an accident out on his farm. He's sent his lass over to fetch you. It sounds like he'll need stitches in his hand.'

'Oh!' Annie was relieved it was nothing worse. If it'd been someone from Heath Place, then... 'Of course, coming right away.'

There wasn't anything she could do to stop the enemy planes dropping hellfire across the capital, but she could do this at least. She could help in her own small way.

Still in her uniform, she picked up her bag and took Mr Bishop's daughter back over to the farm on her motorbike. In the farmhouse kitchen, she cleaned and assessed the wound. Deciding she could stitch and bandage Mr Bishop's hand herself rather than send him to the doctor or a hospital, she set to work.

'That's a nice neat bit of sewing,' Mrs Bishop observed. 'I should get you to take my mending back home with you.'

Annie stayed for a little while, enjoying a welcome cup of tea. The Bishops were keen to discuss what had been going on in the village. It was getting dark by the time she said her good-byes, and she wished she'd left earlier so that she wouldn't have to rely on the weakened light of her headlamps in the winding lanes. Not that she was likely to meet anyone.

As she turned out of the long avenue that led from the farm, she heard the whine of the siren over the sound of her engine. She glanced up, scanning the sky. Wisps of high cloud caught the last of the sun's rays, turning orange and purple as they drifted across the early stars. And among them were bright pinpricks of light. She knew at once what they were.

Bullets, fired from planes. Up above Bramble Heath, a dogfight was in full swing. Every second out here on the road was dangerous, with the Spitfires and Messerschmitts fighting for their lives, swooping and banking in and out of the clouds, trading fire as they played cat and mouse with one another. Annie had to reach shelter, but she was welded to the spot, watching the battle unfold.

The flying was astonishing to watch, the skill of the pilots obvious to anyone who saw them. Annie couldn't begin to imagine what it took to hold one's nerve while ammunition flew through the aerial ballet.

Everyone else in the village would've taken shelter by now, though her father would be out pounding the lanes, on the lookout for the tiniest wink of light as the enemy flew directly overhead.

From above, she heard the sound of an engine screaming, and looked up to see a Messerschmitt in a spiral, bearing down on a Spitfire. Smoke poured from the German aircraft as it hurtled towards the Spit, and Annie couldn't believe the pilot had planned the manoeuvre. The Spitfire banked sharply to the right, but the wing of the Messerschmitt scythed through its tail with a sound that she would never forget, as metal tore metal in a white-hot explosion.

She couldn't quite believe what she was seeing. Ignoring the voice in her head that told her she should find cover as soon as she could, she kicked her engine into life and headed towards the planes. As a fireball filled the sky, she looked desperately for a parachute, straining her eyes for the white silk billowing in the dying daylight.

A single figure plummeted from the wreckage, shrouded in fire as he fell. Whether he was German or English, Annie couldn't tell, but, as the parachute opened above him, she knew he would need help. The burning planes tumbled to earth, but her thoughts now were all on the lone survivor. *If* he survived the flames and the fall.

Her local knowledge guided her through the lanes and over the heath, heading towards the spot where she was sure the man must've fallen – on top of the hill above the airbase. The field was choked with exposed chalk and was only used occasionally for grazing. A few scrubby trees, blown sideways by the wind, provided shelter.

The last scraps of daylight had gone now, and the burning wreckage guided her like a beacon. She dropped her bike, not stopping to put it on its stand, grabbed her medical bag and hurried on as fast as she could. She skidded over in her haste, but got back up quickly. Wincing slightly, but unhurt and unafraid, she plunged through the dark field towards whoever was there.

'Hello?' she called out, hoping that the pilot was conscious and able to reply. 'Hello, can you hear me?'

She saw the white of the parachute first, illuminated by the fierce flames of the inferno that had claimed both the Spitfire and the Messerschmitt. The man was sprawled face down on the grass, unmoving, but the fire that had engulfed him had mercifully been extinguished. For an awful moment Annie was sure he had perished, but as she drew closer she heard him give a low moan of pain.

She dropped down beside him. 'I'm Annie, I'm a nurse,' she told him as she reached for the pulse at his wrist. His flying gauntlets were burnt to a crisp, his skin hot, but his pulse was still strong.

'Annie...' he gasped, and she realised that he was English,

though even that simple word sounded as though it took every ounce of strength he possessed. 'It's William.'

'William!' She was so shocked she couldn't speak for a few moments. Then, 'I'm sure help is on its way from Heath Place, but I'll see if I can... ease things a little. Let me turn you over. Can you bear that? Feel free to yell like billy-o if you need to.'

William didn't answer, but instead closed his fingers around hers, holding on for a brief second before his hand fell limp to the grass.

SIXTEEN

Every time Annie closed her eyes, she saw snippets of the dogfight and the crash. The white of the parachute, the fire on the hillside, and William lying face down in the patchy grass.

The medics from the airbase had eventually found a way to get the ambulance close to the crash site, and had stretchered him away. While she waited, Annie had doused his burns in distilled water, using the bottle she kept in her medical bag. She had looked around for more water, wondering if there was a trough nearby, but she hadn't wanted to leave his side. Now, as she sat in the rocking chair back home, giving Clara her bottle, a heavy regret weighed on her.

I could've done more. I should've had more water with me. Anything, even milk, would've done. I could've done more.

It didn't matter that the medics had thanked her for the treatment she had given him in that dark, hellish field. All she could think of was the moment when his grip on her hand had gone limp, when he'd slipped into unconsciousness.

Once the medics had taken him away, the firefighters from the airbase had come and put out the flames. They barely noticed Annie, who was still crouched on the grass where

William had lain. The creamy white silk of his parachute was still there and, wanting to do something but not knowing quite what, she'd collected it up and put it in her motorbike pannier.

He might want to marry his girl when he's better. She could make a super dress with this.

When he's better, she kept telling herself. Not *if*. The parachute was now in a sack in a cupboard.

From the kitchen she heard the sound of the back door opening and two voices, speaking softly. One was her mother's, the other belonged to Betty.

'Annie?' Betty whispered as she popped her head round the door. 'I thought I'd come and see if you and little Clara wanted a bit of company.'

'Oh, Betty, thank you for coming. I...' Annie paused as she looked down at Clara, who was squirming away from her bottle. 'I'm sorry, I'm not much use for anything now. Clara's full, and I hadn't noticed.' She set the bottle down on the table and put Clara over her shoulder, rubbing her back.

Annie was wearing William's cravat. She had told her parents it was because it matched her uniform. But that wasn't why at all, and she was sure her parents knew. 'Have you heard anything about William? I was going to head over to Heath Place, but... I'm not sure I can bear it.'

'I've not heard a thing.' Betty stooped to kiss Annie's cheek, then dotted a kiss to the top of Clara's head. 'Look at her, cuddling that little stork. I keep asking around, but... Oh, Annie, what a thing for you to see!'

'It really was dreadful but, do you know, I'm actually rather pleased I was there, because it meant that I could help him.' Annie went on rubbing Clara's back. 'I only wish I could've done more. He was in a terrible state. I've never seen anything like it.'

'You did more than any of us could.' As Betty spoke, Norma pottered in and put a cup of tea down for each of the women.

She gave Annie a smile, then returned to the kitchen, closing the door behind her. 'You look tired out; has Clara been keeping you up?'

Annie shook her head. 'No, she's an angel really. She cries for her bottle, but Mum does most of the night feeds. I just...' She watched the steam rise from the surface of the tea. 'I just lie in bed, and close my eyes, and it's all I can see. The flames, and... and everything.'

And the lack of information was just making it worse. The pilot of the German aeroplane hadn't survived, but William's fate seemed a little less certain. At first, to Annie's horror, word had gone around the village that the wing commander was dead, followed swiftly by gossip that he was alive, but only just. Nobody seemed to know what to think, or what the truth was. It was like being in limbo.

'You know you can talk to me about it any time,' Betty assured her. 'I just keep thinking about you and little Clara, and about Wing Commander Chambers... Neil thought the world of him, you know. He really did.'

'I'm sure he did.' Annie sighed. 'I'm so sorry, Betty. You lost your brother, and here I am moping because William's injured. I've no right to be so upset about it, especially in front of you.'

But Betty shook her head. 'How long have we known each other? You're like a sister to me; you can mope all you need to. Heaven knows, you've been through it these last few weeks!'

The kitchen door opened again and Norma peered into the room.

'Mrs Glinka's here,' she said, apparently as surprised as Annie and Betty at a personal appearance from Ewa. 'You girls don't mind if she joins you, do you?'

'Not at all,' Annie said, trying to conceal her amazement. She wondered what had prompted the visit. Had something happened in the hamlet? 'Come on in, Ewa,' she called.

The Polish woman was buttoned into a heavy coat, her arms

folded tight over her chest as ever, though this time a shopping bag hung from one bent elbow. She sat down, looking from Betty to Annie and Clara, but she didn't take her coat off, nor did she seem to relax. Instead she perched on the edge of the armchair, straight-backed, with the bag in her lap.

'She's a pretty little thing,' she said, though her face was as straight and drawn as ever. Then, to Annie's surprise, she gave the barest hint of a smile. 'My grandmother used to call me her little *zabko*. Little froggy. Are you a *zabko*, Clara of the hatbox?'

Clara stuck out her bottom lip, and all three women chuckled.

'That does rather make her look like a frog, doesn't it?' Annie said, wondering again why Ewa was here. Could Clara's mother be one of the Polish women? After all, Ewa *had* lost her ration book. But Annie couldn't prove it was the one in the hatbox, and maybe Ewa was taking an interest in the baby simply because she cared. She smiled down at Clara. 'Look, it's Auntie Ewa, she's come from the hamlet. She helps me when I go to visit people there. We like Auntie Ewa, don't we, Clara?'

Was it Annie's imagination, or did Ewa look rather touched by that admission? Surprised, but touched.

'I have news about Wing Commander Chambers,' Ewa said, taking a little notebook from her coat pocket and peering at a page inside. 'Mateusz has heard for sure this morning that he is alive and in hospital. The Queen Victoria Hospital in East Grinstead.' She closed the notebook. 'Ward III.'

'Oh, thank heavens for that – he's in hospital!' Annie repeated, as if Betty hadn't heard what Ewa had just said. 'And he's... Gosh, hang on. That's the burns ward, isn't it? I read in *Nursing Times* that there's a very clever chap there who can do all sorts of marvellous things with people who've received burns. That's a relief. Oh, it really is. Will— Wing Commander Chambers is in the best place.'

Even though it meant his injuries were as bad as she had

feared. If not worse. She hadn't been able to make out much in the darkness and the inconstant light from the leaping flames of the wreckage, but it was obvious from what she'd seen of the crash that he had been severely burned.

'The women of the hamlet have sent this for Clara.' From the bag, Ewa took a folded blanket made of a rainbow of crochet squares. As she stood to offer it to Annie, Norma returned to the room and set down an extra cup of tea for her visitor. 'May I hold the little one? For a moment, perhaps?'

'This is beautiful, Ewa. Thank you.' Annie passed Clara to Ewa as she took the blanket. She marvelled at the squares, each in a different pattern and colour. It was a special gift from a community who had left behind almost everything they owned.

'When I ran from Poland, I had nothing. Not even Mateusz; he and I found each other again later.' Ewa held Clara close, speaking to the baby rather than Betty and Annie. 'You will always have everything, *zabko*. You will never have to run.' Then she whispered something to her in Polish, the words soft and soothing, and Clara sighed and rested her head against her shoulder.

'You're good at that!' Annie said. 'I don't know what you're telling our little froggy, but she's enjoying every word.'

'I am telling her that she will be loved.' Ewa settled back onto the chair, as straight-backed as ever. 'That she *is* loved.'

Betty gave Ewa a gentle smile. 'I'm sorry about my brother. He and those squirts he pals about with don't speak for anybody else at Bramble Heath, you know.'

This time Ewa's reply was one of those one-sided shrugs. 'He will learn,' was all she said.

'I hope so,' Annie said. 'I'm embarrassed at how they behave towards you. They don't seem to grasp that we're all fighting against the same thing – that silly little man in Berlin who's... who's...' She swallowed down her rage. No one needed to witness it. But if it wasn't for that silly little man, William wouldn't be on a burns ward, and thousands of other people wouldn't have been killed or wounded.

'Your brother was flying with 319 Squadron.' Ewa was addressing Betty. 'I know Jamie believes the Polish pilots could've done more for him, but he is mistaken. We have all lost people we love.'

Betty nodded, but Annie already knew that nobody blamed the Polish pilots for Neil's death. It didn't matter whether the men who flew out of Bramble Heath were Polish or British, they were still a family.

'Oh, Ewa,' Betty sighed. 'Nobody but Jamie thinks that the lads from 319 were to blame. I'm not making excuses, but our dad... well, he wasn't a kind man, and, when he died, Neil was like a father to Jamie. Jamie's grieving, but he won't admit it to anyone. It's just made him so angry.'

Annie nodded. 'It's true. It's impossible to get through to him, because he won't even admit it to himself. All that sadness is turned outwards into vitriol aimed at everyone else. But it doesn't make anything better, does it? It just spreads unhappiness.'

'We are only trying to make a home,' Ewa said. Her voice betrayed no emotion, but Annie could see the sadness in her eyes. 'We would like to make it here.'

'You're welcome here,' Betty assured her. 'And Jamie better get used to it.'

SEVENTEEN

Although it was Annie's day off, she was leaving early. She wanted to fit in a few visits to her patients before she left for East Grinstead and the hospital where William had been for the past week.

A nurse going to a hospital on her day off – what a busman's holiday!

As she reached the front door, she spotted an envelope on the mat. She picked it up, expecting it to be for her parents, but then realised that it said *NURSE RUSSELL* on the front in careful capital letters.

She opened it, wondering if it was a note left by someone who needed help. Instead, it was a card with a bluebird on it holding a ribbon in its beak. Across the ribbon it said *Thank you.*

Annie smiled. She'd become a nurse because she wanted to help people. The thought had never crossed her mind that she would receive praise for doing a good job. But she did get the occasional card or gift from her patients. Wondering which of them it could be, she opened the card, and found a message written inside in the same capital letters:

THANK YOU FOR CARING FOR MY BABY. KISS MY LITTLE GIRL FOR ME. BLESS YOU AND YOUR PARENTS. AND BLESS WING COMMANDER CHAMBERS.

Her hand shook, and she almost dropped the card. Clara's mother had written it, hadn't she? Annie was certain of it. She turned the card over, wondering if there was something on the back, an address, *anything*. She examined the envelope too.

But there was nothing.

She went back into the front room, where Clara was propped up on the sofa cushions, clutching her toy stork. Crouching down beside her, Annie showed her the card.

'I think this is from your mum. She's asked me to give you a kiss, so I shall.' She kissed the top of Clara's head. 'I'm going to see Uncle William. I'll tell him you say hello.'

After making her visits, Annie headed through the country lanes towards East Grinstead. She concentrated on the road, but her mind drifted as she thought of the card again. She'd shown it to her parents, who had been just as puzzled as she was; but more than that, all three of them had been touched by the message.

Surely it meant that Clara's mother would come to claim her? And surely it meant that she was a local? Because once again, she had come unseen to the house and left something.

Annie wondered about William being mentioned in the card. There was no thought in her mind that he could be Clara's father – with a background like his, Annie was certain that he wouldn't get a girl in the family way in the first place. And if he had, he would've done something more to help. He wouldn't have wanted history to repeat itself, surely. No, it seemed instead that this was someone who respected him and had heard of his injuries. Of course, everyone in the village knew what had happened, but Annie wondered if William's mention meant that Clara's mother was somehow connected to the airbase.

Could it be a clue? She might be the girlfriend of one of the pilots, or an Air Transport Auxiliary girl. Could she even be a nurse, or one of the WAAF who worked at Heath Place?

Annie was soon at the hospital. It was a modern-looking brick-built place with a wide frontage that overlooked a broad lawn. A tower stood sentinel with a bronze snake coiled around a staff on top of its roof. Patients were dotted about enjoying the sun, and the nurses wandered on the lawn with them, their white uniforms making them look like petals on the grass. A large Rolls-Royce was pulled up outside, and its uniformed chauffeur was leaning on the car smoking a cigarette as he waited for his passenger. No doubt someone rather grand visiting a patient.

Parry had told Annie that William was now allowed visitors and, in light of her being a nurse with an airbase in her district, she had been permitted to spend longer than just visiting hours there. She'd speak to the people caring for William, and other pilots with similar injuries, and find out what she should do if the same thing happened in Bramble Heath again.

After securing her motorbike outside, she headed into the building. It didn't strike her as a military hospital, even though she knew that servicemen occupied many of the beds. In the reception, she saw two men sitting on a sofa, one in his RAF uniform, the other in a linen suit, laughing as he tried to pour tea with a bandaged hand.

Annie wondered if she should rush forward and help him, but she didn't want to ask. She sensed an independence of spirit here, unlike in other hospitals she'd been to where the patients were treated like children, whatever their age.

After introducing herself to a nurse, she was led along a

bright, sunny corridor and into William's ward. Her heart hurried in her chest. She hated to think of him being injured so badly, and wondered what she'd see.

But he's alive. He made it. That's the most important thing.

A gramophone sat in the middle of the room with a stack of records beside it, and a bookcase stood under one window. Every windowsill had a vase of flowers. Beds were lined up on either side of the room, some men looking rather unwell, attached to drips and half asleep. Several were barely visible under their bandages. One man sat on top of his blankets in his dressing gown, half of his face hidden under wrappings as he read a paperback. He was still wearing his moustache, and what Annie could see of it was kept well trimmed.

'Good morning!' he greeted her cheerfully. 'You must be a new nurse!'

'I'm visiting,' Annie explained with a smile. 'I've come to see Wing Commander Chambers. I don't suppose you know where he is?'

The man pointed. 'Oh, yes! Billy's over there. Must say, he's doing very well for lady visitors this morning!'

She looked around, her gaze landing on a bed at the far end of the room. An elegantly dressed woman sat beside a heavily bandaged patient. She was the only woman in the ward who wasn't in uniform. The dark beady eyes of her fur stole caught the sunlight, and as she moved her head the perfectly curved feather on her silk hat trembled.

Heavens! That must be William's girl!

Annie thought back to the Rolls-Royce outside the hospital. Was that her car?

'Wing Commander Chambers!' she called cheerily as she approached his bed. 'Have you room for another visitor?'

Georgie – for who else could it be? – flicked her head round, her gaze sweeping over Annie in that appraising way ladies of a certain class seemed to be so skilled at. She rose from her seat and extended one gloved hand, upon which a diamond ring glittered.

Annie was surprised to see Georgie's engagement ring on display like that. It wasn't exactly etiquette, yet Annie tried to be kind.

She wants it to be seen. It is beautiful. And surely she must be proud to be William's girl?

'Darling,' she trilled, her voice so loud that Annie wondered if the crash had damaged William's hearing, 'there's a young lady here to see you!'

'Annie?' Within the bandages, William turned his gaze towards her. His voice was rasping, damaged by the smoke, but she could still recognise it. Where his hands rested atop the bedsheets, the skin was red and angry, despite the protection his gauntlets had offered against the inferno. 'What're you...?'

'It's my day off, and Dr Parry said you could have visitors, so here I am!' She stood at the opposite side of the bed from Georgie. She wanted to take William's hand, but she was wary of hurting him. 'Isn't this a wonderful place? Do you all fight over what to play on the gramophone?'

Georgie threw back her head and laughed. 'Imagine!' She chuckled as she took her seat again. 'You're the young lady who found William, I believe? I've certainly heard your name a few times. You're practically a heroine to the gentlemen in here.'

'Oh, yes, I found him,' Annie said. She glanced at William. 'But I'm not a heroine. It was just lucky that I was passing when... when it happened. And also that I know my way through the fields. That motorbike of mine is the heroine really!'

'A lady on a motorcycle!' Georgie exclaimed. 'Of course, *I* wanted to stay in London just like our dear king and queen, but Daddy won't hear of it. He's squirrelled the household away at the Sussex house. It's *such* a bore!'

Annie did her best to smile politely, but Georgie's words grated on her nerves. She thought of all the families who'd been bombed out in the East End, people who didn't have a second house in the countryside to run away to. *They* wouldn't have thought it was a bore to nip off to Sussex.

'They're having quite a time of it in London,' she said. 'But brave chaps like Wing Commander Chambers have been doing a fabulous job and it really could've been a whole lot worse.' She looked back at William, a man who had nearly made the ultimate sacrifice for the good of people he'd never know. 'How are you, anyway? Clara says hello. Everyone in Bramble Heath does too!'

'Will you send my regards?' William asked quietly, each word an effort. 'And give Clara a hug from—'

Georgie patted her hand on the edge of the bed. 'Aren't you going to tell her your good news?'

William shifted his gaze over to his fiancée, but even that simple movement looked painful. He shook his head and murmured, 'I don't have any good news.'

'Oh, Wing Commander, I'm sure there must be something.' Annie tried to be jolly, but there wasn't a great deal that was good about William's current situation. 'Go on, tell me what it is.'

'William, really!' Georgie clasped her hands together and announced, 'They're awarding him the DFC! Isn't that marvellous? He should be telling everybody, but instead it's left to me to do it!'

William gave a heavy sigh and shifted beneath the blankets. He looked to Annie and held her gaze silently, but she saw his fist clench briefly atop the bedclothes. The angry red skin grew white across his knuckles, just for a second, until his fingers relaxed.

'Congratulations,' she said, her tone not as effusive as Georgie's. She knew that William, who cared so much for his men, wouldn't be comfortable about getting an award. 'I'm glad you're being recognised, Wing Commander. Although if I had my way, you'd all get the DFC, as you're all terribly brave.'

'Couldn't get out of the way of a Messer... I don't deserve a medal,' he muttered. 'Nothing brave about being a bloody idiot.'

Georgie tutted. 'William!' she admonished. Then she curved her lips into a smile and chanced a surreptitious glance at the silver watch that shone on her narrow wrist. 'A DFC for my chap. We're all so terribly proud.'

'If you don't mind me saying so,' Annie said to William, 'I saw some of that dogfight. You could've turned around and run off, but you didn't. You stuck it out. I didn't see anything idiotic from where I was standing.' She looked at Georgie. That glance at her watch seemed rather rude. What could be more important at that moment than to be at her fiancé's bedside, giving him moral support?

Her expression must have shown some of her distaste, for Georgie explained smoothly, 'I don't want to tire the patient.' She kissed her gloved fingertips and tapped them briefly against William's hand. 'I'll leave you to rest. I'm sure Nurse Annie here has all sorts of medical business calling her away too, don't you?'

William shook his head. 'I'm poor company anyway.'

'Oh, you're not at all,' Annie told him, doing her best to smile even as she worried about his state of mind. It wouldn't be at all surprising for a man stuck in a hospital bed to feel gloomy. And she resented Georgie trying to surreptitiously dismiss her like a servant. 'I've got *pots* of time to spend with you, don't worry.'

'I'll be along at the weekend, or Monday at the absolute latest.' Georgie rose to her feet. 'I have *stacks* of letters to send about the DFC; everyone'll be wildly proud!' She glanced at Annie. 'Absolutely lovely to meet the lady who saved my chap. Cheerio, both. Remember – don't tire him out!'

'I'm not a damned child!' William barked, earning a pout from his fiancée, who wagged one finger.

'You're already too tired!' She kissed her fingertips again, but didn't touch him this time. 'Toodle-pip!'

Annie watched her go, the feather on her hat bobbing with each confident step, then turned back to William. As the silence between them grew, she wasn't sure what to say, and all her words tumbled out at once.

'I thought... I didn't know... but you were alive when I found you, and I hoped... Someone said... but I didn't believe them. I didn't *want* to believe them, then Mrs Glinka came round, and she told me you were here, and I knew you'd be all right then because this is such a marvellous place. I'd read about it, you know, and...' She stopped, almost out of breath. 'I'm so sorry. You don't need me talking nineteen-to-the-dozen like that, do you?'

William's fist clenched again, putting Annie off saying more. There was another heavy silence, but eventually he whispered, 'I wish... I... Why didn't you just let me die, Annie?'

She blinked at him in astonishment. This was so unlike him. Was he angry with her? Angry because she'd done her job? 'That's not what I do,' she said eventually. 'I'm a nurse. I care for people, look after them. I saw the parachute, and I knew I had to find whoever it was – whether our chap or the enemy. I couldn't just run off home.'

'I don't want to live like this,' he murmured. 'Like a... a freak.'

A freak? The word wrung Annie's heart.

'You're not a freak,' she assured him kindly. 'I can see you're all bandaged up, but it's still William under there, isn't it? And if you're in pain, you really ought to ask the nurses for some medicine. No stiff upper lips, please!' she added, trying to make him smile.

But even as she thought that, a horrible notion occurred to her.

Can he smile if he's been so badly burned?

Surely every man in this ward had been through the same thing? The men who were now chatting and laughing like old friends, on whose tables sat bottles of Scotch and clusters of glasses as though it was a gentlemen's club. None of them had escaped with minor burns, or else they wouldn't be here. Annie had made an effort not to stare, but the merest glimpse as she had passed the cheery patients had shown her the results of the ward's pioneering surgery. These were men who were being rebuilt, who had lost limbs, whose faces bore skin grafts, their eyelids and lips lost to flames, their ears and hair burned away. Everybody here must know to an extent how William was feeling at this very moment. It was a blessing that he'd been brought to East Grinstead.

'A cuppa for the lady.' The booming Yorkshire voice belonged to a man in RAF uniform who had arrived at the bed with a cup and saucer. He looked as though he was wearing an opera mask, but Annie recognised immediately that he had undergone one of the hospital's much-discussed skin graft procedures, replacing the damaged flesh around his eyes with healthy skin. His hair was sparse, the scalp beneath pitted and angry, but if he was self-conscious he showed none of it. 'Flight Lieutenant Piggy Hammond, miss, lovely to meet you! Wing Commander Chambers is already sick of the sound of my voice, but I make it my business to welcome new chaps and pretty young ladies. It's a rather scary place for the first few days, but we try to make the boys feel as much at home as we can – Boss McIndoe insists!'

Annie smiled at him as she took the tea. She wondered if William had told Piggy that he felt like a freak. She couldn't imagine the Yorkshireman would have much truck with *that*. 'Pleased to meet you too. I'm sure William will adjust, but you've all been through a lot. It's not at all surprising that it's a bit of a shock to the system.'

'What did I tell you when they brought you back from theatre?' Piggy asked William brightly. 'That you've now got the biggest, most reprobate bunch of brothers any fellow could ask for! And the prettiest visitors too.'

'Miss Russell's a nurse,' William murmured, settling his gaze on Annie again. 'She was the lady who helped me when... The accident... She helped me.'

'Then, Miss Russell, you must forgive me.' Piggy laughed. 'Some of the prettiest *nurses*, who are busy racing about the countryside saving downed Spitfire boys!' He dropped into a courtly bow, revealing more of the seared scars across his head. 'You've made this doughty Yorkshireman very happy, Nurse Russell.'

Annie chuckled. 'That's kind of you to say so. You've made me feel very welcome. I was on my way back from stitching up a farmer's hand, and... well, it was just luck, really, that I was there. Then the medics from the airbase came along, and this is the first time I've seen him since. You're looking a lot better now, William, I must say.'

'He won't believe you.' Piggy leaned over to briefly pat William's hand. 'The world hasn't ended, chum. It just feels that way at the start.'

With that, he strolled away, leaving William and Annie alone again.

'Everyone in Bramble Heath has been wondering how you're doing,' Annie said, trying to sound bright. She dived into her bag and took out the card she'd found on the mat that morning. 'And guess what? This came through the letter box. It's from Clara's mum, and she mentions *you* in the card.'

As she held it out to him, she glanced at the stand beside his bed. He'd received several get-well-soon cards, some with black cats for luck, others with flowers, and a hand-drawn one with a long-legged, long-beaked bird on it.

'She wrote, "bless Wing Commander Chambers",' she told him. 'That's lovely, isn't it?'

'So she *is* keeping an eye on her daughter. We thought she would, didn't we?' That was the first time he'd sounded anything other than despairing, Annie realised. It was a start.

'Yes, we did think so, and we were right, weren't we?' She grinned at him. 'And don't be too hard on yourself. It's not easy being stuck in hospital, especially not for a chap like you who's used to being up and about all the time. Do you know, I remember when Dad had to go to hospital, and he lay in bed grumbling for a few nights before deciding to solve the mystery of who was stealing grapes from the ward!'

She chuckled, hoping that William would enjoy the story.

His eyes twinkled within his bandages as he said wryly, 'The law never sleeps, eh?'

'It doesn't!' She laughed again, glad that he seemed to be perking up a bit. 'Unfortunately, he couldn't arrest the culprit. And do you know why? It was a mouse!'

'No shortage of those,' William murmured.

Annie smiled at him. He sounded tired, and she watched as the tension began to leave his body. It didn't take long before he was dozing. She sat there for a moment after his eyes had closed, then left the ward, thanking Piggy for her tea as she went.

In the corridor outside, she spotted a man who seemed strangely familiar. She realised where she'd seen him before – he was the well-dressed man who'd been up at Heath Place. And he was heading for William's ward.

EIGHTEEN

Annie had a little time to spare before going to speak to the medical staff, so she went outside into the sunshine to gather her thoughts. There were patients sitting playing cards together or reading newspapers. One was at a table with some paints and brushes, working on a vivid red picture of a poppy.

She found a bench to sit down on. It saddened her to think that William was so despairing about his condition, but what she could do? No one could be forced to be happy or to accept their lot. That sort of thing took time.

She watched as some of the men set up a game of cricket on the lawn, and a few nurses joined them as fielders. These men, like William, had scars that would never fade, but they were laughing and joking, limbering up for their match. Surely some of them – perhaps even all of them? – had arrived at the hospital feeling just as low as William did now. But they had come through it, and Annie hoped with every fibre of her being that he would too.

She thought about Georgie, who had kissed her gloved hand and briefly tapped that of her fiancé; who had preened and cooed over the medal he would be awarded, and who had looked at her watch when she wasn't looking at a spot over William's shoulder. She must be in shock herself, Annie decided, or at least that might be a charitable way of explaining her disinterest, though Annie wasn't sure Georgie knew what shock was.

Please don't let him down, she thought to herself. But Georgie's reluctance to spend time with him was clear enough to Annie. Surely it hadn't passed William by either? He must know her better than anyone.

And to think I saved his parachute for her wedding dress.

That gave her an idea. If she met Georgie again, she could tell her that was what she'd done. It had to help, surely. What could be more romantic than getting married in a dress made from the parachute that had saved the groom's life?

'Miss Russell, I believe, of Bramble Heath?' A man's shadow fell across the grass in front of Annie.

Australian? No, isn't that a New Zealand accent?

She looked up and saw a jovial-looking man wearing round horn-rimmed spectacles. She knew who this was: Archibald McIndoe, the surgeon who was pioneering the sort of surgery William and his fellow patients were enduring.

'Yes, that's right.' She stood, extending her hand to him. 'I'm a friend of Wing Commander Chambers. He's not been with you long. I've just been in to see him, but I think I must've worn him out. He's asleep now.'

McIndoe gestured towards the bench for Annie to sit as he said, 'The more rest Wing Commander Chambers gets, the better. He's been through quite an ordeal.'

Annie smoothed her dress over her knees. She wanted to hear all about the techniques McIndoe used, the walking stick grafts and everything else. But she wanted to ask him something else first.

'I know you're a terribly busy man, but...' She paused before deciding to go on, no matter how hard it was to broach. 'I fear

William's in a bit of a state. Up here.' She tapped the side of her head. 'He said he wished I hadn't...' *Saved him*. She couldn't say it, though. She took her handkerchief from her pocket and gripped it tightly, not wanting to cry in front of such an important man as McIndoe.

He settled onto the bench beside her and gave a long sigh, then said, 'The men in Ward III are facing a future they hadn't even considered.' He looked out over the grass, where the cricketers were playing as though this was any village green on any Sunday. 'But we won't let them mope. We're going to get them all back on their feet.'

'I'm glad to hear it,' Annie said, before adding hesitantly, 'I was so relieved that he was alive that I didn't think about him being scarred. He's all bandaged up, so I don't know... How badly was he burned, Mr McIndoe? If it's not too nosy of me to ask?'

'It's a long road, but he's not alone,' McIndoe replied. 'Sister Meally is keeping a weather eye on young William.'

'I'm glad about that,' Annie replied. 'And I'm glad you're looking after him. When he comes back to Bramble Heath, *I'll* look after him too.'

But *would* he come back? she wondered.

'That sounds like the right sort of medicine.' McIndoe smiled. 'We don't make them stay in bed or potter about in pyjamas. A fellow feels like he's healing once he's got his civvies on – or his uniform – and has had a wander around.'

On the grass, a wicket fell and a cheer went up. McIndoe paused for a few seconds to give the bowler a round of applause. The young man bowed a thank you and waved one heavily bandaged hand.

'Not bad for a chap with one hand in a mitten!' McIndoe chuckled before he went on. 'Wing Commander Chambers will be paying us some visits over the next few months once he's discharged, and, as district nurse, you'll be playing a part in his ongoing care too. I can see he'll be in the safest of hands.'

Annie beamed at him. That a man like him, pioneering in his treatment of such damaged men, should consider her a safe pair of hands was praise indeed.

Once the surgeon had gone back to his rounds, Annie returned to Ward III and found Sister Meally.

'Sister, could I have a quick word?' she asked her.

'Of course, Nurse,' Sister Meally replied in a breezy tone. 'You're the lady we have to thank for William, aren't you? Never underestimate us nurses, eh?'

'We're a force to be reckoned with!' Annie chuckled. 'Yes, I found him, and... Sister, has he said anything to you? He sounded in despair when I spoke to him, and it worries me.'

Sister Meally's demeanour grew more serious as she said, 'We see that in a lot of the patients, but we don't let it take hold; we pride ourselves that we're a family, and that's at the heart of our work. I can promise you, Nurse, I'm looking after your friend.'

'Thank you,' Annie said, resting her hand on the other woman's arm for a moment. She glanced down the length of the room to William's bed. He was still asleep, poor chap. 'You know, I'm so happy he's here. That he survived something so dangerous, and that now he's in the best place. I'll come and visit whenever I can, if you think it might help him get better.'

'Oh, I'm sure it would.' Sister Meally smiled. 'And if he's on your rounds when he goes back to work, I'll be very happy with that.'

As Annie headed off to her motorbike, she saw the well-dressed man again, in the corridor. She tried to be nonchalant, but too late, as her gaze had locked with his.

Oh dear, this is rather awkward.

'I'm terribly sorry, haven't I seen you before?' she asked him.

'Heath Place. You're the nurse who raised the alarm when

Wing Commander Chambers went down.' His words were clipped and businesslike, and he made no effort to remove his hat in greeting. 'Wyngate, Ministry.'

'Oh, yes, that's me.' Annie held her hand out to him but, if he was the sort of man who wouldn't remove his hat, she was fairly sure he wouldn't shake. 'Miss Russell. And you're from the Ministry of...?'

Wyngate glanced down at her hand but didn't take it. 'Wing Commander Chambers *will* be coming back to Bramble Heath, despite what he says. I assume that means he'll be your patient?'

Annie kept her hand extended, determined to get a shake out of the man. 'I'm so glad to hear that. You know, he's really taken to countryside life. And yes, he'll be my patient. They have medics at Heath Place, as you know, but I still go up there to help.'

His reply was a curt nod. For a moment there was silence, before Wyngate said, 'Good job with Chambers, Miss Russell, you showed a hell of a clear head back there.' At last he took her hand and gave it a very, very brief shake. 'Now back to work, Nurse.'

Annie blinked, taken by surprise.

'Back to work,' she said with a grin.

NINETEEN

Over the next few weeks, as William underwent his treatment at the hands of Mr McIndoe, Annie visited him as often as she could, riding to East Grinstead and sitting by his bedside. After one of these visits she decided that, with her investigations in the village coming to nothing, she would drop by Miss Clara's hat shop. It was worth a try at least.

Miss Clara's Millinery occupied a double-fronted shop on East Grinstead's main shopping street. Through the criss-crossed tape on the windows, Annie couldn't help but admire the items on display on long-necked stands. The hats themselves weren't large, but the trimmings were beautiful. Long feathers drooped from small felt bases, and brooches glittered on turbans. There were small straw hats decorated with wax fruit and flowers, and prettily swathed net veils on little velvet cloches.

Dotted through the display were Miss Clara's hatboxes, and the sight of them sent a rush of emotions through Annie. She was in the very shop that had produced the box that Clara had been abandoned in. At that moment, she felt close to Clara's mother. She was, perhaps, walking in her footsteps, and she felt that unknown woman's fears.

Inside, the shop was lined with display stands featuring even more wonderful hats, along with dressing tables where customers could try on Miss Clara's wares. A long counter ran down one side, with a large brass till, and pads bristling with hatpins.

She knew Miss Clara at once, because who else could the tall, graceful lady behind the highly polished counter be? She was older than Annie, perhaps as old as her mum, but looked as though she might once have been a fashion model. Poised and elegant, she greeted Annie politely.

'Good day to you,' she said.

'Hello there,' Annie replied. 'You must be Miss Clara. What a splendid shop!'

Miss Clara's smile grew warmer. 'Thank you, Nurse! I'm rather fond of it myself.'

'I'm after a hatpin,' Annie said, coming over to look at one of the collections. She didn't really need another one, but she hoped that buying something would give her time to talk to Miss Clara, and maybe find out something that might be useful. 'Maybe this one, with the pearl on the end? You must sell lots of them. It's very elegant.'

'Hatpins will always brighten up an outfit,' said Miss Clara with an air of fashionable authority. She carefully removed the pearl-headed pin from the black velvet cushion in which it sat. 'We may have to make do and mend, but one can't begrudge a little treat here and there.'

'Your shop must be keeping a lot of people happy at the moment,' Annie said. 'I live over in Bramble Heath. Do you know it? I often see your boxes around the village.'

'Bramble Heath,' Miss Clara repeated. 'It might ring a vague bell somewhere...'

'It's not a big place,' Annie told her. 'No one had ever heard of it really until they decided to put an airbase there. Now the village is full of airmen!'

Miss Clara raised an immaculate brow. 'Then I'll be sure to have plenty of wedding options available!' she teased.

'Yes, I think you'll need to!' Annie chuckled, even as she thought of how desperate Clara's mother must've been. There probably hadn't been a wedding for her. 'I'm sure my friend Mrs Glinka shops here. Her husband's a pilot...'

It was a bit of a punt, but she was thinking of how Ewa Glinka was always nicely dressed, with elegance rather than flashiness. Many of the hats in the shop would suit her and, if she had indeed left her ration book with Clara, then the hatbox could have been hers too.

'Mrs Glinka...' Miss Clara repeated, furrowing her brow. 'Is she a Polish lady?'

'Yes!' Annie smiled. *Finally, a lead!* 'Yes, she is. There's a whole Polish community in Bramble Heath now, and Mrs Glinka is like their mayoress.'

'Ah, yes.' From the knowing and rather amused look on Miss Clara's face, Annie was certain that she remembered Ewa. 'Yes, she bought a rather lovely piece from me last Christmas. I remember her husband had been promoted and she wanted to look her very best at the Christmas services. We do have a lot of Air Force wives among our clientele, from every corner of the world, it seems.'

'I remember that hat,' Annie said. And what relief she felt. She could definitely tie Ewa to the shop where the hatbox had come from. 'Everyone was complimenting her on it. It was so lovely, with those red glass beads that looked like holly berries, and the dark green velvet... It was gorgeous!'

A disheartening thought struck her. Ewa's visit had been a while ago – nearly a year had gone by since then. Even if

Clara's mother had been here with her, the shop owner was hardly going to know it was her with no signs of pregnancy.

But what if she had come here since Ewa's visit? Annie didn't know how to ask, because what could she say? *Did you have any pregnant customers come in during the summer?* Surely someone trying to keep their pregnancy a secret wouldn't have gone hat shopping? Still, she had to know.

'I'll take the hatpin, please,' she decided. It was silly, really, but she felt it would give her a connection to Clara's mother. While her purchase was being rung up, she continued pushing for information. 'There's another friend of mine who I think shops here. She's one of Ewa's friends too. She had a baby a couple of months ago, and she was wearing a lovely straw hat in the summer – I'm sure it must've been one of yours. Do you remember her? She was out here!' She mimed a pregnant belly with her hands.

'Oh, you must mean Mrs Lincoln,' said Miss Clara. 'I was taking tea with her just this past weekend. Such a bonny little boy she's had... Isn't he adorable?' She placed the hatpin in a neat little box even as she went on rhapsodising about Mrs Lincoln's blessed event, but Annie barely heard a word. Mrs Lincoln certainly wasn't Clara's mother. As Miss Clara closed the box, she added, 'I think ladies in the family way are a little more careful when it comes to buying hats in wartime. Every penny seems to be stretching as far as it can, don't you think?'

'Yes, of course, and who can blame them? It must be difficult getting everything together that mums need for a baby when things are in such short supply,' Annie replied, but her thoughts were elsewhere.

Had Clara's mother set foot in the shop at all? Perhaps she'd somehow concealed her bump? But how would she have got all the way to East Grinstead without *anyone* spying her? On the other hand, so many of the residents of the hamlet kept themselves to themselves; if it was one of them, it wouldn't be difficult to stay out of sight of the Bramble Heath villagers.

Her mind reeling with more questions than answers, Annie said goodbye and left the shop. But at least she now knew that Ewa had definitely been there. She could only hope that the Polish woman would open up to her about Clara's mother.

TWENTY

On Annie's next visit to William, she caught sight of a tube of his skin running up from his shoulder to his face, disappearing out of sight under his bandages. But as he didn't mention it, she didn't either. Instead, she brought him news from the village, and of her investigations into Clara. Although she now knew that Ewa had lost her ration book, and that several months earlier she'd been to Miss Clara's in East Grinstead, it didn't tell her who Clara's mother was.

'She changes every day,' she told William as she showed him a photograph of the baby that Norma had taken. 'See, doesn't she look different from when you last saw her?'

As soon as the words were out, she wished she could take them back. Clara wasn't the only one whose appearance had changed.

'I'm liable to give the poor lass nightmares,' he sighed, but there was humour in his tone. Just a little, but it was there. 'And you've had no more trouble from those social workers?'

'The only thing that would give Clara nightmares is if the milk ran out,' Annie told him with a smile. But it soon faded as she realised she'd have to tell him what was happening with Social Services. 'Oh, William, it's not good news, I'm afraid. They sent a very formal-looking letter asking if we'd found out who Clara's mother is, then they made a surprise visit, as if they thought the house would be an insanitary pigsty with a booze-fuelled party in full swing with Clara in the middle of it! Mrs Southgate reminded us very sternly that it's only a temporary arrangement. She said it can't go on indefinitely.'

William gave a tut of disapproval. 'Would you like me to ask some of the chaps here to write on your behalf? Piggy loves to organise a project, and Mrs Southgate wouldn't dare say no to a ward full of pioneering surgical wonders, would she?'

'That's such a sweet idea,' Annie said, glad that William seemed to be feeling more at home at the hospital. 'But I don't know. She even said – goodness, it still makes me cold to think of it – would we mind prospective adoptive parents coming to the house to visit Clara?'

'Some of them are quite decent folk, you know,' he said gently. 'No note from her mum either?'

Annie shook her head. 'Not a sausage. But you know, it's the strangest thing – maybe I'm just being paranoid, but sometimes it feels as if someone's watching the house. Perhaps it's because I know it's likely Clara's mum has been there on at least two occasions. I just wish she'd come forward, I really do.'

'I'll have a word with Pigs. Gives me something to do,' William decided. He reached over to the bedside table and picked up a small envelope. 'Ma and Pa were here earlier. They left a note for you. They get over as often as they can. Ma's still rather emotional.'

'I'm so glad they come to see you. All this Blitz business makes getting about rather a chore,' Annie said. She wondered if Georgie was coming to visit too. Annie hadn't bumped into her since her first visit. She took the envelope and opened it.

Thank you for saving our son.

Tears threatened to rise in her eyes as she read the words. She'd only been doing her job, hadn't she?

'I was in the right place at the right time,' she said. 'But will you let me have their address, and I'll write to them? And how's Georgie?'

'Oh, you know... busy, busy. She pops by when she can, but she has her commitments, even though she's hidden away from the bombers in the countryside.' William glanced across the ward at the sound of voices raised in laughter, then settled his gaze on his hands, which rested atop the bedclothes. 'Let me write down Ma and Pa's address. I think they'd love to hear from you.'

'That would be wonderful, thank you.' Annie opened the drawer of the locker beside his bed and found a pen and paper. Her voice gentle, she told him, 'You know, they were talking in the village about having a dance to celebrate winning the Battle of Britain. And I thought of you and all the chaps here, and I wished you could come along. Because it wouldn't have been won if not for fellows like you, would it?'

'We had a little – well, not that little – celebration here,' William admitted as he wrote out the address. 'But we didn't want to overdo it, not with London taking the bombardment it is. I've had a lot of letters from Brambles... a few requests to visit, too, but I'd rather they didn't. Those boys really are fearless, aren't they? I'm proud to have flown with them.'

'They're a marvellous bunch,' Annie assured him. 'And I know for a fact that they're ever so proud to have flown with *you*. Maybe... couldn't one or two of them come to see you?' She wondered if she had overstepped the mark, and added quickly, 'Not that you're starved for airmen around here!'

He gave a brief shake of his head. 'No, not yet. One thing at a time.'

Annie realised it was best not to force the issue, and smiled at him. 'All right. There's no need to rush into everything at a hundred miles an hour, is there?'

As it was still Annie's day off, she decided to take Clara for a walk in the pram when she got home. Autumn was approaching, bringing a chill in every gust of air, and the lanes around Bramble Heath rattled with the golden husks of fallen leaves. Clara didn't seem to mind, though, and cooed happily. Annie had to keep stopping to rearrange the blanket as the little girl kept enthusiastically kicking it away.

She paused at the mill cottage again and took Clara out of the pram to show her the ducks in the stream. Now that she was a little older, Clara could properly take them in. It was amazing how fast babies grew. She hadn't been a tiny newborn by any means, and now she was even bigger. But still adorable.

Annie heard someone coming down the lane, and she looked round to see Ewa. 'Hello!' she called. Ewa was wrapped in a heavy coat, her hands thrust into the pockets and her head bowed. She looked like a woman with something on her mind, and Annie wondered if she hadn't heard her call. Only as she drew closer did she look up.

'I am unwell,' she said, blunt as ever. 'I need your help, I think. Advice.'

'Oh, of course,' Annie said sympathetically. She wasn't surprised that Ewa wasn't feeling well, seeing as she didn't have a ration book and couldn't buy meat. She put Clara back in the pram, then turned back to the other woman. 'Please, just ask me. I'll help you if I can.'

'Monthly.' Ewa leaned over the pram and dabbed her fingertip to Clara's nose. Clara smiled. In the sunlight, Annie could see that Ewa was paler than ever, her eyes encircled with shadow. 'I bleed very badly. I'm very tired... what do I do?'

'I'm sorry to hear that, Ewa,' Annie said. 'It sounds like you might have anaemia. Do you have any other symptoms? A hurrying pulse sometimes, dizziness? Do you feel irritable?'

Even Ewa had to smile at that. 'Always,' she replied. 'Dizziness, yes. And a light head? I need to lie down more than I stand. This is anaemia?'

'I think it could be, yes,' Annie replied. 'We need to get some more iron into your diet. But forgive me, Ewa, I know you don't have your ration book any more.'

'It was lost,' Ewa said quickly, though Annie was sure that she knew precisely where it had gone: into Clara's hatbox. 'And they will not give me another unless I can prove I have exceptional hardship. How can I prove such a thing?' She shrugged her characteristic shrug.

'I can write a letter,' Annie explained. 'Having anaemia is a medical matter, so they'll have to replace your lost book.' She pictured the ration book, in a drawer in the kitchen dresser. But she knew there was no point in handing it back to Ewa.

Ewa nodded. 'Thank you.' Then she smiled and asked, 'I have an excuse to eat steak now, huh?'

'Yes, you do!' Annie chuckled, glad to see a crack in Ewa's shell with that flash of humour. 'But there's lots of other things you can eat too. Eggs – I can ask at Gosling's farm to see if they can spare you some – spinach, even chocolate and liquorice if you can find them. I'll bring some iron pills round for you the next time I'm at the hamlet. You can't take them for ever, but they'll definitely help.'

Ewa nodded. 'And it is something that will go? It's not dangerous?'

'As long as you start increasing the amount of iron you eat, it should be fine,' Annie explained. 'Unfortunately for us ladies, there's no magic wand to stop our monthlies – well, apart from having a baby or reaching fifty!'

Ewa replied with another sharp nod, then asked, 'And how is our little girl? She is growing so big!'

'Isn't she?' Annie replied. As Clara had kicked the blanket off again, she decided to lift her back out of the pram. 'Would you like to hold her?'

'I would,' Ewa admitted, accepting Clara from Annie's arms. She cradled the little girl against her coat, whispering softly to her just as she always did when they happened upon one another. 'And your family. You are still happy to care for her, yes? Our little gifts are helping? We spare what we can.'

Annie nodded. 'We're more than happy to care for her, and your gifts are so kind and welcome. The only thing is...' she sighed, and stroked Clara's soft blonde hair, 'Social Services seem rather keen to find her a permanent home.'

She thought of William, how happy he'd been with his adopted family. It wasn't the end of the world, but it seemed wrong for Clara to disappear and gain a new name and a new family without her mother's approval.

'No.' Ewa gave a sharp shake of her head. 'She is happy *here*. Her mother has placed her with you for safe keeping. Too many of us have lost our homes. She will not. I *know* her mother will come for her, I feel it!'

'I know, Ewa, it's hard,' Annie replied. 'Clara loves the village – and the village loves Clara. I just wish her mother would come forward. That's all she has to do. We can help her look after her child.'

Ewa whispered to the little girl again, then placed a soft kiss on her hair.

'This is her home,' she said. 'That is all that matters.'

After Ewa had put Clara back into the pram, Annie sent her home, insisting she get lots of rest. As Annie wheeled Clara through the village, something undefined gnawed at her thoughts. A feeling that something was off.

Why was Ewa so insistent that Clara stay in Bramble Heath? It made Annie wonder even more if Ewa knew who Clara's mother was. And that would mean that the woman was probably in the hamlet, a member of the Polish community. It would make sense, wouldn't it? Because the Polish were refugees who had fled the Nazi invasion with little more than the clothes on their backs, yet not a week went by without Ewa presenting Annie with a gift for Clara on behalf of the community.

And yet Annie wondered if she was adding two and two and making five hundred and three. The things she had found certainly suggested that Ewa knew more than she was letting on, but what actual proof was there that she knew Clara's mother? Her concern for little Clara was clear. But wasn't it just as likely that a woman who had lost her homeland would empathise with a baby who had appeared on a doorstep seeking shelter? And didn't a baby, so new and innocent in a world turned dark and frightening, offer everyone hope for a better future?

Time was passing, and winter was approaching. Clara seemed to be growing day by day, changing and learning to do new things. It was wonderful to see, but Annie and her parents were sad that the little girl's mother was missing out on seeing her daughter grow up. Or at least creating memories herself, as Annie still suspected she was watching from a distance.

Henry continued to ask around, and Annie kept an eye out, but they still couldn't identify who Clara's mother was. Neither Ernie or Henry had been able to find out anything further from the other shopkeepers, apart from the fact that Ewa was the only person in Bramble Heath and the hamlet who'd lost their ration book. Annie was sure that she had carefully plotted that – it would've been too obvious to put the ration book belonging to Clara's mother in the hatbox.

Annie had taken the exceptional medical circumstances letter to Ewa, which would mean she could get a replacement ration book, and kept dropping off iron pills for her, hoping they would help. And if they didn't, she would recommend that Ewa saw a doctor.

The boys in Ward III had kept their promise to write to Mrs

Southgate, and once again Clara received official permission to remain in Bramble Heath. It seemed that even such a stern woman daren't say no to Piggy and his pals. This time, though, it was clear that there would be no more extensions. Once Social Services had dealt with the consequences of the terrible bombing campaign that was bombarding London night after night, it would be time to decide Clara's future. She had a place with the Russells for now, but definitely not for ever.

Norma had made rock buns for Ward III as a thank you for intervening. Annie didn't have time to take them personally, as her days off had become a rarity thanks to the increased bombings and the casualties left in their wake. And even when she did have some time to spare, she still had to check that William would be able to see her and wasn't lying on another operating table or recovering from the latest round of surgery. But it wouldn't be for ever; they'd see one another again soon enough.

All of Bramble Heath was ready to welcome back their returning hero, and news of his medal had been received with the sort of warmth that the village did so well. It was little wonder that William had taken to this little slice of England, nor that it had taken to him.

The village street was quiet when Annie arrived at the post office to send the rock buns off to the boys. She pushed open the door, her arrival announced by the cheery jingle of the bell – one of the few the village heard these days. Betty and her mother were behind the counter as usual, enjoying a cup of tea.

'Morning, ladies!' Annie greeted them.

'Morning!' Betty beamed. She glanced over her shoulder as the door from the family sitting room opened and Jamie strolled out, swaggering as usual.

He greeted the women with what he clearly thought was a manly nod, then told his mother, 'I'm away out with the lads.' As he passed Annie, he said, 'Not got your kid with you today, then?'

'Jamie!' snapped his mother. 'Don't you dare, young man!'

Annie was glad she was being stern with him, but whether it would make any difference remained to be seen.

'Clara is at home with my mother,' she explained, putting the box of buns down on the counter. She smiled at Betty and Mrs Farthing. 'Mum's made rock buns for the boys up in East Grinstead. I promised William some, and now he can enjoy them with all the other chaps too!'

Jamie snorted and swaggered out. Turning from frowning at her brother, Betty softened her expression as she looked at Annie, before saying, 'I don't know if this is true, but I think William might be back at the airbase. A couple of the boys came in this morning and said they think he's in his rooms, but they haven't been told officially.' She added carefully, 'They haven't *seen* him either...'

Annie blinked in surprise. 'Really? I knew there was talk about him being ready to come back, but I...' She drummed her fingertips on the box of buns. 'I rather thought he might've mentioned it when I last saw him. I guess that was a few weeks ago, though, as I've not had time to visit. And, of course, the military are terribly hush-hush about everything, aren't they? He might've not known until the last minute.'

'Don't blame yourself for not being able to see him regularly, Annie,' Mrs Farthing said kindly. 'You've always been a hard worker, but... well, this business is a disgrace; you've not a moment to rest, with bombs dropping and who knows what. That rotten little creature in Berlin's got a lot to answer for!'

'I'd like to go over there personally and kick him in the rump!' Annie told them. 'I only get a half-day off here and there, and it's exhausting, but then I think of how drained the chaps were during the Battle of Britain, and I remind myself that at least I *do* get a half-day. Those boys never stopped.'

'And they won it!' Betty beamed. 'The likes of Woolly, Jarek and William... they're real heroes.'

'Aren't they just?' Annie smiled. 'I'm so proud to have known Woolly and Jarek. And William... well, he's the bravest person I know. I hope it doesn't take him too long to adjust to living in Bramble Heath again. You know how hard some people can find it if they're away for weeks or months in hospital.'

'Dr McIndoe's a marvel,' said Betty. 'I'm ever so glad it was his hospital that William went to. It sounds like he's good as new!'

Not quite, as Annie knew. But Betty was right, McIndoe *was* a marvel. And thanks to him, her friend was back in the village.

After posting the box of buns, Annie rode over to Heath Place. She had patients to see anyway, and on her journey she had time to mull over what Betty had said. What if William really had come back? She thought he would've written to let her know, but then the military moved at lightning speed sometimes, and she realised that it might've been as much a surprise to him as it was to her.

And maybe he just wanted some time to settle in. *That* wouldn't surprise her at all.

The weather was too cold now for the men to sit outside in the garden, but some hardy chaps had put their RAF greatcoats over their dressing gowns and were walking in the grounds, pipes clamped between their teeth. Inside, Flight Lieutenant Barker, with his legs and arms in traction, was serving as a card table for his friends, and had somehow managed to join in the game too.

'Hello, Nurse Russell!' he said cheerily.

'I see you're keeping yourself occupied!' Annie joked.

'I'm a very lucky sort of card table,' he explained. 'I might take it up for a living when the war's over!'

The men sitting around him laughed. Barker had baled out of his stricken plane, but had landed in a tree. The bough had snapped and his parachute could do nothing to slow the rest of his fall to the ground. But he'd decided he was fortunate nonetheless.

She looked around the room, wondering if she'd see William there. But there was no sign of him. Then again, if he'd recovered enough to leave the hospital, he didn't need to be on the ward.

'Miss Russell, good afternoon!' Dr Parry announced as he strode in. 'I was going to call on you later, but here you are!'

Annie smiled. 'As ever. What did you need to talk to me about?' No doubt there was a new patient on her list and Parry needed to discuss the case with her.

'Oh, just a general update.' He smiled, but Annie sensed there was more to it than that. 'Have you time to pop along to my office?'

'Of course,' she replied. 'I can come along now, before I get started. I wouldn't want to interrupt that card game,' she teased.

Parry gave a hearty chuckle, then led the way to the end of the ward and the cluttered little room that seemed to get untidier with every visit. To Annie's surprise, however, when they stepped into the office today there wasn't so much as a paper clip out of place. Instead, it was pristine, the desk empty other than an in-tray and a silver pen stand, while the files that were usually piled up on every surface were gone, no doubt into the row of cabinets where Dr Parry used to store his tea leaves.

'Gosh, you've been busy,' she commented. 'Although you do know it's the wrong time of year for a spring clean?'

'I've had a couple of visits from a gentleman from the Ministry in preparation for Wing Commander Chambers' return.' He gestured to a chair and waited until Annie had settled before taking his own seat. 'It became swiftly apparent that he likes a tidy ship. Hence we now have to clean this place up.'

Annie chuckled. Then she remembered the well-dressed man. 'Would that be a Mr Wyngate, by any chance?' she asked.

Parry nodded. 'You've met him,' he said with a wry smile. 'I told a little white lie, I'm afraid. I really want to talk to you about Wing Commander Chambers.'

Annie knitted her hands on her lap. 'There's a rumour in the village that he's back, you know. I have no idea if it's true or not. Have you heard how he is? I know he was hoping to be allowed to recuperate here.'

'He arrived back in Bramble Heath two days ago,' Parry replied. 'And as far as I know, nobody but myself and Group Captain Conway has seen him since. Obviously I'm not privy to the finer points of strategy, and nor should I be, but I believe he's already back in service, as it were. He won't be flying again, obviously.'

Annie beamed. 'Oh, I'm so glad he's back. That's wonderful news, isn't it? And how is he? I expect he's rather relieved not to be up in the air any more. He had a rather close squeak, didn't he?'

That was an understatement, she knew. But he was back at least, and her mind was already full of all the things she'd tell him and the places she'd show him. He had to see Clara too, of course, and how much she'd grown.

'I've spoken to Mr McIndoe, and Wing Commander Chambers will have to make regular visits back to East Grinstead,' Parry explained. 'But it seems the powers that be were keen to have him back on the base. Mr McIndoe doesn't seem to think he'll need much immediate medical aftercare, but he has asked me to keep an eye on things. The chap's had some fairly serious surgery, as you know.'

Annie nodded. 'They've explained some of the medical side of things to me on my visits. It's extraordinary what they can do.

Wing Commander Chambers didn't talk about it much, but I know he's been in and out of theatre.' Annie had never seen him without his face in bandages. 'And you know I'll help with his aftercare, Dr Parry, whatever he needs.'

'Friendship,' the doctor said simply. 'I'll admit I'm a little concerned that he has kept himself to himself; he used to be a social sort. The lads are keen to see their pal again. I know you and he have become friends, and I wonder... Just keep an eye on him. Mr McIndoe is sure – and I have to say, he has me convinced – that keeping patients in good spirits is as important as looking after their physical injuries.'

'Oh, I agree,' Annie said. 'They make so much effort at the hospital to help them stay jolly. And I'm more than happy to be a friend to William.' She shrugged. 'See? We're already on first-name terms. I am his friend, and I'll look after him, I promise. Do you think he'd mind if I drop in on him today? I'd love to see him again.'

'Not at all, if you've the time.' Parry smiled. 'He's up on the first floor, all the way to the end. Lucky blighter looks out over the rose garden.'

Annie got to her feet. 'I'll pop in to see him on my way out. I'm sure he wouldn't want me to drop everything and make a fuss. Thank you, Dr Parry, for trusting me with him.'

She went off on her rounds, checking on the men who had become her patients. But all the while there was another patient she was thinking of more than anyone else. She tried not to, because no one wanted to be treated by a nurse whose mind wasn't on the job in hand, but she was overjoyed at the thought of seeing her friend again after so long.

Once she'd finished, she went up to the first floor. She'd only been up here a couple of times before, when calling on the house's previous residents, before the Ministry of Defence had requisitioned it. The place still looked very grand, even if the more rare and valuable antiques had been put into storage.

She walked to the end of the corridor and knocked on the door. 'Wing Commander Chambers, are you free?' she called. There was no answer from within, but she could hear the quiet strains of classical music. He was in there, she was sure, but if he had heard her he wasn't answering.

This isn't a good sign.

She knocked again. 'William?' she said, thinking he might appreciate her dropping formalities. 'It's Annie.'

Still there was no answer, but she wasn't about to be put off. She had the feeling that Mr McIndoe and his team wouldn't be, after all. If she had to stand here all afternoon, she would.

'I'm afraid to say I can't lure you with the promise of rock buns,' she said conversationally, as if the door wasn't there. 'Mum made some, as I told you she would, to say thank you to Piggy and the chaps, and I posted them to Ward III this morning. I didn't know you were back – I would've saved one for you otherwise!'

She heard footsteps approaching the door, then William's voice as he said, 'That's very kind of you both, thank you. Do thank your mother... I'm sorry I won't be there to enjoy them.'

Annie rested her hand against the door. If only she could reach through the wood to take William's hand.

'Dare I say I'm rather glad you're not?' she admitted. 'Because the fact that you're here means you're doing really well. Oh, William, it's so good to hear your voice again.'

'The lads in Ward III sent a gift for Clara,' he told her. That struck Annie as tremendously kind, that they would think of Clara despite their own trials. 'Look, I'm a frightful horror, so you might prefer to wait outside, perhaps?'

A frightful horror? No, William, you could never be that.

'I'd much rather come in,' she told him. 'I haven't seen you in an age, and besides, this corridor's rather draughty!'

'Right... well...' She heard the sound of a key turning, then footsteps hurrying away from the door. 'Come in. But... well, I don't look like I did, Annie.'

But she had to see him. He was her friend, and she couldn't support him through a door.

'Here I come,' she said.

She turned the handle, and the heavy old door creaked open. William was standing over by one of the room's long windows, with his back towards her, looking neat in his blue RAF uniform. She took in his room, full of family photographs and books; there were even a couple of little balsa-wood mock-ups of houses on the shelf. A record spun on the gramophone as the orchestra finished its piece, then it fell into static.

'What a lovely room.' Annie wasn't sure how much space William wanted. She didn't rush over to him, but stood in the middle of the rug. 'And you must've got a lovely view, as well.'

She wished she could take back the words as soon as they were out. *A lovely view? What a glib thing to say.*

She heard William take a deep breath, and a moment later he turned to face her.

The light from outside was so bright that for a moment Annie could only see his silhouette. But as her eyes adjusted, she found herself looking at the new version of William, the damaged, rescued and repaired version. Her gaze ran across his face, even though she didn't want to stare.

She thought of the men on Ward III. But she hadn't known them before their accidents, so she couldn't compare them to how they had looked before. William had been a handsome man, she would admit that. And now he'd changed. His hairline had receded, and his skin looked stretched and waxy in places, pink and new in others. His eyes were narrower, and his lips were slightly twisted to one side. There were lines from stitches across his cheeks.

'I'm sorry, William – you must think I'm so rude!' She came further into the room, her hands outstretched to him, no longer seeing the old version of him that she remembered. 'It's just so wonderful to have you back. You know, up on that hillside, I thought... But I hadn't lost you, had I? Because here you are!'

'A rather sorry version of me,' he murmured. He winced. 'If Mr McIndoe could hear me, he'd have my guts for garters.' A hint of his old smile crept onto his face, before a brief flash of pain brought a shadow back to his expression.

'He certainly would.' Annie gently took his hands. 'And you're not a sorry version, you're just different. You've undergone a sea change, as Shakespeare said. I just... I just remember seeing you fall, and it's a wonderful sort of miracle that you're here.'

That you're alive, she wanted to add, but held back.

'Hardly. No more flying for me... not until we've won this bally thing. I'm supposed to be in some sort of strategic role or some such ridiculous thing.' His voice was shaky, and Annie realised what a moment this must be. Away from the hospital for the first time since the accident, away from the supportive men who had been through exactly what he had, away from the medics who had been there beside him every step of the way. 'How can I possibly advise the lads on strategy looking like this? Nobody would take a word that came out of this... this twisted face seriously.'

'I don't suppose any of them will be thinking of how you look,' Annie tried to assure him, but it was difficult. She wouldn't expect someone who was depressed to suddenly laugh and smile just because she'd told them to cheer up; in the same way, she couldn't expect William's anxieties about how the men would respond to him to vanish simply because she'd told him not to worry.

'I met that Wyngate chap, you know,' she went on. 'He strikes me as terribly important, and I don't think for one minute he'd give you this sort of strategy job if he didn't think you could do it. And the men will just think, here's our terribly brave wing commander, and we're jolly glad he's back.'

'I don't know if I should even *be* a wing commander any more... I won't be flying, after all, but apparently I'm to retain the rank.' He looked down at their joined hands. 'Dr Parry said the lads wanted some sort of welcome-home bash, but I said I'd rather not. It's enough with Georgie showing off the DFC all over London. I don't want any more fuss.'

Annie grimaced. 'Oh, dear, is she?' *You'd almost think she was the one who was flying the plane.* 'You don't have to have a party if you'd rather not. But remember, everyone in the village is ever so proud that you were awarded the DFC as well. I suspect that once news gets round that you're back, you'll be invited to every tea table in a five-mile radius.'

She wondered what he'd make of that. Would popping round for tea, like the Ward III men did with the East Grinstead locals, be something he would want to do?

'I don't think I will, once they've had a look at me,' he said with another little smile.

Withdrawing his hands carefully, he crossed to the mantelpiece and picked up a parcel. It was wrapped in brown paper and tied with a pink ribbon, to which a little card had been affixed.

'From everyone at the sty.' He held it out to Annie. 'That's what we call the ward, sorry. From the chaps to little Clara. We hope she likes it.'

'I'm sure she will.' Annie took the parcel. She felt choked up as she looked at it, thinking of the men who'd been through so much and still had much more to endure, but who cared for a little girl they'd never met. 'Can I open it now? I'll wrap it back up again for Clara.'

William nodded. 'Of course. Did our letters reach the Social Services people?'

'Yes, they did.' Annie did her best to smile, even though the news wasn't entirely what they'd hoped. 'Thanks to the chaps, we've got another extension, but I'm sorry to say it's still a temporary arrangement. Social Services are very busy at the moment, what with all the carry-on with the Blitz, but it means we've got more time to find Clara's mum. And now you're back in the village, I feel like we've got a much better chance of tracking her down.'

She dropped onto a chaise longue that stood under the window, and patted the seat beside her. 'Won't you sit down?'

He settled beside her, but he was as tense as ever. She would behave perfectly normally, though, because this was her friend and nothing would change that. What mattered was that he was here next to her, alive, which seemed like more of a miracle every time she remembered his figure tumbling from the Spitfire, wreathed in fire.

She read the card – *To baby Clara, love from the chaps on Ward III* – then tugged at the pink ribbon, the brown paper falling open to reveal a collection of little hand-painted planes on string. For a moment she wondered what it was, then she held up a long, curved section of wood that the strings were attached to, and realised it was a mobile of Spitfires and Hurricanes to hang over Clara's crib. Each plane had different markings and letters and was beautifully detailed.

'It's wonderful,' she gasped. 'What a thoughtful thing to make for her. I'll write a letter to thank them. And I can thank you now, of course, seeing as you're right here! Go on, show me, which one did you make?'

He tapped his finger against the Spitfire that hung on the lowest level of the mobile. The two neatly inscribed letters on one side of the roundel read *AC*, while the third, on the other side, read *W*.

'For Annie and Clara, you see.' He sounded a little bashful as he explained. 'From William.'

Annie beamed at him. 'That's so lovely of you, William. I'll tell her that – I'll point it out to her so that she knows you made it. And of course I'll tell her that the other planes were made by the chaps who've convinced Mrs Southgate to let her stay a bit longer. I do hope you'll come to see it in action over her crib.'

But even as she said it, she had the distinct feeling that he wouldn't. Or at least not without a little encouragement. But Annie had plenty of time to make sure her patient wasn't allowed to retreat too far.

'I'll do my best,' was his reply.

'I know you will,' she told him. 'Because you always do.'

TWENTY-TWO

The next day, Clara lay on her back in her crib, stretching her little arms up towards the aeroplanes that dangled above her. Annie had sat beside her for a good half-hour that morning telling her all about the men on Ward III, how William had been one of them and that he had made one of the Spitfires.

Not that Clara could understand, of course, and Annie wondered if she even remembered William. He had, after all, been absent from the village for most of her life. But even if the conversation on Clara's side consisted of coos and gurgles, Annie was certain she was saying something profound in her own way.

'You be a good girl for your Auntie Norma, won't you?' Annie leaned down into the crib and kissed Clara's cheek, and the baby cooed in reply.

'That means "have a lovely day, Auntie Annie, I'm going to have my nap now", doesn't it?' Annie beamed. 'And don't worry, if I happen to see Uncle William I'll tell him you said hello.'

She softly closed the door and went downstairs. When she went into the kitchen to say goodbye to her parents for the day, her father said, 'If you see William, tell him I'd like to take him to the George and Dragon for a pint.'

'I'll let him know,' Annie replied. 'But it might not be for a little while.'

'Mrs Miller was saying that she's not seen hide nor hair of that young man when she's been doing her cleaning rounds.' Norma looked up from the pan of potatoes she was peeling for dinner that night. 'The boys are worried about him too.'

'He's adjusting, that's all,' Annie said. 'Back at the hospital, he was surrounded by other men who'd been through the same thing as him. Now he's back at Heath Place, he's the only chap there who's got such significant burns. He does look different, there's no getting around that, but once you're talking to him you don't notice at all. All *I* thought was how glad I was that he'd come through.'

Norma gave a gentle smile. 'Invite him for tea next time you pay a call,' she said. 'He's always welcome here, especially after he spoke up for little Clara. I'll admit, I wondered for a minute or two if... Well, you know. But I don't think he's the sort of gentleman who'd shirk his responsibilities.'

Annie chuckled. 'You're not the only person to wonder that. I did too!' And her father's sudden cough seemed to indicate that he'd speculated the same. 'But he's not her dad. And I will ask him round for tea. I've told him that everyone in the village will want to invite him over. You know, once he's sat in some-one's parlour, laughing and chatting, it'll give him so much confidence, but it's taking that step that seems to be so terrifying for him.'

'Poor chap,' Henry said. Without realising, it seemed, he touched his own cheek, as if wondering what it was like for William. 'But I *will* be buying him a pint one day!'

'Your dad said he'd buy me a pint once,' Norma chuckled to Annie, as she picked up the peeler again. 'And look where we ended up!'

'Yes, look!' Henry puffed out his cheeks as if he was exhausted, then laughed. 'And I wouldn't be without you, Mrs Russell!'

Annie climbed onto her motorbike and rode to the hamlet. She had another bottle of iron pills in her bag. Ewa had still looked pale last time she'd visited, and Annie wondered if stress was making her anaemia worse. After all, she'd been through so much, and she hadn't had time to rest, as she was forever called on to act as translator and mediator.

As she turned the corner, she spotted some lads standing about in the lane. A stone dropped into her stomach as she realised it was Jamie and his gang. Hadn't they anything better to do on a Saturday morning?

But maybe I'm jumping to conclusions and they've come here to help out.

Jamie watched her approach, scuffing his shoe on the ground insolently as she came closer. Then he turned to his friends and went on chatting as if she wasn't even there.

Annie stopped her bike. 'Is there a particular reason why you're down this way?' she asked them.

Joe ran his sleeve under his nose. 'Free country, ain't it?'

Jamie glanced over his shoulder. 'We've every right to stand here if we want. Not doing you any harm, is it?'

'It's not *me* I'm worried about,' Annie told him. 'Don't think for a moment that I've forgotten what you lot got up to down here, harassing the Poles. Let them live in peace, won't you? At least, as much peace as any of us can find at the moment.'

'So stop picking a fight and crack on,' Jamie told her. He nodded towards the little row of houses. 'On your way.'

You rude little toerag!

'I'll be telling your mother and your sister about this,' Annie told him. 'How dare you speak to me like that.'

And with that, she started her motorbike again and rode into the hamlet, trying her best to stifle her annoyance at Jamie and his gang.

She reached Ewa's cottage and parked up on the path before knocking at the door. A minute or so passed before it opened and Mateusz emerged in uniform, looking rather strained. Ewa stood behind him, her face thunderous as she spat something after her husband in Polish. At the sight of Annie, he gave a smile and said, 'Just the person I needed to see.'

'Mateusz,' Ewa warned darkly, shaking her head.

'Ewa's losing weight,' he said. 'And she cannot afford to. Talk to her, Annie, please.'

'Of course I will,' Annie replied, trying to avoid sounding too concerned. Patients didn't like nurses and doctors to sound worried. It didn't do much for their confidence. 'I brought you some more iron pills, Ewa. They should help.'

'Go on in,' Mateusz told her, an invitation Ewa hardly ever issued, no matter how many times Annie visited. Then he gave Ewa a smile and said, '*Kocham cię!*'

Ewa shrugged one shoulder, but twitched her lips into a half-smile and replied with the same words before Mateusz strolled away, no doubt headed for the airbase.

Annie went into the cottage, wondering what her next steps should be with Ewa's treatment. She didn't want to frighten her, of course, but she was concerned that Ewa's illness might be more severe than she was willing to accept.

'I would ask how you are, Ewa, but Mateusz has already answered that for me,' she said. 'You do look rather pale still.'

'Rationing. Because I lost my book,' was Ewa's explanation, but Annie could see that she had lost weight. And she was hardly plump to begin with. 'How is Clara?'

'She's doing very well,' Annie told her. 'The men at Wing Commander Chambers' hospital made her a wonderful present. Lots of little planes to hang over her crib. She was trying to grab them this morning when she should've been settling for her nap. I think it's safe to say she likes them!'

Ewa gave another of those all-too-rare smiles. 'She is happy, yes?'

'Very happy,' Annie assured her, glad to be able to give her some good news.

As Ewa opened her mouth to reply, there came a raised voice from outside. Annie recognised it at once as old Mr Sobczak, who always took great pride in being a martyr to his bunions when she made her rounds. Ewa bolted for the door and wrenched it open to reveal Jamie and his gang clustered around Annie's motorcycle, with Mr Sobczak loudly berating them in Polish. He waved his walking stick towards the boys, who met his annoyance with jeers of amusement.

Ewa addressed the old man in their own language, listening to his furious reply before telling Annie, 'They were trying to let the air out of your tyres.'

'Were we heck!' Jamie protested. 'This old blighter was about to take your bike for a spin round the village. You're lucky we stepped in to protect it! He's a nutter, this one!'

Annie looked from Jamie to Mr Sobczak. How on earth could anyone believe that *he* would try to steal a motorbike?

'Jamie, stop fibbing and trying to shift the blame. What a ridiculous thing to say! Ewa, could you translate for me, please?' Annie's gaze returned to Jamie and his gang. 'Could you thank Mr Sobczak for stopping the boys? I do appreciate it.'

Mr Sobczak listened to Ewa's translation, thanking Annie with a nod. When he began to speak again, though, Annie's heart clenched. She might not understand his language, but she recognised the stricken expression on his face all too well. He had come to England with nothing and no one but his wife. The couple had trudged miles through conditions the likes of which Jamie, God willing, would never know, hoping to reach safety. And now here they were being jeered at and mocked by a brat.

'He says you should be ashamed,' Ewa told the boys fiercely, but they met her anger with stony indifference. 'You are a disgrace to your families, all of you! You think this man would have come here if he could have stayed in his home? The place he was born? You think he would have left that life if the Nazis had given him another choice?'

The boys looked shamefaced for a moment, but as they exchanged glances their expressions transformed into smirks. Annie sighed inwardly. She hadn't even had time to speak to Ewa about her health issues, and they were having to deal with this nonsense.

'I'm so tired of the lot of you,' Annie said. 'I've got a job to do, you know. I have to go around the area looking after people, and I need my bike to do it. It horrifies me that you'd even *think* about letting the air out of the tyres, let alone actually try to do it. And to blame someone else... Do you think you're clever, doing this? Coming into the hamlet and causing trouble?'

'We didn't do anything,' Joe claimed. 'Everyone picks on us, especially *this* lot.' He gestured towards Ewa and Mr Sobczak.

'We was saying just now,' Jamie said, 'poor old Chambers went up like a Roman candle and none of their lot were anywhere to be seen. Same as our Neil. Whenever there's trouble, the so-called Polish Air Force take off quicker than a bunch of scalded cats! Yeah, they hang about for the medals and the glory, but not when our lads are in trouble.'

This was the last thing William and Neil would want, Annie knew. They were brave, kind men, not the sort who'd allow idiotic boys to speak on their behalf. Jamie was taking after his boorish late father, it seemed, rather than the brother who had tried so hard to become the role model he needed.

'Jamie, I want you to listen to me,' she said, her tone shifting from stern to gentle. She *had* to find a way to get through to him somehow. 'I miss Neil so much. He was my friend, and I wish we could bring him back. And I wish Chambers hadn't been injured. But the Polish pilots were doing their best fighting the enemy. You can't blame them for what happened. I *saw* Chambers as he was shot down, only I didn't realise it was him. I went to the field where the wreckage ended up, and I didn't know if the man I'd seen falling from the sky was one of ours or a German. But I went because there was a human life in jeopardy. Don't you see? If I can go to help someone when I don't even know if they're friend or foe, why must you be so hateful towards all these people here? People who are on our side?'

'What's the point of their lot being over here?' Jamie asked, his words an angry garble. 'They should be looking out for us, but where were they, eh? Where were they when the Krauts were shooting seven bells out of Woolly or Neil or your mate?'

'Ask Jarek where they were.' Ewa's voice was flat. 'You insult every man at Bramble Heath when you talk that way. You insult every man who has died.' She jabbed her finger towards Jamie and added, 'You insult your brother.'

Jamie flew forward, only the swift intervention of his friends preventing him from reaching Ewa as he bellowed, 'You don't ever say that, you bloody bitch! Don't you dare!'

'That's enough!' Horrified, Annie stepped in front of Jamie, barring his way. 'If I tell my father what you've just done, you'll be in a cell in seconds for a breach of the peace. Is that what you want? Go home, the lot of you. Go and find something useful to do with your lives, because you're very lucky to have them.'

'Leave 'em to it!' Jamie spat, but Annie knew that she would have to speak to his mother again, for all the good it did. The boy simply refused to listen, and heaven knew where he might end up. 'C'mon, lads.'

As the young men sloped away, Ewa took Mr Sobczak's arm and whispered soothingly to the old man. Annie wasn't sure she'd ever seen her being quite so tender, other than when she was with Clara. But after Jamie's outburst, a little calm was exactly what was needed.

'I will take Mr Sobczak home,' Ewa said. 'He says if that boy doesn't change, he will end on the gallows.'

Annie sighed. She felt so helpless. Maybe if Jamie didn't have his entourage following him about, he wouldn't feel so brave, but he'd just as likely wage a one-man vendetta instead. If nobody could get through to him, his future looked anything but bright.

TWENTY-THREE

After sitting down with Ewa and checking that she was all right with her tablets, Annie went to speak to Mrs Farthing about her son. At least in Ewa's case she knew the steps that needed to be taken now to get to the root of the problem and settle on a course of treatment. But when it came to dealing with a hateful boy who wouldn't stop causing trouble, she had no idea what to do.

Her father had his thoughts on the matter and went to see Mrs Farthing too. That, Annie hoped, might help everyone to see how serious things had become, but would the realisation get through to Jamie?

A few days later, she snatched a spare couple of hours to go to the village to do some shopping. She was grateful for the fact that shortages weren't too much in evidence out here in the countryside, but it was clear that things were beginning to pinch. There were gaps on the shelves in the grocer's, and some of the potatoes looked a little green. When she realised she was about to have the last of the butcher's sausages, she stepped aside in favour of Mrs Hubbard, who had just come in and who had four small children to feed. There's nothing wrong with tripe and onions, she reminded herself as she left the shop.

As she looked up the road, she saw someone she thought she recognised. Not that that was unusual in Bramble Heath, but this was a woman Annie had only ever seen outside the village before.

Georgie.

She was dazzling in a white suit and matching gloves, the diamond glittering on her engagement finger just as it had in the hospital and the beady eyes of her fur fixed not on Annie, but on her chauffeur. Her arms were folded and she was tapping one immaculate foot as the middle-aged driver struggled down to his knees to examine the very flat front tyre of the sleek black Rolls-Royce that Annie had last seen parked outside the hospital in East Grinstead.

Annie went over to speak to her. 'Hello! Do you remember me? Miss Russell, we met at the hospital.' She glanced down at the tyre. 'Oh, dear. Looks like you're in a bit of a fix. Do you want me to find someone to give you a hand?'

Georgie narrowed her eyes for a second, then a look of recognition dawned on her face. 'The nurse! How *are* you?' She glanced down at the chauffeur. 'Do you need help, Jones?'

'I wouldn't object, ma'am,' came the reply.

She rolled her eyes and gave a theatrical sigh. 'If you have some frightfully useful local chap, do send him Jones's way.'

Annie nodded. 'Just bear with me a moment.' She went over to the pub on the other side of the street, where a group of older local men who could fix a tractor in seconds were drinking with some off-duty pilots. Having explained what had happened to Wing Commander Chambers' fiancée, a group of men came out, bringing their pints with them.

Annie tried to not to chuckle as the men crouched down around the flat tyre and conversed with the chauffeur. What would the well-bred Georgie think?

'Does the village have anywhere a lady might wait?' Georgie asked, watching the men with a frown. 'I don't go into public houses and obviously I'd rather not stand by the side of the road. Honestly, Daddy will be furious when he knows Mummy let me use the car... and this is *not* going to help my case!'

'There's the tea rooms,' Annie suggested, pointing a bit further along the street. She decided to use the opportunity to see how Georgie was taking William's return to Bramble Heath. 'I could do with a nice cup of tea myself, actually.'

Georgie glanced towards the car again, twisting her engagement ring as she seemingly turned the decision over in her mind. Then she gave a decisive nod.

'Tea.' She smiled. 'My treat, of course. Shall we?'

'Lovely!' Annie led the way up the street, noticing the curious glances of passers-by as the elegant Georgie walked at her side. When she opened the door to the tea rooms, she glanced back and saw quite a crowd of men and boys around the Rolls-Royce now.

She spotted a table free in the bay window. 'How about here? There's a lovely view out to the fields.'

'I've been rather naughty,' Georgie said as she settled down into one of the seats. 'I've been jollying back to London for the odd night on the town whenever Daddy's working. I would go simply *mad* if I were trapped in the countryside for the whole war!'

Annie wondered how Georgie could be so blasé about the Blitz raining down on the city. So many people would've loved to be able to get away from London, and yet she was deliberately going back. 'I take it you're going to bars and clubs that have got shelters?'

'Only the occasional party at the Ritz, and they wouldn't let us get bombed, would they?' Georgie gave Annie a bright smile.

'Isn't this adorable? We used to pop along to a little shop just like this when I was away at school!'

Annie smiled, even though she quailed inside at how patronising Georgie sounded. Some of the regulars, stalwarts of the local WI, were watching the glamorous woman. She picked up the menu. 'Yes, it's a lovely place. Shall we share a pot?'

'Let's,' said her companion, knitting her fingers atop the table as she gazed around.

Rose, the waitress, came over and Annie ordered. For once, Rose didn't take her presence as a chance to regale her with her family's every sniff, sneeze and ache. Annie suspected she didn't want to say anything so common in front of the dazzling Georgie.

Once they'd ordered and Rose was back at the counter, it was time for Annie to broach the subject of William. 'So you've been down to see Wing Commander Chambers?'

'Yes,' Georgie said, but she suddenly seemed a little less effusive than she had. Or a little less theatrical, at least. She twisted her engagement ring again and gave a long sigh.

'How did he seem to you? I've been up to Heath Place to see him since he's been back. He's... well, he's doing well, considering,' Annie said, before the pause became awkward. She wouldn't admit how difficult William was finding things. Not yet, anyway. Besides, Georgie would've seen as much with her own eyes.

'I didn't stay long,' Georgie admitted. 'Please don't think I'm awful, but... well, William isn't easy to look at any more, is he?'

Annie swallowed. She had seen several times in her career how hard family and friends found it to accept loved ones' illnesses and disabilities. 'Well, he looks *different*, I can't claim otherwise. But he's still William, isn't he?'

Rose appeared at that moment with a tray. It seemed to take her for ever to unload the tea service and pour their drinks. 'Will there be anything else?'

'No, thank you,' Annie said politely, waiting for the girl to leave again before turning back to Georgie. 'He's still William,' she repeated.

'Of course,' Georgie said, a little too quickly. 'If I spoke to you, Miss Russell, are you bound to keep a confidence?'

Annie sipped her tea, wondering what the other woman was about to say. She was finding it difficult accepting the dramatic change in William's appearance, that much was obvious. 'Yes, it goes with the territory, being a nurse. It helps to talk, doesn't it?'

'William is a lovely man.' Georgie picked up her cup and blew across the surface of the tea. 'But he and I... He's absolutely adorable, but we're not really from the same world. When I saw this dashing chap at the aerodrome, it never for a moment occurred to me that I would be *Mrs* Chambers one day!'

'And yet you're engaged to be married.' Annie nodded towards Georgie's ring. She wondered how long it had taken William to save up the money to buy it, the man who came from a different world from Georgie. 'Things change, don't they?'

'The war, you see.' Georgie put her cup down. 'One could hardly abandon a chap when he was about to lay down his life for his country, could one? And as I said, he is a lovely man, but... Oh, dear. Will you think me dreadful if I admit that I simply can't look at that face for the next sixty years?'

Annie lost her struggle to keep a smile. 'But his recovery is still a work in progress. He hasn't finished his treatment yet. I know he won't go back to looking exactly as he did, but... but...' Her words sputtered out.

She took a fortifying swallow of tea this time, instead of a dainty sip. The engagement had perhaps been doomed as soon as Georgie decided she couldn't call things off when the war started. And yet William didn't need this, not now. Not when he was so convinced that the world wouldn't want to look at him.

'I don't think it's dreadful, no,' she said, 'because you fell in love with a man who looked one way, and suddenly he looks another. But that DFC you're rightly proud of, that came at a cost. No one's unscathed by the war. Even if William hadn't been injured by the crash, he would have changed inside anyway.'

'But... do you think it might almost have been kinder to let him go?'

Annie stirred her tea, even though she hadn't added anything to it. She could hear William's voice again, rasping and smoke-damaged, declaring that he was a freak, and wishing she had left him to die.

She shook her head. 'He's still a well-respected man who is more than capable of working for the war effort. He's still in uniform, even if he's not going up in planes any more. He survived against the odds, and I think that's a marvellous thing, you know.'

But Georgie wasn't twisting the ring any longer. Instead, she was removing it, sliding the diamond along her gloved finger until she could lay it on the tabletop next to her cup and saucer.

'I was going to write,' she said, 'but that seems suddenly terribly impersonal.' She lifted her handbag onto her lap and opened it, withdrawing a black purse with a shining silver clasp. 'I know William thinks so highly of you. Would you tell him that I'm most awfully sorry, but I really can't marry him? I'm sure he'll understand.'

Thunderstruck, Annie dropped her spoon with a clatter. 'I... I can't. I'm not a messenger. Surely it would be best coming from you? He's ever so down in the dumps at the moment, but that'll change. Don't do this to him now. He just needs time, that's all. Please reconsider. *Please.*'

Georgie met her gaze and held it as she said again, 'That face... imagine looking at it for the rest of your days. I'm sorry, Miss Russell, but I simply can't do it!' She dropped a handful of coins onto the table and rose to her feet. 'You're a nurse, you've dealt with all sorts of things. Do tell William I'm sorry, and I wish him the very best of luck.'

And with that she stalked away across the room, leaving Annie and the engagement ring behind.

TWENTY-FOUR

That evening, Betty came round to see Annie. They got together when they could to listen to the wireless together, but there'd been precious few occasions lately. The new series of *Howdy Folks* was airing, and Annie couldn't wait to listen in and spend time with her friend.

'Howdy!' she joked as she opened the door for Betty.

'Howdy, folks!' Betty waved her hand, then gave Annie a quick hug. As she began to unbutton her coat, she said, 'I'm glad to be out tonight. Mum and Jamie are having a proper barney!'

Annie winced. 'I'm glad your mum's taking him to task, but will he ever listen? Honestly... trying to deflate my tyres, leaping at Ewa and calling her a you-know-what in the middle of the street... I've had a heck of a day too, I must admit. Let's enjoy the show and take our minds off things!'

Her gaze wandered to the cupboard, where she'd stowed William's parachute. She felt a pang as she realised there would be no wedding now. And even worse, she had been forced to be the bearer of Georgie's bad news.

She shook her head, trying to dislodge her gloomy thoughts. She took Betty's coat and hung it up for her on the stand, then ushered her into the front room. Picking up Clara's toys, she cleared a space on the sofa for her friend.

Clara was reclining in a nest of cushions on the armchair, and Annie passed her the stork, which she grabbed tight in her tiny hands.

'For a small person, you make a lot of mess!' Annie laughed, and gestured for Betty to sit down. Betty paused at Clara's chair first to stoop and kiss her on the cheek, receiving a gurgle of amusement for her trouble.

'She looks like the queen sitting there on her throne,' she chuckled. She picked up the cup of tea that was already waiting and took a sip. 'Have your folks taken themselves off for a well-deserved drink? I bet they didn't expect to have a baby in the house so soon...' She assumed a disapproving air and said in a high-pitched squawk, 'And you not even married, Miss Russell!'

'It's Dad's night off, so they've gone to the George and Dragon. It's just us three girls here tonight.' Annie laughed. 'Gosh, if Clara *was* my baby, imagine the scandal! Mum and Dad hope to be grandparents eventually, but they know it won't be for a while, seeing as I'm incapable of keeping a boyfriend for longer than a dance or two!'

But that word *married* rang in her ears. They had some time before *Howdy Folks* began, so she said, 'Betty, something horrible happened earlier. Not a medical thing, but... something I can't quite get my head around.'

Betty furrowed her brow, then quickly stuck her tongue out at Clara, who chuckled again. 'What's happened?' she asked. 'Are you still fretting about William? Some of the lads came in today and said he'd given a briefing to the base. They didn't say too much, but... well, poor man!'

'Yes, it's William.' Annie picked up her teacup but didn't take a drink. 'I suppose they told you how bad it is? It was a shock, seeing him for the first time, but it's still William for all that, even if he doesn't really feel quite himself.'

Betty nodded keenly. 'But they're so proud of him, Annie. Do you know *why* he won the medal?'

'He's never spoken about what happened,' Annie said. 'Why, what did he do?'

'The chap he was in the dogfight with was an ace,' Betty replied, widening her eyes. 'One of the Luftwaffe's best, Chalky said. The boys were headed out to intercept a German bomber and escort that was on the way to London, and the fighters came out of nowhere. Well, these Germans were swatting our boys for six and William drew their ace commander off... Ginger said he'd never seen anything like it. If not for William, the lads wouldn't have been able to get one over on the escort and the bomber would have made it to London. Not to mention that we'd have lost men if the wing commander hadn't been buzzing Jerry to break their formation.'

Annie'd had no idea. 'He took him on alone? That's incredible. Lured him away, and... Well, the dogfight I saw was just astonishing. It's awful it ended like it did, though, but I suppose up there the men don't think of themselves. Poor William – what a brave man. What a sacrifice to make.'

And yet Georgie, after making such a fuss about his DFC, could still walk away from him.

'Did you know he hasn't even kept the medal at Brambles?' Betty asked. 'He sent it home to his mum and dad. Isn't that sweet?'

'Oh, it is,' Annie said. But had he sent it back to them because he couldn't bear to see it? 'I saw Georgie today, William's fiancée. She'd come to visit him, and her Rolls got a puncture – I suppose you must've seen the crowd it attracted?'

'Oh, did I!' Betty laughed and rolled her eyes. 'Jakub came to ours for tea and he talked about that Rolls-Royce so much I asked him who he was walking out with: me or the car! That's what I get for falling for a mechanic, I suppose.'

'Well, it *is* a beautiful car, but not as lovely as you,' Annie chuckled. 'It's just a shame about the woman who turned up in it. Do you know what she did, Betty? We went to the tea rooms while the Rolls was being sorted out, and she took off her engagement ring. She's breaking up with William. And not for anything he's done, just for what's happened to him.'

Betty's hand flew to her mouth and she gasped, 'She's given him the elbow because he's had an accident? What a nasty cat!'

Annie nodded. 'She's a cow and a half. Said William "isn't easy to look at". What a thing to say, really! The poor man... After everything he's gone through, how can she do this to him? I pleaded with her not to break off the engagement, not now at any rate, while William's trying to get back into the swing of things. But she wouldn't listen.'

Clara cooed from her cushions, evidently aware of the emotion in the room. Annie picked her up and took her to the sofa, holding her tight.

'So she did it today?' Betty asked. 'I'll tell Jakub that William might need looking out for.'

'That's kind of you, Betty, thank you,' Annie said. 'But no, she hasn't done it today. She's really put me on the spot, you know. She's... well, she's made me her messenger.'

She took her handkerchief from her pocket and unwrapped the engagement ring. The diamond glittered in the lamplight. Betty's mouth fell open and she breathed, '*Oh!*'

'William doesn't deserve to be treated so badly,' Annie said. 'I don't want to do it, Betty, but I can't see what else I can do. It wouldn't be right for me to enlist one of the men at Heath Place. That'd make me almost as bad as Georgie!'

'I just can't believe anyone would be so cold,' her friend said sadly. 'And to just dump the ring like that, not even have the guts to tell him – oh, that poor man! As if he's not got enough to cope with! How can you love somebody and say, that's it, I can't look at him?'

But Annie suspected that Georgie had never really loved

William. She'd just gone along with the engagement for the look of the thing – and because of the war.

'I'm sure you don't need me to tell you that injuries like William's need healing on the inside as well as outside,' she said. 'Even though he's clearly going to be better off without Georgie, this is going to set him back. I look after people, Betty. The thought of having to hurt him is just awful.'

'Are you going to do it? Can't we get her back here and...' Betty shook her head. 'No, of course we can't. Women like her make me so angry. What a... what a cow!'

Annie shrugged. 'I'll have to do it. Georgie's grown up with servants to do everything for her, so why should breaking up with her fiancé be any different? Poor William – why did he have to get engaged to someone who's as shallow as a puddle?'

'He's got a good pal in you.' Betty smiled. 'We all have.'

TWENTY-FIVE

The next day, Annie left the house to go on her rounds, taking the engagement ring with her. She would've sworn that she could feel the coldness of the metal and the stone through her pocket, and it seemed to weigh ten times what it actually did.

She tried her best to smile for her patients, but the burden she was carrying exhausted her.

Once she'd finished seeing the men on the ward at Heath Place, she asked Parry where she could find William, and it didn't surprise her when she was directed up to the first-floor room again.

She knocked on the door. 'Afternoon, Wing Commander!' she called, trying her best to sound cheerful.

'Miss Russell.' William opened the door almost immediately. He looked far brighter, and she wondered if it was after his first briefing with the boys yesterday. Her heart went out to him, though, as she remembered her dreadful task. 'It's lovely to see you again.'

'And you too.' Annie did her best to smile, even though she wanted to run as far away as she could. *I really, really don't want to do this.* 'I was here on my rounds and I thought I'd pop up and say hello. How are you doing?'

'Dare I say a little better?' He moved back so she could step into the room. 'Georgie came to see me yesterday, and – you'll be very proud of me – I had to brief the boys. I was utterly terrified, but I did it. And they all came home safe and sound.'

'I'm so glad they're all back. See, you can do it, I knew you could! You're a bloody talented chap, William. And... erm... Georgie?' She tried to sound casual as she asked. 'How did that go?'

'Are you allowed a little snifter?' William asked, deftly changing the subject. 'The chaps clubbed together and got me a very nice brandy.'

That's not a good sign.

'I've finished my shift,' she said. 'I can leave the bike here, as I'll be back again tomorrow. So why not?'

And as William opened the brandy bottle, Annie got the distinct impression that he wasn't going to say another word about Georgie. Which really said a lot.

'Do sit down,' he told her. 'How's your little charge today?'

Annie sat down on the chaise longue. 'She's doing very well. She misses her Uncle William, though.'

'Did she approve of her mobile?' He handed her a glass. 'I do hope so.'

'She absolutely loves it! She lies on her back and stretches up, trying to reach the planes.' Annie took a sip of the brandy. It was delicious, just as William had promised, and she hoped it would give her courage for what she had to do. 'She watches them moving about and gurgles away at them. It's the *perfect* present. I need to write to the chaps on your old ward and thank them.'

The corner of William's mouth twitched into a smile as he settled into a chair opposite. 'The boys at the briefing were all very careful not to notice my face yesterday. I was grateful for that.'

What a shame we can't say the same thing about Georgie.

She nodded. 'That's good. And you must know, they have so much respect for you, they're not really looking at your face. They're looking at *you*, if that makes sense.'

'They're putting a lot of trust in me. Everyone is.' William took a sip of brandy and Annie knew that he wouldn't say any more than that. They all knew that careless talk cost lives, but the shadowy presence of Wyngate from the Ministry was proof enough that William's strategic role was of some importance.

'You're very good at what you do,' she assured him. He needed to hear that before she delivered Georgie's message. 'I don't suppose you heard about Georgie's car, did you? Some of your chaps at the George and Dragon lent a hand. They didn't put down their pints, though!'

'I did hear,' he admitted. 'I'm not sure it was the best use of petrol, but I haven't seen her for so long... She could only spare an hour or so.'

Annie took another sip of the brandy. Her gaze drifted towards the door. She wanted to run, but that would be cowardly.

'I'm sorry she wasn't able to stay longer,' she said. *Because then maybe she could've done this herself.* 'While her car was being fixed, she and I shared a pot of tea, you know, and... and...'

Oh, bother, this is making this dreadful business even worse.

Her throat tightened and she couldn't say anything more. She looked up at William and tried to grin but, despite having feigned a smile all day, it now failed her.

'Did she say something?' And when William asked that in his guarded way, Annie had the feeling that he already knew what was coming. Or at least he knew that something had been said, something about the accident and his scars. Because he knew Georgie well, and somewhere in his heart perhaps it wasn't a surprise.

'Yes, she did.' She put down her glass. 'Do you know, it's funny, but I kept your parachute. After the ambulance came, I collected it all up and took it home, because even someone as wealthy as Georgie will struggle to find silk for a wedding dress. And it seemed only right that she should have it. Seemed rather perfect to me, that she'd get married in a dress made from the parachute that saved your life. Only...'

She gasped back a sob. Something inside her was breaking. 'I'm so sorry, William. I really am. I begged her not to, but she'd made up her mind.'

William swallowed and gave a tight nod. Then he drank what was left in his glass in a single gulp and said in a clipped voice, 'So she asked you to do it, did she? I half expected her to leave it up to her poor bloody driver.'

'Yes, she asked me,' Annie replied. 'I didn't want to. I think she's a dreadful coward, William. It really isn't right for her to do this to you. But... you suspected, then, when she came to see you?'

He gave a mirthless laugh. 'No! No, have you ever heard anything so damned ridiculous? When she arrived, I was ridiculously happy to see her, but... I may be ugly, but I'm not stupid. I know when someone can't even bear to look at me.' He rose from the chair and strode to the window. 'And she didn't want me to kiss her goodbye, because she has a *cold*.'

'She wouldn't even...?' Annie shook her head. 'Oh, William, you're not ugly. Don't let her make you think that.'

She got up and followed him to the window but stayed a step back from him. Their reflections looked back at them in the old rippled glass.

'Not ugly?' He turned to look at her. 'I look like something out of a damn nightmare, Annie! I think I need to be left alone.

I'm sorry she saddled you with breaking the news to her washed-up cripple of a fiancé.'

'You look like a man who came back from the dead,' Annie told him. 'A little bashed about the edges, but who wouldn't be after what you survived? You're a walking miracle, William. Look at you, leading your men! And they all came home safe, remember? How can you *possibly* think you're washed up after achieving that? Just because of her – Miss Hoity-Toity, going to nightclubs during air raids because heaven forbid people not see her in her fancy clothes and her fancy car and forget she exists! She's just an expensive clothes horse, William, and you're better off without her.'

'A few weeks ago, I was a Spitfire ace with a fiancée who loved me,' William said simply. 'And what am I now?'

'You're William, and you're a hero, that's what you are,' Annie said gently.

'She sends back my ring, and they dump me back here to look at Spits I'll never be allowed to fly again,' he said bitterly. 'To work on a mission where I'll be asking my lads to put themselves in the sort of danger *I* should be sharing. Please, Annie, go home.'

'I think you've had your fair share of danger. Anyway, I ought to give you this.' Annie reached into her pocket and took out the ring. It glittered mockingly in the fading autumn light. 'Make sure the next girl you give it to deserves you.'

'The next girl,' he scoffed. He settled his gaze on the ring, regarding it as though it was a dangerous snake for a moment before he reached out and plucked it from her palm. 'Whatever this fetches, I'm sure the war orphans will be glad of it. And more deserving too.'

There will *be someone else. Not everyone's as shallow as Georgie, you know.*

But Annie held the words back.

'Are you sure you want me to go?' she asked, hoping there

was something she could do or say that would make everything better. William balled his fist and turned back to the window, and his view over the rose garden. For a few seconds he was silent, and when he spoke again his voice was firm and angry.

'Leave me alone,' he said. 'I've been humiliated enough for one day.'

Annie went silently back to the chaise and picked up her medical bag. She headed to the door and opened it, but before she went out into the corridor, she turned back. 'Take care, William, won't you?'

In reply, he gave her a curt nod, his back still turned and the engagement ring still held in that tightly clenched fist.

TWENTY-SIX

The next morning, an official-looking envelope arrived on the doormat addressed to *Mr and Mrs H. Russell*. Annie looked at the return address on the back, and her heart sank as she saw that it came from Social Services.

She took the post through to the kitchen, where Henry was eating his breakfast and Norma was giving Clara her bottle.

'Mum, Dad?' She held up the letter to show them. 'I think this might be from the fragrant Mrs Southgate.'

'Maybe she's changed her mind and Clara can stay as long as ever she needs to?' Henry said hopefully.

'She's welcome here,' Norma said gently, rocking the little girl. 'Go on, love, what does it say?'

Annie opened the envelope, humming a tune under her breath that she'd heard on *Howdy Folks*. She took out the letter and read it aloud.

Dear Mr and Mrs Henry Russell,

I hope this letter finds you and Baby well.
    The local Social Services Board have made the decision to

remove Baby into a children's home on Thursday 2nd January 1941. The current temporary arrangement cannot be sustained without the permission of the child's mother, as per for instance the evacuation of children into countryside accommodation. As this permission is impossible to obtain with the ongoing refusal of Baby's mother to come forwards, Baby must be removed.

The Board is very grateful for all you have done to care for Baby under difficult circumstances.

Sincerely,

Mercy Southgate (Mrs)

Annie threw the letter down onto the table and folded her arms. 'Mercy... what a joke.'

'*Baby*,' Norma scowled. 'Clara has her own name! Well, this does it for me. We've got to find her mam, because if she didn't want her she wouldn't have sent that card. Let's make sure the village knows what's to do, so word gets back to that poor lass.'

Henry nodded. 'I've got the morning off, but do you know, I'm going door-to-door again. I don't care a tinker's toss if I get reprimanded for it; I'm doing them a favour by getting back into my uniform as it is!'

'That's the spirit!' Annie said. 'I usually try to drop Clara into conversation when I'm on my rounds, but now we've got a date it might help Clara's mum get her courage up. First day back after the Bank Holiday. How bureaucratic.'

'Think hard, love, you know most of the ladies in the village,' Norma said. 'Is there *anybody* who's been acting out of character? Anybody you haven't seen for a bit, maybe?'

'I've been wondering about Ewa, in the hamlet,' Annie admitted, thinking of the lost ration book and the hatbox. 'She's a rather stern sort really, but lately she's been unwell. She said it was anaemia, but I'm sure she's burdened down with something. I think she must know who Clara's mother is.'

'The interpreter lady?' Henry said. 'It's worth a try, isn't it?'

Norma nodded. 'She's not much of a talker, but... Oh, it must be hard coming to a new place. I don't think I'd be much of a talker either.' She dabbed Clara's chin with a handkerchief. 'She might be glad of a friendly ear if she *has* got something on her mind.'

'You're quite right,' Annie said. 'I'll go over and see her now.'

Annie had left her motorbike at Heath Place yesterday. She hadn't wanted to ride home on it, not with brandy and anger in her belly. And she was angry now as well, thinking of Clara vanishing into the system when her mother was still out there. Fuelled by her frustrations, she walked at quite a clip to the hamlet and knocked at Ewa's door.

'Ewa, are you there?' she called.

'Who is that?' Ewa called from somewhere inside the little cottage. 'I'm busy!'

'It's Annie! It's really urgent!' Annie replied.

'A minute!' Ewa shouted in response, but, as Annie waited in the autumn cold, it seemed as though much longer than a minute passed. Eventually the door opened a little and Ewa peered out at her. 'What is it? Is someone unwell?'

'I need to speak to you,' Annie said, trying to glance around Ewa into the cottage. Even more now she had the impression that the other woman was hiding something. 'Can I come inside? This isn't something I want to discuss in the street.'

Ewa glanced back over her shoulder, then gave a reluctant nod and stepped back.

Annie went into the house. She didn't bother taking off her coat, just thrust out Mrs Southgate's letter.

'Ewa, I'm pretty sure you know who Clara's mother is,' she said carefully. 'I know you lost your ration book, and I know you had a Miss Clara hatbox. You did what you could to help a friend in need, didn't you?'

Ewa took the letter and read it, but her fixed expression didn't change.

'I had a sister once. I would have done anything for her,' she said as she folded it and slid it back into the envelope. 'When we fled Poland, the winter was harsh. My sister did not survive the journey.'

Maybe I'm wrong. What a terrible thing to live through, and I'm standing here flinging accusations around.

'I'm very sorry, Ewa,' Annie said gently. 'I didn't know. That's awful.'

'Betty is like *your* sister, yes?' Ewa held out the letter.

Annie took it. 'Yes, she is. It'd be dreadful to lose her.'

'And if your friend asked you to keep a secret for her, wouldn't you keep it? Even if you thought maybe you shouldn't?'

'Yes, I would,' Annie said. 'Ewa, you're trying to tell me something, aren't you? You *do* know who Clara's mum is! Look, you've made a promise and you don't want to break it. I understand that. But you *have* to tell Clara's mum about this letter. She has to see that this is her last chance. New Year's Day is the last day Clara will spend in Bramble Heath before they take her away.' She snapped her fingers. 'Then it's too late.'

There was a flicker of something in Ewa's eyes, but Annie wasn't sure what. Could it be compassion, she wondered, or sadness at the memory of her lost sister? Whatever it was, she blinked it away and said, 'I must keep my word, Annie, but I will share the letter with the community here.' She met Annie's gaze. 'I will make sure that what needs to be told is told.'

'Thank you, Ewa,' Annie said. 'And if it helps – whatever her circumstances are, whether she's a widow, or unmarried, it doesn't matter. You saw how the village helped when Clara first arrived. People care.'

'People care for the baby, perhaps. Even if there was a mother with no husband?' Ewa shrugged one shoulder. 'Maybe not so much.'

Annie knew she was right. People were judgemental. But she shook her head. '*I* care. My mum and dad, they care. Not everyone's keen to wag a finger. And you care too, don't you? Because you wouldn't be standing here looking so worried and strung out if you didn't.'

Ewa smiled. Just a little, but it was a smile.

'I will remember the letter,' she promised.

TWENTY-SEVEN

After Annie had finished her rounds for the day, she decided to take Clara out to get some fresh air. Even though it was getting dark and the autumn breeze was chilly, she needed to keep going. She hadn't stopped all day, because every time she so much as paused she saw Mrs Southgate's letter before her eyes. But maybe now that Ewa knew how serious the situation had become, Clara's mum would realise she couldn't hold back any more.

Every time Annie took Clara out in her pram, she felt as if the little girl's mother was watching from a distance. She pleaded silently as she followed the stream from the mill cottage, *Please come forward, please claim Clara before she's taken away for ever.* Her anxious thoughts didn't seem to fit with the peaceful route, which was beautiful whatever time of year it was, with golden and bronze leaves hanging above her in a canopy.

It was difficult to believe that the country was at war when she was in a place like this. It felt a million miles away from the Blitz that was raining down on London. But as those simple new graves in the churchyard showed, death was as close to

Bramble Heath as it was to anywhere. The sirens would sound again and they would all run for cover, and so it would go on until the war was won.

The ducks were making a racket as they settled for the night but, through their noise, Annie heard the sound of raucous lads. She was starting to wish she hadn't come out in the fading light after all, but she didn't want to be scared to walk around her own village.

'... and I said to her, listen, you give me any more squawk and I'll give you a hiding, just like Dad used to!' It was Jamie's crowing voice, filled with swagger as his gang laughed along. Nobody had really mourned at his father's funeral, but Jamie had only been a little boy. If he'd truly known the sort of man his father was, he wouldn't even dream of emulating him. 'If I want to go out, I'll go out. And if I want to go to school, I'll go. And I bloody well don't, do I?'

There was laughter and whooping and the sound of... was that a bottle hitting the path? Annie's blood ran cold. There was a drunken edge to Jamie's voice.

Oh, heck, I'm not walking into this.

She tried to turn Clara's pram, but it was heavy, and one of the wheels was caught between two stones in the path. Too late she saw Jamie and his gang rounding the corner ahead.

'... and then some bloody Polish runt turns up and starts running her gob off to my bloody mother, giving it all...' Jamie fell silent as he saw Annie. He lifted his beer bottle to his lips and took a swig. 'Speaking of runts,' he sneered, 'here's our very own village bastard!'

'Go home, James Farthing,' Annie retorted, trying to muster all the authority she could. His gang jeered at her as they came closer. 'And your friends too. And how dare you use bad language like that in the street – again!'

'They're our streets!' Jamie sneered. 'English streets. All them bloody Poles out with our Neil and not one of 'em could help him out? Pull the other one... they look out for their own. They ran over here fast enough, didn't they? They look out for themselves.'

Annie tried to turn the pram again, but still the stony path scuppered her attempt. The boys came nearer, step by step.

'Just stop it, Jamie!' Annie didn't want to sound frightened, but her voice had risen in pitch, betraying her fear. 'You're spewing hateful lies, don't you see that? You go on and on about your brother, but he'd be disgusted with your behaviour. He'd be disgusted with the lot of you!'

Clara started to whimper, and Annie bounced the pram, trying to calm her, but the little girl only cried all the more.

'You know what I think about your bastard baby?' Jamie kicked a stone past Annie as he advanced, followed by his friends. 'I think you and one of them Poles knocked her up between you. Even our Betty's fallen for 'em. Birds round here are a right bunch of bloody idiots!'

He took another step forward, and Annie retreated, instinctively tightening her hands around the handle of the pram.

'We live here, love,' Jamie crowed, almost nose to nose with her now. He prodded her in the shoulder with the bottle. 'Not like your foreign mates. Maybe they should all get back to where they bloody well come from and leave the defence of our country to the lads that were actually born here!'

'Don't you dare touch me!' Annie snapped, even though she was frightened of what this horrible boy and his friends could do. She had been trusted with Clara by her unknown mother, and had taken the baby straight into danger. 'You think *you* should be defending the country? You're just little boys out being loutish and scaring a baby! I'm very glad the Poles and the Czechs, the Jamaicans and Indians and everyone else are here! The more the merrier!'

Everything seemed to happen at once then. Annie could hear footsteps moving fast and stones tumbling from the pathway behind her. She even felt the rush of air as Jamie's hand came up to slap her as she instinctively tried to shelter the frightened baby in her pram. The slap didn't land, though, because another figure came between them, seizing Jamie's hand before he could strike her.

'You leave them alone!'

William.

Annie reeled back a step. She hadn't expected anyone to come to her rescue.

'Bloody hell,' Jamie murmured. *'Jesus!'*

Annie's stomach turned over. As far as she knew, she was the only person from the village to have seen William since he'd returned from the hospital. And now Jamie, who'd just been so vile to her and Clara, was standing there staring at his damaged face.

'This is what bravery looks like,' Annie told him.

Jamie twisted his arm free and took a few steps back. He looked like a boy again in that moment, and so did the lads who were always there, jeering behind their leader. Nobody was jeering now, though, least of all Jamie. He blinked once, then blinked again, and Annie knew before he spoke that he was desperately trying to recapture his swagger; but it had already deserted him.

'Then bravery's bloody ugly,' he retorted. He looked back at his mates and crowed, 'Right, lads?'

The boys were silent for a moment, before Joe shook his head.

'No, Jamie,' was all he said.

The others shifted uneasily. 'That's not a nice thing to say,' one of them muttered, and with that it was obvious that Jamie's gang, who'd followed him through thick and thin, had finally decided he'd gone too far.

Jamie spun to look at them. Then he jerked his head and said, 'Let's leave them to it.' He glanced back at William and hissed, 'She's never going to fancy you, mate,' before he hurried off along the path.

His gang looked awkward for a moment.

'Sorry he was so rude,' Joe mumbled, then he and the rest of the boys turned and ran off, in the opposite direction from Jamie.

Annie didn't say anything for a moment. Clara's crying had quietened, but she was still whimpering, so Annie leaned over the pram, giving her her finger to grip.

'I'm so sorry you had to hear that from Jamie,' she said gently. 'He's ungovernable. The things that come out of his mouth, and the way he behaves... Thank you for rescuing me – again.'

'I'm still a long way behind you in the rescuing stakes,' William said softly. 'Are you all right? Clara sounded terrified.'

'I... I think so.' Annie clucked soothingly at the little girl. 'I remember what his father was like, a drunken bully. Jamie's turning into him, it's horrible, and I was scared what he'd do. He said some dreadful things about Clara, and he was getting closer and closer. I tried to turn the pram around, but the wheel was stuck. It was stupid of me, really, I shouldn't have come out when it's nearly dark, and what a daft thing to do, bringing a pram onto an uneven path like this. And I shouldn't have snapped back at him, but I was scared. I didn't know what to do.'

William dropped to one knee, and Annie heard the clatter of stones. He was dusting his palms together as he rose to his feet. 'You were wedged in tight. All free again now.'

'Thank you!' she said.

Clara wasn't whimpering now, but cooing instead, her arms stretched up.

'What is it, little girl?' Annie asked her. 'It's your Uncle William. Do you want to say hello to him?'

'I'm afraid she'll scream all the louder if she catches sight of me.' William was aiming for humour, but Annie could hear the effort it took. Jamie's words had stung, and she hoped that he hadn't put William off leaving his rooms again. This might be his first trip out into the wider world since coming back to the village, after all.

But Clara was still cooing, and had kicked off her blanket in her enthusiasm.

'You do know that when Clara was a newborn, she couldn't see a lot?' Annie asked him. 'She's old enough to see much better now, but she doesn't know what you looked like before. Babies can hear very well, though. They recognise voices. And she recognises yours.'

William met Annie's gaze and held it, as though he were trying to fathom whether she was being honest or just kind. He cocked his head to one side. 'She won't be frightened?'

Annie shook her head. 'Everything's new and exciting to her. Mum said she saw a man with a moustache in the grocer's the other day and was fascinated by it! All Clara knows is that she recognises your voice and that it's the voice of her friend, so your face will be a friendly one to her.'

She could sense William tussling with himself as he looked from her to the pram. He drew in a shaky breath, then finally peered past her to where Clara was kicking her legs and gurgling a welcome.

'Hello, young Miss Clara,' he said gently. 'I've had a bit of a scrape...'

Clara waved her arms at him, and went on gurgling as her large blue eyes tracked his face.

'She does that to everyone,' Annie explained, hoping William wouldn't think that the little girl was staring. 'Look, it's Uncle William! He's been away because the other nurses and the doctors were patching him up, but now he's here, look!'

Clara beamed at him.

'She wants you to pick her up,' Annie prompted him gently. William glanced at her doubtfully.

'Are you sure?' he asked. 'I wouldn't want to alarm her.'

'You won't,' she promised. 'She's smiling at you! She's very happy to see her Uncle William again.'

With another glance towards Annie, William leaned into Clara's pram and gathered her up. He lifted her from her tangled blankets, watched by the cheery gaze of her little rag-doll stork.

'You've grown since I last saw you,' he told her. 'I think Miss Russell's family have been looking after you!' He blinked at Annie over Clara's head. 'I take it the ration book held no clues? And no more cards from her mum?'

Annie shook her head. 'No, there's been nothing else. Although... I went to see Ewa earlier, and she as good as admitted she knows who Clara's mum is.' She swallowed, not wanting to upset William when he already had so much else to deal with, but he needed to know. 'Time's running out, William. They're taking her away after Christmas.'

'The boys back at Brambles haven't a clue,' William sighed. 'But you think it's one of the girls in the hamlet? I wonder... If Ewa knows, might Mateusz?'

'I'm not sure,' Annie replied. 'She said she'd promised faithfully to keep it a secret, but surely Mateusz would've noticed if something was going on. They were having a row when I turned up the other day. I wonder if Mateusz was telling Ewa that she can't hang on to her secret any longer.'

'I'll be seeing Mateusz tomorrow.' He lifted Clara high into the air, much to the baby's obvious delight. 'I can ask him. He's a straightforward sort of chap. If he knows, I think he'll tell me.'

Annie hoped so, although Ewa was a very determined sort of woman. Some might even say stubborn. If she was keeping a secret, then she was keeping a secret, and nothing would change that.

'He must've seen Ewa's behaviour change,' she said. 'If Ewa is hiding Clara's mother, she must be feeding her too, even though Ewa doesn't have a ration book.'

'She doesn't have...' William began. Then he said with dawning realisation, 'Because she put it in the hatbox to help whichever friend is Clara's mum?'

'Yes, exactly,' Annie said. 'We know that Ewa had a Miss Clara hatbox, because we know she went to the shop. And we know that she sacrificed her own ration book to help her friend and the baby.'

'And all that's achieved is leaving them with less food to go round,' he sighed. 'I wonder if Mateusz has noticed food leaving their house, perhaps? Or maybe even one of Ewa's friends behaving oddly?'

'I'm sure he'll tell Ewa that you've asked him,' Annie reflected. 'And if *she* tells Clara's mum, then she'll realise that more and more people are trying to find her, because... We just want you to see your mum again, Clara, don't we? And you're ever so glad to see your Uncle William, aren't you?'

She beamed up at Clara, who was gazing down at William and gurgling. It plainly didn't occur to the baby that there was anything wrong with William's appearance. He was her Uncle William, and he was back, and that was all that mattered to her.

'I know it's not easy to face,' William told Annie gently, 'but perhaps she's made her decision. If she really can't look after Clara, it's a decision that we should respect. After all, I don't think I could've wished for a better family than the one that adopted me.' He swooped Clara in a gentle arc, just like the planes that used to swoop overhead in happier times. 'My mother took me to the orphanage and left me there: she'd made her decision. But then I keep thinking... Clara's ma *hasn't*. Maybe it's wishful thinking, but what if she left Clara with you because she knew you wouldn't rush her off to Social Services without a second thought? I'm glad you're in her corner, An— Miss Russell.'

'Annie, please,' she insisted. 'I sometimes think she's watching. Maybe she is now.' She looked up and down the lane, and called, 'Are you there? Are you watching? Please come forward. Your little girl needs you.' But there no was no reply, apart from the sighing of the wind in the trees. Feeling a little silly, Annie looked back at William. 'If she turned up and said, "I really can't look after Clara, I need to give her up to become part of someone else's family," then I would respect her decision. But she hasn't said that, has she?'

'No, she hasn't. And if she heard how those boys spoke to you, it's no wonder she won't come forward. It's a very hard world sometimes.' He pecked a kiss to Clara's cheek, then laid her in her pram and covered her with the blankets. Clara gazed up through the twilight, utterly content after her escapades in the air, and William asked Annie, 'Since it's dark enough for me not to frighten the villagers, could I see you home?'

'Clara and I would be honoured,' Annie replied. 'Do you want to pop in and see Mum and Dad? Although if you're not ready to, it's perfectly all right.'

'I don't think I'm quite there yet,' he admitted. 'But I do owe you an apology. I behaved appallingly about Georgie, but that wasn't your doing.'

'Mum and Dad will understand. And you really don't need to apologise,' Annie said gently. 'Would you give me a hand to turn this pram around?'

William took hold of the pram's handle and turned it with what seemed like very little effort at all. As he did, he said, 'The worst thing is, I'm not sure why I was surprised. She couldn't look at me in the hospital, you know, even when I was bandaged up.' He shook his head. 'She couldn't look at any of my pals either.'

Annie tried her best to be charitable. 'Some people accept

and carry on. Others can't. She just didn't know how to cope with what'd happened. I feel sorry for her, because I think you're smashing, and now she won't have you in her life any more.'

'I think you're rather smashing too,' he said cheerily, surrendering the pram to Annie. 'And little Clara, of course.'

Annie was glad it was getting dark so William wouldn't be able to see her blush. She gripped the pram's handle and they walked back along the lane. The mill cottage soon appeared, the water wheel still turning.

'It's lovely, isn't it?' she said. 'It's used for storage now, but I sometimes think it'd be fun to live there, just like people did in the past.'

'It looks a little sorry for itself,' William observed. 'But it just needs someone to show it some love, don't you think? It'll make a lovely family home one day.'

Annie nodded. 'Oh, wouldn't it? Imagine being a child growing up in that house. You'd feel like you were in a story every day. I suppose you'd know how to fix it up so someone could live there? I have to admit, I saw the little balsa-wood houses in your room.'

'Just something to while away the time in hospital. I made some for the boys to send home too,' was his bashful reply. 'But I must admit, I'd love to have a crack at that little mill cottage.'

Annie smiled at him. She was glad he sounded more positive now. 'You'd do a marvellous job of it too.'

They carried on along the path and Annie took him through the lanes she knew would be the quietest, so he wouldn't have to worry about anyone seeing him. The closer they came to the village, the more she could sense his trepidation growing, but still he walked alongside her. It would take courage just to do this, she was sure, now that he wasn't among the new friends who had been on the same journey and could understand all too well what he had faced. Mr McIndoe had started them on this path, but there were some steps that he couldn't take with them, and those must be the most frightening of all.

'You're very brave,' Annie reminded him. 'It must be rather unnerving going out and about again.'

'It's terrifying,' he admitted. 'But I have to brief the boys every day, there's no getting out of that. We lads from the ward keep in touch too, so we can buoy each other up a bit.'

'They're good chaps up at the airbase,' Annie observed. 'And I'm glad you're still in touch with the men from Ward III. It helps to know you're not alone in the grand scheme of things, doesn't it? Have you seen McIndoe since you've been back?'

William nodded. 'He's created quite a little club from us misfits.' He glanced towards her, his tone more serious when he spoke again. 'I... I never thanked you. For saving my life.'

Annie's thoughts returned to how William had reacted when she'd first gone to visit him in the hospital. She didn't want to remind him of how despairing and bitter he'd been.

'You saved me when that German plane came down,' she gently reminded him. 'So I was returning the favour. I will never regret the fact that I was there that night, because not many people get to save their friend's life, do they?'

'No, no, they don't,' William replied softly. 'When I was in those bandages, I never thought I'd feel a breeze on my face again. I don't think I cared, if I'm honest, but Mr McIndoe doesn't have much time for thoughts like that.' He gently kicked a stone along the silent path. 'Between your visits, Mr M and his team, and the lads on the ward, I found I started to miss the breeze and the sun, and... Well, it's still going to be a long road, but I'm on it. Going slowly, but on the path.'

'Why rush?' Annie said, as the silhouette of her cottage appeared up ahead in the shadows. It was nearly time to say goodbye. 'It's *your* path, and you need to go at your own speed. Dad is still insisting he's taking you out for a pint, but he knows you'll tell him when you're ready, whether it takes two weeks, two months or even longer. And you know that beer is going to taste *amazing*.'

They reached the garden gate. The night was still and quiet, even though Annie knew that over the cities of Britain it would be a very different story.

'Goodnight, William.' She opened the gate, then turned to him with a salute. 'Sweet dreams, Wing Commander!'

He returned her salute with a sharp snap of his wrist. 'Sweet dreams, Nurse Annie,' he replied.

Annie grinned at him, then turned and pushed Clara along the path to the front door. Now that night had fallen, and the blackout meant that no light leaked out from anywhere, William was only a shadow among all the others. But she knew he was there, and the knowledge of his presence made her feel safe.

TWENTY-EIGHT

NOVEMBER 1940

The kitchen hearth at the Goslings' farm was lovely and warm, but the friendship of Betty and the Land Girls was warmer still. They were planning a Christmas party for the village, pulling together everything they could think of to give them all – locals, pilots and the newly resident Poles alike – some much-needed fun and entertainment. It was a nice distraction for Annie, who still hadn't got any further trying to find Clara's mother over the past couple of weeks.

Becky, one of the Land Girls, was drawing up a list. 'So we'll be good for music, then?'

'Oh, yes, if we can convince everyone to join in!' Annie told her. 'There's a piano in the village hall, and we've got trumpet players and goodness knows what else in the village.'

'And we have excellent singers in the hamlet,' Natalia said. 'We can sing some Polish Christmas songs for you. Mr Nowak even managed to find a fiddle from somewhere. He loves to play.'

'Excellent,' Annie said. 'I'll ask Wing Commander Chambers if there are any musicians up at Heath Place too.'

'How is he these days?' Nicola asked as she added a little

more tea to their cups. 'We haven't seen him since he came back from the hospital. Is he doing all right?'

Annie was glad she had asked. The other girls all looked concerned. 'He's keeping to Heath Place mainly. He rather feels he's the odd man out at the moment. He's worried people'll stare.'

Annie glanced at Betty. They'd spoken on the way up to the farm about Jamie's behaviour. As Betty was such a good friend, Annie had initially been reluctant to go into every detail. Betty was just as disgusted with Jamie as Annie was, though, so soon Annie had explained everything that had happened on that evening walk. As ever with Jamie, though, the question remained: what could anyone do about him?

Betty met her gaze and offered a smile.

'Jamie ran into him,' she told the others. 'And he behaved like a little hooligan. Mum and me are at the end of our tether. We had a nasty piece of work for a dad and he's going the same way. It'd break Neil's heart.'

Annie reached out and closed her hand around her friend's. 'I know, Neil'd be devastated. But Jamie's young still. Maybe there's time to stop him turning out bad?'

'That poor wing commander,' Becky sighed. 'Tell him we said hello, won't you? If he ever wants to come up here for a cuppa, he's always welcome.'

'And to come to the hamlet also,' Natalia said.

'I'll tell him,' Annie assured them. 'And I'd love for him to come to the party, but we can't put him on the spot and expect him to get up and give a speech or anything. If we can convince him to just be there and have a wonderful time, it'd be a big step for him.'

Nicola nodded. 'And I think we should send him a note to say congratulations on the medal they gave him. Some of the boys were saying he doesn't make anything of it, but he should!'

'That's a lovely idea,' Annie said.

Frances, another of the Land Girls, who was a quiet sort usually, said, 'I could get hold of some cardboard from somewhere and paint a DFC on it. Hang it on the wall of the village hall. And if I can find enough cardboard and paint, I'll do a Polish flag and a Union Jack sort of crossing over, and some Spitfires and Hurricanes too.'

Becky was already writing it down. 'Perfect!'

'We'll have the party on a Sunday afternoon,' Nicola decided. 'And if Hitler sends his rotters over that day, they can answer to me!'

'Blimey, he won't know what's hit him!' Becky joked. 'And we'll need food, of course. If everyone clubs together with their rations, we'll have enough, won't we?'

'And bring Clara too,' Nicola instructed. 'Her first party!'

'She wouldn't miss it for the world!' Annie said, doing her best to smile even though she knew that if Clara's mother didn't come forward, it'd be the little girl's first and last party in Bramble Heath. 'If... if Clara has to leave the village, it'd be lovely for her to be there so everyone can see her before... you know.'

'We'll all adopt her ourselves if we have to,' Betty replied, squeezing Annie's hand. 'They can't take her away. She's a little Brambler!'

'She belongs in this village,' Annie said. 'I just wish the powers that be thought so too.'

Natalia didn't say anything, and Annie avoided glancing at her. If Ewa knew who Clara's mother was, then might Natalia too? But now was not the time to grill her about that. And maybe Natalia would go back to the hamlet and try to encourage Clara's mother to come forward before she lost her daughter for ever.

'A baby corner!' Becky said, writing it down. 'If everyone's coming to this party, that means babies too. I've no idea what they need, though.'

'Don't worry, I'm sure my mum won't mind organising that!' Annie grinned. She could already see Norma bustling about gathering everything for the little ones. It would be a wonderful way to bring the different parts of the village together. Jamie didn't speak for Bramble Heath; he barely spoke for his own gang any longer.

Annie was in a good mood as she headed home. After everything that had happened, the party was something fun to look forward to. But when she opened the front door, she heard an unfamiliar voice.

'She's perfect!' a woman cooed.

She hurried to the door of the front room and looked in. Clara was sitting on Norma's knee. Mrs Southgate was on the sofa, looking very pleased with herself, and beside her were a well-dressed man and woman. They were holding hands.

Who on earth...? Oh, no! Are they here to see Clara? Mrs Southgate moves quickly!

'A lovely little thing, with those big blue eyes and blonde hair,' Mrs Southgate said indulgently.

'Hello,' Annie said, walking into the room. She folded her arms. 'Mrs Southgate, this is a surprise.'

'Miss Russell,' Mrs Southgate said, 'may I introduce Mr and Mrs Ashford? They are very keen to adopt a child, and I wanted them to come and meet Clara.'

Annie was at a loss. She could see from Mr and Mrs Ashford's expressions how taken they were with Clara, and she thought of William's adoptive parents. She couldn't imagine how painful it was to desperately want a child and not be able to have one. And here was a little girl who'd been left in a hatbox on a doorstep. If they could give her a good home...

But no. Clara's mother was still out there. No one could waltz off with the little girl yet. They still had time.

TWENTY-NINE

A few days later, Annie went up to Heath Place. As she made her way from patient to patient on the ward, she spotted several men outside again, but one in particular, wrapped up against the cold on a bench, caught her eye. Once she'd finished with her last patient, she bundled herself up in her coat and scarf, pulled on her gloves and went outside to see him.

'William?' she asked as she approached him. She was smiling at the thought of seeing him again.

His attention was focused on the sheaf of paper clipped into a cardboard folder that he was holding in his gloved hand. At the sound of her approach, his head snapped up and on instinct he pulled his scarf higher, muffling his face to keep it from the sight of whoever was drawing near. On seeing Annie, though, he lowered it back to his chin and stood to greet her.

'Miles away,' he said with that little smile he could just about manage through the tightened skin. 'Rounds all done?'

Annie nodded. 'All done. I'm ready to head home. But seeing as *you're* here... Do you fancy a walk around the garden? Although you do look rather busy.' She gestured to the folder.

'One of those things we're not allowed to talk about.' They

both knew there was no need to say anything else. The war was full of *those things*. He tucked the folder into the inner pocket of his greatcoat. 'I'd love to go for a stroll, if you're sure you can spare the time.'

'Of course I can, for you,' she assured him, and took his arm. 'And I've got lots to tell you. Good *and* bad.'

'Which do you want to tell me first?'

'The good!' she said, as they wandered along the path. In the flower beds on either side, frothy pink sedums and delicate anemones gave the garden some colour among the glossy dark evergreens. 'You'll have heard about the party, won't you? I've told all the boys in the ward here, and Dr Parry knows too. They're going to make paper chains, and there's a sign-up sheet on the noticeboard in the hall asking for volunteers to join the band and to help out. I think everyone in Bramble Heath could do with a party, don't you?'

She wondered what William would say, but she had deliberately avoided telling him that he had to come. She didn't want to pressure him.

'The boys'll be glad of it,' he assured her. 'These last few months have been hell for them. It's all been rather relentless, hasn't it?'

'It really has,' Annie replied. It was all too obvious to her that William was talking of others enjoying the party, not himself. 'You're invited too, you know, but I perfectly understand if you think it might all be a bit too much and only intend to be there in spirit.'

He patted his coat in the place where he had tucked the folder away.

'Busy, busy,' he said, but she knew that even he would have time to socialise if he wanted to. 'I'm not ready, Annie. The thought of walking into a hall filled with people... The lads all know, but... I don't need to explain it to you, do I? You've been nothing but kind.'

'You're right, you don't have to explain it,' she said. 'I'm sure the boys will enjoy it, and'll raise a glass to you anyway. Of orange squash, naturally!'

'I've been invited back to East Grinstead for their Christmas bash,' he told her. 'But I don't know... We'll have to see how things go here before I make party plans.'

Annie smiled. 'How lovely of them to invite you. And do you know, I rather think it'd do the chaps good to see someone like you who's left and gone back to work.'

'Perhaps.' But she already had a suspicion that he would make his excuses. And a suspicion that his friends from the hospital wouldn't accept his apologies lying down.

William looked up as a plane soared overhead, banking in low towards the airfield. It was one of theirs, Annie knew, and she watched with him as the pilot brought the Hurricane down behind the trees, where the airstrip lay.

'Go on,' he prompted once the plane had disappeared from sight, though he had dropped his gaze away from it long before that. 'Bad news time.'

'It's about Clara,' she told him. 'I came home the other day, and guess who was there? Mrs Southgate, and she had turned up with a couple who want to adopt a baby.' She looked up at him. 'I feel so sorry for them, wanting a baby and not being able to, but they *can't* have Clara.'

'Oh, Annie, I'm sorry.' He stopped walking and looked at her. 'Can she just... *turn up*? We have a few weeks left yet, there's still time. It feels a little premature to be making plans.'

'I don't think she's supposed to,' Annie replied. 'But then I dare say *she'd* declare that we're not supposed to be looking after Clara. That poor couple – it's like waving a banquet in front of someone who's starving. I reminded Mrs Southgate that there was still every chance that Clara's mother would come forward, but I did feel rather as if she was trying to give us a push. You know, meet a couple who want a baby, then we feel guilty for saying no to them.'

William nodded. 'I'm sure they understand the situation,' he said carefully. 'And I'm sure they'll give a baby a wonderful home. I did ask Mateusz, but he doesn't know anything. He said Ewa's been anxious, but he puts it down to Jamie and his rotten pals.'

Annie gasped. 'Good heavens! Ewa really is a tough nut to crack, isn't she? I really don't know what we can do, William.'

'Neither do I,' he admitted. 'Short of knocking on every door in the village and the hamlet. If Ewa does know her ma, she'll pass on all the messages, and then it's up to Clara's mum. But Clara is cherished, which is more than some are.'

'I know,' Annie replied. 'And we don't know what position her father is in either. Did he know about the baby and refuse to have anything to do with it? Or did he never know, so he never got the chance to take responsibility?'

'Did she lose him?' William asked softly. 'I don't know if I prefer that to him being a bounder, but... she must've been desperate, whatever the situation.'

Annie nodded. 'You know, Dad's still going door-to-door asking if anyone knows anything. He's just as determined to find Clara's mum as we are, but...' She shrugged. 'Between us all, we'll make sure that little girl has a wonderful Christmas. Speaking of which – are you staying in Brambles for Christmas, or visiting your parents?'

'I'll be staying, I think.' They strolled on again. 'It depends how this strategic job of mine pans out. When I was in the air, I felt as though I was doing something useful... *contributing*. Now I'm stuck on the ground risking the lives of my friends instead of my own, and it's the hardest thing I've ever had to do – tougher even than lying in that hospital bed.'

'But you *are* contributing,' Annie said. 'And bearing in mind you're still having treatment, you *could* still be on sick leave.

You mustn't be so hard on yourself, William. You've risked your life, and you nearly didn't come back. Those friends of yours will be ever so glad to have someone like you on the ground looking out for them.'

'An ace in a day,' William sighed, his voice wistful. She remembered the chipper man who had visited their home a few months ago to have the wound on his neck dressed; how full of bravado and fight he had been. Now he was a shadow of that man. It was hardly surprising, but Annie wished there were more she could do to help him escape the doubt and seclusion that had claimed him. 'I felt invincible up there, you know. It never occurred to me that... Well, look at me. How could this happen to anybody outside of a nightmare?' He swallowed hard and shook his head. 'Some of the boys at Grinstead have gone back to their kites, but not me. Not with these grafts. Instead I'm stuck here, moving planes around a map and letting my friends take all the risks that *I* should be taking.'

'I know it must be hard,' Annie said gently. 'You didn't ask to change your role, it's been forced on you. But you're not just moving planes about – think of all the civilians in the cities you're protecting. Besides, you'd never put your lads in danger. I'm sure there are some strategy types who don't think of pilots, soldiers and sailors as human beings. They're only chess pieces to them – like in the last war. But you're not like that, not a bit.'

He gave a nod of understanding, then said, 'Clara and I are very lucky to have you in our corner. You're quite a warrior on the quiet.'

Annie chuckled. 'Do you think so? Boadicea on a motor-bike! I rather like that, don't you?'

'I do,' William admitted. 'Hitler better watch out!'

THIRTY

DECEMBER 1940

The year was drawing on, and Christmas was approaching. The second Christmas at war, with bombs dropping from the sky. But everyone was trying to be cheerful. As soon as December arrived, the ward at Heath Place had been decorated, and the men were happily talking about the village party.

Annie had gone up to the house on her usual rounds. The beds never seemed to be empty for long: as soon as one patient got back on his feet, another appeared in his place, with broken bones, or minor burns, cuts and bruises.

After seeing her patients, she put on her coat and scarf and headed along the corridor that led to the front hall. A flow of uniformed RAF and WAAF staff strode past, reminding her that even a district nurse was a cog in a vital machine; what she did supported the war effort, and that made her feel proud.

A door banged open, and the well-dressed man from the Ministry appeared, almost knocking Annie off her feet.

'Good afternoon,' she said, suspecting he wouldn't remember her.

'Miss Russell!' he barked. 'Would you say Chambers is a friend of yours?'

She wasn't surprised by his complete lack of preliminaries. She *was* surprised that he'd used her name, though; indeed, that he had remembered her at all.

'I... Well, yes, of course, Wing Commander Chambers and I are friends, yes,' she replied. Feeling rather put on the spot, she added, 'Gosh, I'm terribly sorry if it's not allowed.'

'Right.' He gave a very sharp nod. 'Get in there and talk some damned sense into him!'

Annie thought back to William's sense of failure that by not flying he wasn't contributing to the war. She nodded. 'Don't worry, Mr Wyngate, I'll have a word with him. Is he feeling glum again that he's not to fly any more?'

But why would that warrant a visit from the man from the Ministry?

'You've heard this nonsense before?' he asked.

'As a matter of fact, I have,' she replied. 'I did try to convince him that he's doing a splendid job on the ground these days. They also serve, and all that. We do our bit as best we can, don't we?'

'If he steps down, he *will* regret it.' Wyngate's voice was low and urgent. 'And so will every man on this base. The only men who'll have cause to celebrate will be flying in the bloody Luftwaffe. Do you understand?'

Steps down? Annie went cold. 'Yes, I do understand. Don't worry, we nurses are experts at giving pep talks. But they only work if people are willing to listen.'

She glanced at the door through which Wyngate had emerged, wondering if William was behind it, aware that he was being discussed. Wyngate pointed towards it and gave her a nod, which she took as a prompt.

She knocked on the door and the sound echoed in the corridor. 'Wing Commander Chambers? It's Miss Russell. Can you spare a moment?'

Wyngate rolled his eyes and strode away as William opened

the door and said, 'Careless talk doesn't apply to men from the Ministry, I see.' He gave a heavy sigh. 'Come in, Annie.'

The room appeared to have once been a gentleman's study, with green leather wingback armchairs in front of a fireplace adorned by a painting of a racehorse. Long windows looked out over the garden, and a heavy wooden desk with green light shades stood to one side. But there was no mistaking that it was now an office at an airbase, with several maps hung up on the walls, and two battered tin filing cabinets flanking the elegant windows. A typewriter sat on a rickety metal table.

It suited William, somehow, that the room was a blend of two different styles; traditional but at the same time prepared for the fight.

Except... he wasn't any more.

'How are you?' Annie said, and gently touched his arm.

'Wrung out.' He sank down into one of the armchairs and put his face in his hands. On the mantelpiece an ashtray still smouldered with the remains of the cigarette Wyngate must have left there, and a thin plume of smoke snaked up into the gloom.

'You must be so busy,' Annie said sympathetically, as she took the armchair opposite him. 'I collided with Wyngate in the corridor just now. He said you're thinking of standing down.' She tipped her head to one side. 'Is that true, William?'

He shook his head and murmured against his palm, 'I'm not thinking about it...'

Astonished, Annie said, 'You... you've already decided, is that what you mean?'

She left her chair and sat down on the footstool in front of William. She took his hands in her own and held them gently.

'Do you know, I have a theory,' she told him. 'People who are actually very good at what they do often don't realise it. Because they just *do* it. And they don't need to go about telling the world about how wonderful they are. You are doing a very difficult job, William, under very difficult circumstances. You were even chosen for it by Mr Suits-and-Cigarettes. He really doesn't seem the type to give the job to just anyone, I'm certain.'

'When you're scrambled, it's an instinct. You don't have time to think, you just do what you have to do,' William told her. 'But this... There's so much that could go wrong and so much time to think about it. And every time I catch my reflection, it's a reminder that I was never half as good as I let myself think I was. I can't risk making a mistake and having the boys pay the price.'

'But you were up against one of the Luftwaffe's best,' Annie pointed out. 'Besides, if you walk away from this job, what sort of danger are you putting the chaps in then? This airbase will have lost its best strategist. The RAF will really struggle to find someone as good as you.'

He gave a hollow laugh. 'Did Mr Wyngate tell you that?'

Annie shook her head. How could she convince him? 'He didn't, but isn't it obvious? Why would he be so keen for you to do this job if he thought for one tiny fraction of a second that you were putting men at risk? He's a very direct fellow. I don't doubt he'd soon tell you if you didn't cut the mustard. And yet quite to the contrary, what is he saying? That he doesn't want you to resign, that's what!'

'I'm so afraid of making a mistake,' William admitted in a whisper, but Annie couldn't help feeling that it wasn't his decision to make. If the men on the base and the bosses in Whitehall or wherever they were didn't trust his judgement, he wouldn't be here in Bramble Heath. Yet he *was* here, and, by his own admission, the friends he had seen had welcomed him back without a moment's hesitation.

She held his hands tighter. 'You've been to hell and back, William. It's no surprise that you feel like this. You said yourself you felt invincible up there in the sky, then one day you found out you weren't. But that didn't happen because of a *mistake*. It happened because you had the presence of mind to lure that ace fighter away from the pack and see to him by yourself. You saved the other men you were up there with and stopped a whole heap of bombs landing on London. *You* did that, William. Because you're a dashed clever man. And it's not just me that thinks that. Wyngate thinks so too, and his bosses. But most importantly of all, the men who get into planes and zoom off down the runway each day from Bramble Heath think you're clever. No – more than that, they *know* you are. And they trust you, William Chambers.'

William clung to her hands and bowed his head. After a few seconds he met her gaze and whispered, 'What if I get it wrong?'

Annie smiled gently at him. The poor man was terrified. His accident had shaken his confidence down to his bones. 'Everyone gets things wrong sometimes, but some people, arrogant types, they're the worst, because they don't take the time to think things through properly. And I don't think you would make a mistake, but if you did, it'd probably just be putting sugar in someone's tea when they'd rather just have milk.'

'Anyone seen the skipper?' she heard a man call from the garden. 'We need our boy Billy's spin if this match is going to last more than five bally minutes.'

'Cricket...' William murmured indulgently. 'In December. I ask you.'

Annie let go of his hands. She chuckled as she got to her feet. 'Keeps you fit, I suppose! Go on, William. Your men need you.'

'Still got my bowling arm.' He smiled as he stood. 'Thank you, Annie. Your friendship means an awful lot to me, you know.'

'Oh, William...' She glanced down at the carpet. She was rather worried she was blushing. 'I'm so very pleased to have you for a friend too. Knock down some stumps for me, won't you?'

'You're welcome to join us,' he teased. 'We never said no to a nurse making up team numbers at the hospital.'

'Are you sure?' Annie grinned at him. He gave a keen nod, the keenest she'd seen from him in a long time.

And with that, she followed him outside to the grounds, where the men were setting up for their game.

THIRTY-ONE

The morning of the Christmas party arrived. Norma and Henry were busy in the kitchen, keeping an eye on Clara as they made jam tarts and cheese whirls. There was a knock at the door, and Annie's heart jumped. Could it be Clara's mother? Surely it had to be. Surely she knew that there was precious little time left.

'I'll get it!' She ran to the door and opened it. But instead of a woman on the step, it was the elderly postman.

'Morning, Annie!' he said brightly. In his gloved hand he held an envelope. 'This one's for you. Marked urgent, so I wanted to be sure you got it straight away.'

'Thank you. And merry Christmas!' Annie said, grateful that he had made the effort to knock. She took the envelope. It wasn't from Mrs Southgate again, was it?

She opened it on the way back to the kitchen. It was a Christmas card with a robin on the front, just like the ones the Farthings sold in the post office. But the contents made her gasp.

Thank you again for taking care of my little girl. Happy Christmas to you all.

Annie had spent so long staring at the first card, wondering if it'd yield up any clues, that she'd come to know the handwriting. Now, as she read this new message, she was stunned by the change. It was the same handwriting, but it was unsteady and blotchy. Clara's mum had evidently struggled to write it.

If only Ewa would tell what she knew, because it looked as though the unknown woman was struggling. It wasn't only Ewa and Natalia who were exhausted, it seemed.

'Mum, Dad?' She held the card out to them. 'Look – it's Clara's mum again.'

Norma peered at the card, her face creased with concern.

'She doesn't look like she's doing very well, does she?' she said gently. 'And Ewa's not said a word?'

Annie shook her head. 'She won't. You know, William asked Ewa's husband, and even *he* doesn't know anything. Oh, it's awful. Poor woman, writing this card and... and...' She looked at her father, who had draped Clara over his shoulder as he was peeling carrots. Clara lifted her head and gurgled at her. 'Clara's mum only has a couple of weeks to come forward. I just don't know what we can do.'

'If she sees Clara and how bonny she's got at the party, it might bring her out of herself,' Norma sighed. She turned to the little girl. 'Won't it, Miss Clara? Wouldn't you like to see your mummy again? I bet you would!' Clara listened as though she understood every word.

Henry put down his vegetable scraper and danced a jig around the kitchen with the baby. 'And wouldn't that be a happy Christmas for everyone? Do you know, I think her mum might've left a clue there, don't you? Why leave that card on the mat for us today of all days? The day of the party!'

'Of course!' Annie said. 'Everyone in the village is coming to the party, and that includes Clara's mum. I can just see it – she'll come over to see Clara and she'll tell us, she'll say, "This is my baby."'

At least she hoped so. She hoped so with all her heart.

There came a tentative knock at the back door, and Norma lifted the latch to welcome their visitor with a cheery, 'Hello, Ewa! This is a nice surprise.'

'Mrs Russell, hello,' Ewa replied. She had lost even more weight, Annie could see, and looked exhausted even as she held out a parcel wrapped in brown paper. 'This is a gift for Clara, from we women in the hamlet. All of us helped, you understand?'

All of us. Annie understood exactly what she meant by that. *Clara's mum helped too.*

Annie put the card down in the middle of the kitchen table, watching to see if Ewa reacted to it, then took the parcel and opened it. Inside was a beautiful little dress made from red and white velvet. It was hand-embroidered with red poppies and trimmed with rows of ribbon. It reminded Annie of the traditional dress that Mrs Zajac had managed to bring with her from Poland. And to think that Clara's mother had sat there hour after hour, decorating this exquisite dress for the little girl she'd left on a doorstep. 'This must've taken ages to make! What a wonderful gift. Clara will *have* to wear it to the party!'

'These are the flowers of my country,' Ewa explained. 'She will be the prettiest girl in Bramble Heath, I think.' She gave a sharp nod as though to end the sentiment. Then she chucked Clara's cheek and gave her one of her rare smiles before she told the little girl, '*Jesteś kochany* You are loved.'

'I didn't know that poppies were Polish,' Annie said. 'But then they're red like your flag, aren't they?' Her eyes immediately flicked over to Clara's rag-doll stork, and the tiny poppy that someone had so lovingly embroidered on its wing. She was even more sure now that Clara's mother was from the Polish community.

'Your corn poppy is our national flower.' Ewa's gaze

followed Annie's just for a moment. 'In the home I knew before this, from my bedroom window all I could see was a field full of them. They made me sneeze.' She heaved a sigh and shook her head. 'One day I will go home and see them again. And I will be glad to sneeze then.'

Annie chuckled. 'That sounds so beautiful. Next year I'll have to show you where there's a beautiful patch of poppies not far from here. I know it won't be quite the same, but...'

'I would like to see that. Clara should see it too.'

'Oh, Ewa,' Norma sighed. 'Can't you just tell us the name of her mum if you know it? I know you gave your word, but...'

'It is not my decision,' Ewa replied. 'I cannot break my word. Not everyone is so kind as you and we have already struggled enough just to find a home. It is not easy to trust, and if the person we trust breaks their word... well, what then?'

'Would you at least consider it?' Henry asked her. 'It'd make for a wonderful Christmas present, don't you think?'

But Annie knew full well that Ewa was as loyal and as stubborn as they came. Christmas or not, she couldn't see her giving up the name of Clara's mother.

'If Clara had a mother and father who could care for her, they would,' Ewa told Henry. 'But the world is unkind to women who have never had a husband and deliver a child. Perhaps if it was different, the decision could be different.' She cocked her head to one side and folded her arms. 'I shall see you at the party.' With that, she left the kitchen, closing the door behind her.

Women who have never had a husband.

Annie swallowed. Ewa knew Clara's mother, and she knew that she was unmarried. One of the Polish girls. But who could it be?

Clara stuck out her bottom lip and her little face creased up as she started to cry. 'Oh, there, there,' Annie said, and took the child from Henry's shoulder, holding her tight. 'Your mummy loves you, Clara. She just doesn't know what to do.'

'I just hope she doesn't come to regret it,' Norma sighed. 'Because Mrs Southgate isn't going to give her a second chance.'

THIRTY-TWO

When Annie walked into the village hall that afternoon, she was amazed at how the place had been transformed. The men on the ward at Bramble Heath had made yards and yards of paper chains, and the Land Girls had plundered the woods for holly, ivy and mistletoe. There were paintings of village sights, along with Spitfires and Hurricanes, and bunting of alternating Union Jacks and Polish flags.

A long table was set up at one side of the hall, and each new arrival brought something to add to it. The members of the band tuned their instruments and went through a short, spirited rehearsal. Clara, in Annie's arms, looked this way and that, fascinated. She'd never seen anything like it.

Guest after guest arrived, and Annie lost count of how many people were there. The village and the hamlet must've been almost entirely empty, and she was pleased to see that pilots and ground crew from the airbase had been spared to enjoy the party. If the siren sounded to warn of a daytime raid, they'd scramble even as the rest of the village dashed for the shelters, but for now at least the men from the base were able to relax. Those from the hospital wing were determined to make themselves useful too, which came as no surprise to Annie. Some of them had arms in plaster, and others had arrived on crutches, but nothing seemed to dampen their spirits.

Annie went over to help Nicola and Betty. Frances and Natalia were taking cups of tea to the band, and Becky was on the door welcoming everyone in. 'This really is fantastic! We – well, *you* pulled it off!'

'When we say we're going to do something, we get it done,' Nicola told her proudly. She looked at Clara for a second, then crossed her eyes and stuck out her tongue, earning a merry chuckle from the little girl, who waved her toy stork at her new friend. 'There's only one girl here who'll be getting attention!'

'That's as it should be!' Betty laughed. 'Look at your pretty dress, Clara. Is this a new gown I see?'

'Ewa dropped it round this morning. Isn't it gorgeous? The women in the hamlet made it,' Annie said. She lowered her voice. 'And without saying as much, Ewa made it clear that Clara's mum helped. She even sent a Christmas card this morning. She's got to be coming to the party. My eyes are going to be out on stalks looking for her.'

'We'll all keep an eye out,' Betty assured her, and the other women nodded their agreement. 'I've told Jakub to keep his ears open at the base too, but I don't think the men know. If the girls in the hamlet are anything like us, they'll stick together and look after their friend, no matter what.'

Annie nodded. 'I know. I just hope – wouldn't it be marvellous? – that Clara's mum is in this room right now, and she's looking over at Clara and thinking, "That's my little girl, I'll take her back." And any second, she'll come over, and... Oh, it'd make my Christmas!'

What else would make her Christmas would be if William came to the party. She scanned the crowd of jostling people as children ran about, darting between them, but there was no sign of him.

Maybe he'll come later, when it's a bit quieter.

But deep down, she knew that the chances of him coming at all were slim.

He would've loved it, Annie knew. Ewa was at the head of a group from the hamlet, introducing everyone. The children from the hamlet saw the other children running around and dashed off to join them. Soon a melee of children were ricocheting around the village hall, English and Polish alike.

'Just think, in a few years Clara will be running around like that!' Annie chuckled. But what if Clara wasn't in Bramble Heath any more by then? What if she had been adopted and was living far away, where she'd forget her friends here in the village and the friend whose cravat was tied around the handle of her pram?

Annie wouldn't allow herself to think about that today, not when they were having such a lovely time. She scanned the crowd, but nothing struck her as odd; certainly nobody stood out as a woman who might have given up her baby on a pitch-black night during the Battle of Britain. At least Jamie and his gang were nowhere to be seen; the last thing anybody wanted was the sort of trouble they always seemed to bring with them.

The band struck up, playing a jaunty dance number. They'd clearly been practising, and couples took to the floor at once, having to watch out for incoming children running with their arms out like aeroplanes. But no one scolded them; everyone laughed instead.

Annie helped serve up the food. The dishes were certainly inventive. There were even banana sandwiches. Annie hadn't seen a banana for a while, but she recalled a recent recipe for a mock banana sandwich, made from, of all things, parsnips.

She beckoned Ewa to come over with her friends from the hamlet. If anyone needed food, it was them, although she wasn't sure what they'd make of the creative use of parsnips.

'Jam tart?' she offered.

'Thank you.' Ewa took one. 'This is a good party. Clara looks very pretty in her dress, don't you think? A girl should have a new dress for her first party.'

'She absolutely should!' Annie agreed. She glanced at Ewa's friends. She could see Kasia and Agata, Mrs Kubal and Mrs Duglosz. But that wasn't everyone, was it? Annie was sure someone was missing. 'Is... is everyone here from the hamlet?'

Ewa narrowed her eyes and glanced over her shoulder before she admitted, 'One of us was not able to come. But I will take some food back for her, if I may?'

Annie sighed. *How hopeless this all is. Surely Ewa means Clara's mum?*

'Yes, of course, please take some food back for her,' she said. She held up a vivid red sponge. 'How about this? It's cake made with beetroot. And a slice of bread and butter pudding. There's carrot scones... and Mum made some cheese whirls.' Annie felt desperate, as if sending Ewa back with armfuls of food for Clara's mum would somehow convince her to give up her anonymity.

'I'm sorry your friend isn't here,' Ewa told her. 'Mateusz said the men had asked and asked, but Wing Commander Chambers would not change his mind. We all wish he had come; when the Polish squadron came here to Bramble Heath, he treated them like old friends. If not for what he did that night when he was injured, my husband would likely not be here today. I would like to have thanked him.'

'I'm sure you'll get the chance to...' *Soon?* No, Annie wasn't sure of that. Her gaze wandered to Frances's depiction of the DFC that hung on the wall. 'One day in the not-too-distant future. It takes time... And I'm sorry *your* friend couldn't come either.'

'It takes time,' Ewa replied, echoing Annie's words. 'I know she would thank you for all that you have done. We have been through more than you can imagine coming here. I know I am not easy, Annie, but...' And she smiled in resignation as she said again, 'It takes time.'

Annie glanced down at Clara. 'If only we had more of it. It's only a matter of a few short weeks before...'

Before Clara disappears.

'I think Wing Commander Chambers will be sorry to have missed the party,' Ewa replied, deftly changing the subject. 'Perhaps you will give him all of our regards when you see him again?'

'Of course I will, Ewa, you can count on it,' Annie replied, smiling despite feeling deflated. But she couldn't be miserable, could she? This was the Christmas party that she and her friends had worked to put together, a gift for the whole village, even if not everyone had come. 'I'll tell him all about it when I next see him.'

She watched couples dancing, smiling as they whirled across the floor. RAF men danced with local girls, and older folk, even Norma and Henry, were dancing too. Betty and Jakub were giving it their all, laughing as they spun in each other's arms.

If only you were here, William.

She missed him.

The queue for the food table had quietened down, so Annie turned to Nicola. 'Would you keep an eye on Clara for me? I'll just be half an hour or so. Only... only there's something I need to do.'

'Clara's an honorary Land Girl,' Nicola grinned. 'I'll make sure she gets plenty of fuss while you're gone.'

Annie kissed the top of Clara's head, then she pulled on her winter coat and headed outside.

THIRTY-THREE

It was cold out, frost already beginning to sparkle on the ground, but Annie barely noticed as she made her way to Heath Place. She had to see William, even if he wouldn't come to the dance. It just wasn't the same without him. As she'd watched the dancers, she knew that she couldn't have taken to the floor with anyone but him.

She had no idea if he felt the same way. He was such a gentleman, though, that if he'd come to the dance he might have given her a turn or two around the floor then politely left her to herself.

But he hadn't come, and he wouldn't come, because he was hiding. Because, like Clara's mother, he was frightened of being judged by the village. Having lived in Bramble Heath all her life, Annie found it difficult to understand that fear. People gossiped, yes, but there was no one in the village who was malicious with it, unlike in some other places she'd heard about. No one was cruel. Aside from Jamie and his little gang.

At the thought of Jamie, she pulled her coat tighter around herself and hurried her step. She didn't want to encounter him as the wintry afternoon light weakened and eventually faded out.

Her thoughts returned to Clara's mother. She pictured Ewa with her group of friends from the hamlet. She'd recognised them all, even if they hadn't been her patients. She had developed a good memory for faces; it came in handy in her job.

But something was nagging at her.

As she reached the end of Heath Place's driveway, a memory appeared before her mind's eye, as if a cinema projectionist had loaded a film that had started to play. The church, Jarek's coffin by the altar rail beside that of the unknown pilot. Ewa's friends had been there too. Annie had been talking about Clara when behind her someone had dropped their hymn book. And Annie had turned.

She saw the face again. Blonde hair under a dark-coloured hat, and large blue eyes peering through a veil.

Zofia. That's her name. And she hasn't come to the dance.

She ran towards the house, her heart racing. Had she worked out who Clara's mother was? William would be proud of her, wouldn't he?

She took the stairs two at a time, and hurried along the corridor, then knocked at his door.

'William?' she called. She could hear music playing inside, and a few seconds passed before footsteps could be heard approaching the door. A lock clicked and William appeared, looking utterly surprised to see her.

'Has something happened?' he asked. 'You're missing the party.'

She was about to reply, but she was taken aback at the sight of William in his civvies: a shirt and trousers and a cravat. She'd never seen him out of uniform before, other than when he was in his pyjamas on Ward III. She blinked at him.

'I've never seen you in anything other than your uniform!'

she chuckled. 'But then you've never seen me in a party dress before either.'

She suddenly felt rather foolish, appearing out of thin air like a phantom to profess her feelings to him. What could she say?

I missed you and I wished you were at the party?

'I... I just wanted to see how you were,' she stuttered. 'So many people wished you well, and it didn't seem right not to pass it on straight away.'

'That's very kind of them, but you didn't have to leave the party,' he said. 'And I still haven't seen you in a party dress yet. You're wearing your winter coat!'

Annie turned as pink as the beetroot cake on the food table. Could he tell how flustered she was?

She started to unfasten the coat. 'You don't mind me taking this thing off, do you, now that I'm indoors? I didn't want you to feel left out, you see, what with most of the village at the party and you on your own up here. That's why I'm here.'

William looked even more surprised now, but not unhappily so. He helped her to remove her coat and slung it over his arm as he said, 'You look terribly pretty, Annie. Too pretty for a stuffy old place like this.'

Terribly pretty?

Annie blushed a shade darker. 'You're ever so kind to say that, William!' she said, smoothing down her skirt. It consisted of the dark red bodice and black skirt of two separate old dresses, which she'd stitched together and decorated with a trim of velvet ribbon.

He turned away to hang the coat on the hatstand, beside his own greatcoat, and Annie got the distinct impression that he was gathering himself. Eventually he turned back to her and said, 'I'm very glad to see you, honestly. Drink?'

'I'd love one, thank you. And do you know, I'm ever so glad

to see you too. Silly old me – I should've brought some of the treats we made for the party!'

'One good thing about being this ugly is that people are desperate to share treats with you.' He strolled over to the bottles on the dresser, where Annie also saw a cake tin. It was decorated with a cheery Christmas scene and finished with a neat red ribbon. 'The ladies in the hamlet sent me enough to last until New Year, so we won't go hungry.'

'They did?' Annie gasped. 'How lovely of them. Aren't people kind?'

I wonder if Zofia made some too.

Then she smiled at William, because she hated to think that he still thought of himself as ugly.

'I have a very good Scotch,' he said, glancing over his shoulder at her. 'What do you say?'

'That would be lovely,' she replied. 'I have to say, it's not something I drink very often, but every time I deliver a baby the father hands me whisky and asks me to share a drink with him to wet the infant's head!'

'Imagine being a father,' William said as he poured the drinks. He gave a low whistle and shook his head. 'I think I would've liked that, you know, not that I gave it much thought until...' He fell silent and turned to hold out one of the glasses to Annie. 'Let's drink to you being a very persuasive nurse. I'm staying at Bramble Heath.'

Chuckling, she took the drink. 'So no resignation for Wing Commander Chambers, then? I'll certainly drink to that!' She held her glass out, and he tapped his against it and took a sip.

'I'm not a coward, but I came very close to being one.'

'You'll never, ever be a coward,' Annie said. 'I should imagine the chaps are glad, aren't they? And that Wyngate fellow too?'

'The lads never knew I was considering leaving,' William admitted. 'And Mr Wyngate isn't the sort to discuss his feelings.

I know the chaps and I know their strengths; that's going to be very useful in the next few days.'

'The next few...' Annie almost dropped her drink. 'I suppose you can't say anything else, but... gosh, a mission for the chaps? I wish you all well. And if you need me to come up here, just in case, to help out... I'm sure I won't be needed, but you never know.'

'I hope we won't need you,' was all he said.

Knowing he couldn't say anything more, she changed the subject swiftly. 'The ladies in the hamlet made Clara a gorgeous party dress, and do you know, on the way over here – it'll sound ridiculous, but I think I might know who Clara's mother is.'

'You do?' William gestured to the armchairs in front of the fireplace. A low fire burned in the grate, its light reminding Annie of the cosy hearth at home. 'How?'

She took a seat. 'Ewa's brought the whole hamlet with her this evening. I asked her if Clara's mother was there – I thought she might come because we had a Christmas card from her this morning, and it seemed like a hint – but Ewa said she wasn't. And on the way here, I suddenly remembered one of her friends – a young woman called Zofia – and realised she wasn't at the party. The last time I saw her was at Jarek's funeral. She sat right behind me, and she dropped her hymn book when I started talking about Clara.'

She wondered if her theory sounded ludicrous now that she was saying it out loud. It was hardly a fireplace moment in a murder mystery novel. William frowned, his expression thoughtful. Then he said, 'Zofia?'

'Yes. Why, have you heard her name before?' Annie sipped her whisky. 'She's very pretty. Blonde hair, blue eyes – like Clara. Of course, there are a lot of women with blonde hair and blue eyes, but... it stacks up, don't you think?'

'I've heard Mateusz mention her,' he said. 'She and Ewa came to England together, and, reading between the lines, I think it was a pretty difficult journey. I actually thought she was Ewa's sister for a while, they're that close.'

Annie leaned forward in her chair. This was incredible. 'Ewa told me that Clara's mother is like a sister to her – her own sister passed away on their journey over here.' She pondered this for a moment before dropping her voice to a whisper. 'William, it does seem as if Zofia is Clara's mum, doesn't it? But what'll we do?'

'I don't believe Mateusz is hiding anything. I think you're going to have to ask Ewa. Or maybe Zofia herself, if you dare.'

She drank some more whisky, hoping to find courage in the glass. 'I'm not sure I could. I'd have to knock on the door of her cottage and... I'll speak to Ewa, that's the first step, isn't it? Maybe if I'm right, she'll crack. What am I saying? I'm not sure *anything* could make Ewa break her promise to her friend. But it's worth a try.'

'I don't think I've ever met anyone quite like you,' William told her with a smile. 'You're a scrapper, Annie Russell; there's nobody I'd rather have a Christmas drink with.'

Annie glanced at him, the firelight dancing across his face. He certainly wasn't ugly; there was such warmth, such curiosity, such kindness in his eyes. She smiled at him, then admitted, 'Would you like to know why I really came to see you?'

He cocked his head to one side and settled his glass on the arm of his chair. She had a sneaking suspicion that he'd already guessed why she was there, even as he asked, 'Why did you?'

She giggled nervously, then, looking into his eyes, she told him, 'Because I missed you.'

'I'm glad you called by,' he admitted. 'I missed you too.'

'Really?' She glanced down at the hearthrug for a moment. 'Gosh! You see, I was watching everyone dancing – Mum and Dad, and Betty and Jakub – and I couldn't stand there another moment and just *watch*. Because the person I wanted to dance with wasn't at the party. In fact, he's right here.'

She looked up at William and met his gaze.

'Miss Russell,' he smiled, 'would you like to dance?'

'Would I?' Annie giggled again. 'I'd love to!' She put her glass down on the table beside her chair, then stood and held her hands out. William took them and rose to his feet, as though this was the sort of thing he did all the time. And why shouldn't it be? There might be a war on, but that didn't mean the dancing had to stop.

Annie stood close to him, looking up at him as she gently placed one hand on his shoulder and took his other hand in her own. She sensed the strength in his body. It hadn't dissipated because of what had happened to his face; in fact that only made him seem all the stronger.

'Do you like to go dancing?' Annie asked him as they started to move to the music on his wireless. 'Did you, before the war came along?'

'I loved to,' he replied. 'And you must have too, because you're very good at it!'

She chuckled. 'I don't know about that! I can't do all that energetic swing stuff when they fling each other about. But then again, I do rather like this sort of dancing. Only I've never really...'

I've never liked a dance partner before half as much as I like you.

'This sort's better anyway,' William murmured, pressing his cheek to her hair for a fleeting moment.

Annie trembled at his closeness. 'William...' she whispered, 'I liked that. Will you do it again?'

Without saying anything, he let his cheek rest against her hair. It didn't matter that they weren't at the party, dancing to the band that had come together from the village. This was all they needed. Just the music, and the soft light from the fireplace, and each other.

Annie moved a little closer to him. It was marvellous how well they fitted together, like a jigsaw puzzle.

'Isn't this lovely?' she whispered, as the song ended and a new one began. 'More cosy than dancing in the village hall.'

'I think it's the best night I've had in... for ever,' he said softly. 'And the best company.'

'William, can I tell you something?' Annie whispered. 'You're the most marvellous fellow I've ever known.'

'I don't believe that,' was his indulgent reply. 'But it's nice to hear it from a wonderful girl like you.'

She was so surprised, so touched by what he'd said that she turned her head to look up at him. Her lips brushed against his cheek, and she saw such tenderness in his gaze that her mouth moved only a fraction more to meet his lips.

It was rather a clumsy kiss, because she'd never kissed a man before. But it was still a kiss.

She didn't feel clumsy when William returned her kiss, though, hesitantly at first, but only for a moment. Then she felt his arm tighten almost imperceptibly around her waist, holding her closer than ever.

The wireless still played, but they weren't dancing any more, lost in their kiss and in each other. A tremor went through Annie, and she held him tight. She didn't want to let him go. Because she loved him.

THIRTY-FOUR

'I've never done that before,' Annie admitted. 'William, I think I...' But she couldn't say it, and instead she ran her fingertips along William's jaw.

There was a mischievous twinkle in his eyes when he asked, 'But would you like to do it again?'

She giggled. 'Oh, William, you naughty chap! Well, now you come to mention it, I'd *love* to do it again.'

She touched her lips to his once more, and she was still smiling as they kissed. She could very happily get used to this, she decided, and to him, and to lots more afternoons spent in just the same way.

When their kiss came to an end, she said, 'Do you think they'll have noticed that I haven't gone back to the party yet?'

'I'm sure they've noticed. I would,' he murmured. Annie felt him draw in a deep breath, then he asked, 'Would you like me to walk you back to the village before it gets dark? Or are you going to see Zofia tonight?'

'I can't even if I wanted to. I don't know where she lives,' Annie replied, swallowing her frustration. They were so close – but it couldn't be helped.

He nodded. 'We *will* find her. And if Ewa won't help, Mateusz will have to do it.' He gave a bashful shrug. 'Pulling rank has its uses sometimes.'

'It's ever so kind of you to walk me back,' Annie said warmly. 'As long as you're sure. I wouldn't want you to worry about bumping into anyone.'

He shook his head. 'They're all at the party, aren't they?'

She nodded. 'They are. Do you know, I'd like to dance some more. Wouldn't you?' She knew she had to ask. 'William, you said you're not a coward, and I know you're not. You're the bravest man I've ever met. Would you... I know that I'm asking far too much of you, but would you consider coming to the party?'

He swallowed hard, studying her face as he considered the question. He was going to say no, she realised, and he had every right to do so. The moment would come when he felt ready, even if it wasn't today.

'With you on my arm?' he asked.

He hasn't said no. Yet.

She smiled at him. 'Yes, of course. I'll be ever so proud to be on your arm.'

'Give me five minutes to get into uniform.' He kissed her cheek. 'If I'm squiring my girl, I'm not going to do it in civvies.'

Annie couldn't help it. As they walked into the village, she kept pausing to look up at William. He looked so handsome in his uniform, his cap at a rakish angle, his greatcoat emphasising his broad shoulders.

'I'm the luckiest girl on earth,' she said.

'I think a few of the lads might be rather envious of me,' William chuckled. 'Nurse Russell on my arm... who would've expected that?'

'I certainly didn't,' Annie admitted. 'Me of all people, stepping out with Wing Commander Chambers! A hero, no less.'

The sound of running footsteps rang through the empty streets and a young man's voice called, 'Head for the village hall! When that lot get home, I want everyone to know we was nowhere near the place!' The footsteps skidded to a halt as Tommy, one of Jamie's gang mates, rounded the corner. He hadn't seen her and William, Annie realised, as he turned to shout back down the street. 'Come on! We're having no part of that, leave him to it!'

'Tommy!' Annie called, suddenly snapped out of her romantic glow. Jamie was up to something, wasn't he? 'What on earth are you doing?'

His eyes widened as the rest of Jamie's gang hurtled around the corner to join him.

'Nothing!' Tommy said urgently. 'We're right here, all of us!'

'Where's Jamie?' William asked. He glanced back in the direction the boys had come, to the narrow road that led to the homes of the Polish families, where Zofia was very likely alone. 'Is he at the hamlet?' When none of the boys spoke, William seized Tommy's arm and snapped, 'Is he at the bloody hamlet?'

Tommy whimpered. 'Please, Wing Commander, don't take on so. We're nothing to do with it!'

'To do with what?' Annie asked. 'Answer Wing Commander Chambers. Is Jamie at the hamlet?'

Tommy glanced at Joe. All the boys looked terrified. 'If we tell you, you have to remember – it's Jamie what's doing it. Not us!'

'Every single one of you is responsible, whatever he's done, because every single one of you could have told him *no*.' William released Tommy's arm and turned to Annie. 'Will you go to the village hall?'

'I'm coming with you to the hamlet,' she replied. Jamie would be there, and she didn't want William to have to face the little bully alone. William gave a nod of understanding and took her hand, leading her along the road at a clip.

As they ran, she heard Tommy shout, 'We're sorry, honestly!'

'What the dickens is Jamie doing?' Annie gasped as they hurried along. 'What a hateful, nasty little boy! And Zofia – oh, poor Zofia!'

As they neared the row of cottages where the Polish families lived, even in the gathering dusk Annie could see exactly what Jamie's friends had been running from. Across the whitewashed wall of Ewa's home was a painted red scrawl reading *Get back where you came from*. The fresh paint was still wet and ran down the wall in streaks as Jamie stood back to admire his handiwork, as though he was a decorator celebrating a job well done.

'How dare you!' Annie shouted, fury running through every fibre of her being. 'James Farthing, this is shameful! Is there no depth you won't sink to?'

At Annie's side, William was silent, and when Jamie turned to face them she saw his gaze flick immediately to her companion. 'They left Neil to die, and they left you to burn, didn't they?' he said. 'You should hate them just as much as I do!'

William was still silent as he approached the boy. Only when he was a few feet away did he finally say, 'The Polish aircrew on the base are braver than you will ever know. We're a family, all of us, and we look out for each other. Nobody leaves anybody behind, but this is a war. Sometimes it isn't fair, Jamie.'

Jamie narrowed his eyes, then shook his head. 'You're not right any more,' he sneered. 'That fire must've got to your brain. You're not fit to wear that uniform.'

William's hand suddenly shot out and seized Jamie's wrist, eliciting a shriek from the boy. Then he turned and began to stalk back along the narrow road, dragging Jamie along behind him as the teenager twisted and struggled in his grip.

'I will snap your bloody arm if I have to!' William barked. 'I'm not afraid of a bully of a child; this has gone far enough!'

Annie followed them. As they rounded a bend in the lane, she took one last look back at the hamlet, thinking of Zofia there on her own. But there was nothing she could do at that moment, she knew.

'I was Neil's friend,' she reminded Jamie. 'He'd've been so upset by this carrying-on! The men in the hamlet were his comrades, and all you've done is disrespect them.'

'Even your friends have given up on you. And now everybody is going to know what you did,' William added, and it was then that Annie realised he was marching towards the village hall. 'Every single person will know that Jamie Farthing is *nothing* like his brother. And then you can go back there and scrub that wall clean with your bare hands!'

'Don't you say that!' Jamie howled, his face growing paler with every step. 'Don't you dare!'

He was terrified, and Annie knew he must've been thinking of his father, the man who had taken any and every opportunity to slap and hit and beat. When Neil was old enough, he had stood up to him, protecting his mother and siblings, taking a beating for his trouble. But that was Neil – and when the war had started, he'd signed up, because he saw himself as a protector.

'I'm not going in there!' Jamie bellowed as the village hall came into view. He sounded like a frightened child now, his voice rising to a squeal. 'Not in front of the whole village! Don't show my mum up!'

'We're not going into the village hall,' William said, as much to Annie's surprise as to Jamie's. He released the boy's wrist, but Jamie stood rooted to the spot despite being free to run. 'You're going to listen to me, all right? What you do afterwards is up to you, but I want five minutes of your time.'

Jamie sniffed and ran his sleeve across his face. The defeated lad was pretending not to cry. 'Go on then, what do you want to say to me?'

'I know what sort of a man your father was. And I know what sort of man your brother was,' William told him. 'You don't have to be the man of the house, Jamie, nobody's expecting that from a lad who lost his big brother. But you can choose what kind of man you become. Right now, you are closer to following your father. That's the path you're on, and it's a path Neil never chose.'

Jamie sniffed again. 'How do you know about my father?' He glanced at Annie. 'You told him, didn't you?'

Annie nodded.

'Everyone in this blinking village knew,' Jamie said. 'And Neil, he was the best big brother anyone ever had. And then he went and died...'

'I know.' William's voice was gentle. 'But the chap we buried in the churchyard... he was someone's son too, as were Jarek and Woolly and all the friends we've lost since this war started. And every single one of their comrades would've done anything to see them safely home. Neil never thought twice about jumping into his Spit, because he was fighting for you and your mum and everyone who deserves a future free from fear. Please, Jamie, don't throw it all away while you're still a boy.'

Jamie didn't reply at once. He looked up at William for a long moment, then spoke quietly. 'I'm sorry for what I said about your face.'

'It's all right, I said a lot worse about it myself,' William replied kindly. 'Will you think about what I said?'

Jamie looked down at his feet, then nodded. 'Yeah,' he replied.

The door of the village hall opened and a little group of

airmen emerged into the gathering shadows. One of them was offering a packet of cigarettes around to his mates, but at the sight of William he paused and came over.

'Chambers! Good to see you decided to come to the party... Ah, something up?'

'Wait here,' William told Jamie. Then he strolled over to the men and drew them into a close group. From the occasional glance they darted towards the lad, Annie guessed that he was telling them what had happened. Eventually he slapped his hand to the shoulder of one of the Polish pilots, then returned to Jamie and Annie.

Jamie squared his shoulders, but he took a step backwards. His father had cast a long shadow.

'It's all right, Jamie,' Annie whispered to him, and the boy relaxed a little.

'I've explained to the chaps that there's a bit of emergency redecorating needed down at the hamlet,' William said. 'It's getting late, but they think they can sort it before the blackout. I told them we don't know who did it and they don't seem to think it matters anyway. They'd like you to help if you could, though, just to get the job done more quickly. And they all knew Neil, so, if you'd like to hear some stories about him, these are the boys to talk to.'

Jamie looked surprised for a moment, then he glanced over at the men, who waved back at him. He raised his hand in acknowledgement. 'Yeah, I'd really like that! Thank you, Wing Commander Chambers.'

'It's William.'

Jamie bit his lip and held out his hand. Without any hesitation, William shook it, then shot the boy a sharp salute.

'Now get to work,' he said with a smile. 'While Miss Russell and I still have time for a dance.'

Jamie ran over to the airmen, and they absorbed him into

their group right away, patting his shoulder and joking with him. The only thing they didn't do was offer him a cigarette.

Annie took William's arm, and they headed towards the entrance of the village hall. 'Are you ready?' she asked him.

'I'll never be ready,' he admitted. 'But it's not going to stop me this time, because that's not how we do things in 25 Squadron, Miss Russell.'

She giggled and kissed his cheek. Then they walked in through the door.

Everyone was having so much fun that they didn't notice the newcomers at first, but then, one by one, people looked up and saw William. At first there were looks of concern, no doubt as they took in the extent of his scars. But then smiles appeared as the villagers of Bramble Heath welcomed him back.

'Afternoon, Wing Commander,' Mr Gosling said, and patted his arm. 'Good to see you again.'

'And you too,' William replied. 'Nurse Russell thought I needed a change of air, and I daren't say no to her!'

'Who's this, Clara? Annie and William, come to see you!' Nicola was bouncing the little girl in her arms as she approached. She looked William up and down, then asked, 'What'd happen if I raised three cheers for you, Wing Commander? Would you disappear more quickly than my bacon ration if I didn't live on a farm with very plump pigs?'

William considered the question, then said, 'Even more quickly than that.'

Nicola's reply was to laugh and land a solid slap on his back. 'I'll make sure folks know. You've only just got here; we don't want you making a run for it just yet!'

'Thanks, Nicola!' Annie said as Clara gurgled her welcome to William. 'Shall we dance, Wing Commander Chambers?'

William took her in his arms and swept her into the midst of the dancers, losing them both in the music and the crowd. Annie knew the strength it had taken to come this far, to face the people who had known him before the accident, and she didn't think it was possible to be more proud of him than she was at that moment. Yet when she reflected on the mercy he had shown Jamie, she knew that she was wrong; the way he had dealt with the troubled boy made her prouder than she could even begin to say.

THIRTY-FIVE

Annie snuggled against William as they walked away from the village hall, their breath floating in icy puffs on the cold air.

'I wonder if we'll have snow for Christmas?' she said. 'If we do, I'll build an RAF snowman. I'll need to borrow a cap and a cravat, of course!'

'I'm sure I can scare one up from somewhere for you,' he replied. 'Do you think I did the right thing? With Jamie, I mean?'

Annie nodded. She tipped her head just enough to look up at him. 'Yes, I really think you did. You showed him kindness when he's not known very much of it. Even after all he's done, and what he said to you, you forgave him.'

William glanced at her as though sizing her up. Then he admitted, 'I was so angry, Annie. I could've knocked him out, and that's not me. That's never been me.'

'You've never struck me as an angry type,' she admitted. 'Where did all that anger come from? Jamie did a dreadful thing, but then... perhaps he lit the fuse on a powder keg you've been carrying about for a while?'

'I think so.' William gave a long, tired sigh. 'We've all been through so much… we've all lost so much. When you're flying, you don't really stop to think what you're doing, what you're risking. Because if you stop to think about it – that being an ace means you're good at shooting people out of the sky before they shoot you – how could you ever do it again? But you have to do it, because Hitler won't stop unless somebody stops him. Men like that don't.'

Annie nodded. 'We've seen so much death, haven't we? And we've gone without, and we've worked until we're ready to drop. And we've carried on working – you chaps in the RAF especially. Day after day during the summer, I saw so many men, pilots and ground crew, just exhausted from it all. But you all carried on. And on top of that… I don't mean to dwell on it, but to be injured as you were, you've had to draw on every scrap of strength you have. I admire you so much, you know.'

'What would you have thought of me if I'd dragged him into the hall and shown him up in front of everyone?' he asked. 'I don't know what stopped me. I don't think it would've helped him to be humiliated on top of everything else.'

'I think I know what stopped you,' Annie said. 'Giving him a dressing-down in front of everyone would've been revenge. You'd have felt better in that moment, venting at him, but deep down, beneath all the anger, your humanity gave you a nudge. And you knew that that fury you felt wasn't only caused by him. His father would've yelled at him and humiliated him, but not you. Because you're a far better man than that. You're not a bully, William. You don't have it in you to be cruel.'

He chanced the lightest peck to her cheek, then said, 'I think I've been angry for quite a while. And frightened.'

She tightened her grip around his hand. 'Remember I said you could never be a coward? You're very brave to admit to that, you know. There are a lot of men who couldn't bring themselves to.'

'I think I should tell you that I've still got a long road ahead of me. I'm not quite there yet.' He looked down at their joined hands. 'And I wouldn't blame you if you wanted to think again.'

Annie shook her head. 'Think again about walking out with you? Oh, never! I know after what you've been through it's going to take time. And it's a long road. But wouldn't you rather have someone walking that road with you?' She looked up at him and smiled.

'Only if it's you,' he said, returning her smile.

'That can easily be arranged!' she giggled. 'We saved each other, and it means... I know it might sound rather silly, but it means we have a special bond.'

'I think we do.'

At Annie's gate, they paused, hand in hand beneath the darkening sky.

'Do you mind if I come and visit tomorrow, if your rounds allow?' William asked.

Annie beamed at him. He'd been so hesitant about visiting, but today seemed to have changed that; it had changed a lot of things.

'I'd love you to! Why not pop round at twelve?' she suggested. 'I'll be home for lunch then. And don't you worry, I'll be trying to find out where Zofia lives while I'm out and about. Would you mind Mum and Dad being there too?'

'No, of course not,' he assured her, shaking his head. As if on cue, Norma appeared at the window with Clara in her arms. She gave the couple a wave, then pulled shut the blackout curtains she and Annie had sewn. 'I'd better say goodnight before your pa comes out to chase me away. I'll see you tomorrow at noon; thank you for a wonderful day.'

'Thank you too!' Annie reached up and gave him a chaste kiss on the cheek, just in case anyone was watching. 'Goodbye, darling. Take care, and I'll see you very soon.'

He cast a very theatrical glance around, as though he was a thief about to snatch a diamond. Then he scooped his cap off, held it up to shield their faces from the street, and stole a quick peck on her lips.

'Nobody would begrudge a casualty of war a kiss from his sweetheart,' he said mischievously as he popped his cap back on his head. 'Have a good evening, and don't get into any trouble!'

Annie laughed. 'I'll try very hard not to! Goodnight!'

She didn't want him to go, but she had tomorrow to look forward to now. And every day after that, if the universe was kind.

William took a few steps away as Annie opened the gate and walked up the garden path towards her front door. As she turned the handle, he swept off his cap again and dropped into a courtly bow, then stood straight and called merrily, 'Goodnight, Nurse Russell! You're the prettiest dancer I've ever met!'

Annie laughed again, and dropped a curtsey. 'And you're the handsomest *I've* ever met! Night-night!'

'Sweet dreams!' William called. 'Now go inside, before Clara starts to think I'm not a gent!'

'She'd never think that.' Annie blew him a kiss. 'Goodnight!'

She finally forced herself to go inside, but after she'd closed the door she pressed her face against the stained-glass panel and tried to make out William's figure in the lane. Even though they had parted, she didn't feel as though they were apart. Something of him lingered with her, and the thought made her smile.

THIRTY-SIX

On Annie's rounds the next morning, everyone wanted to talk about the party, and about William. Annie did her best not to give too much away, but they were all keen to tell her how lovely they looked together on the dance floor, and she found herself blushing. None of them said more about his appearance than *isn't he looking well?* And that made her happy.

Almost. When she arrived in the hamlet, she glanced around, wondering which cottage Zofia lived in. She thought she saw someone peering around a curtain, but she could hardly run over and demand that whoever it was come outside. At Ewa's cottage, Jamie's hate-filled graffiti was now hidden under a wash of paint, as if it had never been there. Thank goodness William had intervened.

Annie knocked on Ewa's door, as she always did, for her help as translator. But today there was something else she needed the other woman to do.

'Yes?' Ewa's tone was curt as she opened the door. 'Can I help?'

'Morning!' Annie said cheerfully. 'I don't have any patients to visit in the hamlet today. It's about something else, actually.'

Ewa narrowed her eyes. 'I am here to translate. Your *something else* I may not be able to help with.'

'I know, and I'm ever so grateful for all you do,' Annie said. She found herself nervous under Ewa's stern gaze, and braced herself to ask her question. 'It's odd,' she observed, as casually as she could, watching for Ewa's reaction, 'I haven't seen your friend Zofia around for a while. Remind me, which cottage does she live in?'

To Annie's relief and surprise, Ewa lifted her hand and jabbed her finger towards a small cottage in the middle of the terraced row opposite. A moment later, though, that relief turned to despair when Ewa said, 'Zofia has been unwell. She distrusts doctors here, so she is being cared for elsewhere.'

'Would she trust a nurse?' Annie asked hopefully. Zofia had trusted her enough to care for her baby, after all. 'I've got my motorbike, I can easily go to visit her. It wouldn't be any trouble.'

For a long moment Ewa was silent. Then she said, 'She would not welcome you.'

'That's a shame,' Annie said. It was more than that; it was potentially catastrophic. She *had* to find Zofia. 'Where has she moved to?'

'I know you want to help. We all want to help.' It wasn't the reply Annie had been hoping for, but it was more than she'd expected. 'I will tell her you are concerned. But I cannot say where she is.'

'I wish you would,' Annie pleaded, although it felt hopeless. 'I dearly wish you would tell me. *Some* doctors behave as if they're god-like, as if their patients are just an inconvenience. But I'm a nurse. I'm not all bad.' She grinned at Ewa, hoping she could get through her armour.

'Somebody painted my house.' Ewa folded her arms. 'I have not asked why. Should I?'

Annie swallowed. 'Some of the pilots wanted to freshen it

up a bit, as a thank you to you and Mateusz. A Christmas surprise!' Even as Annie told her fib, she knew that if Zofia was still somewhere in the hamlet, she might have seen what Jamie had done and told Ewa.

Ewa narrowed her eyes, then gave one of her sharp nods. 'I passed your messages to Clara's mother. All of them. She thanks you, but... she is afraid for her daughter and what will become of her in a country where she has so little. She loves her child, but she is frightened.'

Annie bit her lip. 'Does that mean... does that mean she *wants* Clara to be adopted? If that is the case, I will leave it alone. But Ewa, people will help, I promise you. She doesn't have to give her daughter away. She doesn't have to be frightened.'

'I know you believe I am not helping,' Ewa admitted. 'But I am. I have tried, but I cannot change her mind. I am still trying. I promise it. Knock on her door, then you will know that I am telling the truth.'

'Thank you, Ewa.' Annie knotted her scarf around her neck, ready to head off into the cold. 'You're in a rather difficult spot, I know. I'll see you again tomorrow, and if anything changes... well, you know where I am.'

She turned away. She'd done her best, but Ewa wasn't giving anything away. She glanced over at the cottage that Ewa said had been Zofia's home. What if Zofia was still there? Annie would go and knock, even though she knew she couldn't hold a conversation with Zofia.

She went up the neat path, past winter shrubs, and approached the door. It didn't look as if anyone was at home, but still she knocked. The sound echoed inside the house. She knocked again and waited for a reply. But none came.

Shaking her head, she admitted defeat. For now, at least. Ewa was telling the truth. As she climbed onto her motorbike, she saw Ewa peering around her curtain. She'd been watching her.

Her heart was heavy. They needed a miracle to convince Clara's mother, and those were rather thin on the ground. Or were they? Surely some sort of miracle had taken place in Bramble Heath just yesterday, when William had faced his fears and danced with her in front of everyone at the party. Who was to say that another miracle couldn't happen in the village?

Annie arrived home just before midday to find her parents had initiated an urgent tidy-up in advance of William's arrival.

'I'm sure he won't mind if everything's not completely spick and span,' Annie told them as she bounced Clara on her knee. The little girl was wearing one of her best knitted ensembles and a frilly bib, clearly prepared to meet William too. 'But I'm sure he'll appreciate your efforts.'

'He's a wing commander,' Norma reminded her, plumping the sofa cushions again. 'I can push the boat out for a hero who just happens to be my daughter's sweetheart too!'

Henry chuckled as he adjusted the tinsel on the Christmas tree. It wasn't enormous, but he had still managed to find one and had helped Clara to decorate it. 'Just remember, you've never had a boyfriend for longer than five minutes before, so there was never time for you to bring one home! And a wing commander with a DFC, too. Cor!'

'But you both know William, you've met him tons of times!' Annie laughed. She knew how important this was for them, though; it was important for her too, and most of all for William.

'If he's my future son-in-law, I'm not having him think he's marrying into a slovenly family,' her mother said. 'And he *might* be my future son-in-law! What do you think to that, Henry?'

Henry looked pleased. 'A son-in-law! He's a very nice chap, I reckon. I think you'll make one another very happy.'

Annie was blushing. 'We only started courting yesterday and it sounds like you're ready to plan the wedding! But... well, he is very nice and we do get on very well, so you never know, do you?'

Although Annie knew it wasn't as simple as that. William still had to overcome what had happened to him. But she knew he could do it. She was sure he could.

'Oh, he's here!' Norma fluttered, darting away from the window. 'I'll go and fetch the biscuits. Henry, come and help with the tea things!'

'Oh, heck!' Henry made a run for the door and nearly collided with Norma. 'After you, dear,' he said, waving her through ahead of him.

Annie let them go, then went to the front door with Clara on her hip. She opened it before William had time to knock.

'Mum wasn't looking out of the window for you, honest!' she chuckled. 'Hello, William! Come on in.'

'Hello,' he said brightly. 'And Clara too. It's dashed lovely to see you both again!'

He was looking very dapper in his uniform, and Annie noticed that he was carefully carrying a parcel under his arm. She stood aside so that he could come in, but stopped him on the doorstep with a kiss on his cheek.

'I'm sorry, I just couldn't wait any longer!' she admitted.

'You'll get no complaints from me.' He kissed her cheek in return, and asked, 'How was your morning?'

'I went to the hamlet,' Annie said as she closed the door behind him. 'Ewa doesn't know about Jamie's graffiti, so I told her the pilots painted her cottage as a thank you. I'm sure she'll find out in the end, though. And I tried to find out if I was right about Zofia being Clara's mother. From Ewa's reaction, I'd say she must be. But Ewa also said something that worries me. Zofia hasn't been well, and won't see a doctor – or me, for that matter. I do hope she's all right. I don't know what we should do. We really don't have much time, do we?'

'There comes a point where one has to charge in, I'm afraid,' William sighed. 'I think you and I should go to see Zofia ourselves tomorrow, and if Ewa still says no it's going to be up to Mateusz to translate. I think it's all we can do now. This is her last chance before Clara goes. In a couple of weeks, that's it.'

'But if we just turn up, won't it frighten the poor woman, if she's even there at all?' Annie asked. 'If she doesn't trust me, I'll make it even worse.' And if Mateusz refused to translate, it'd be hopeless, with Zofia's scant English and Annie's complete inability to speak Polish.

'I'll come by tomorrow and we'll write a note and pop it through her door,' he suggested. 'That's a little bit less frightening. It'll tell her you want to help without you just turning up.'

'I don't know if it'll work,' Annie sighed. 'I knocked on Zofia's door but no one answered. The house looked empty, to be honest, and Ewa says she's gone away.'

'Whether it works or not, we're going to try,' William said decisively. 'Ewa cares about her friend, but we don't have to let her run things.'

'I know,' Annie said. 'She must care so much about Zofia. That's what friends do, though. We always look out for each other.'

She led William into the front room. The Christmas tree stood over by the window, wearing the Russells' accumulated collection of mismatched decorations. Greetings cards were hung on string from the picture rail, and sprigs of holly and ivy were poked here and there.

'Merry Christmas,' Annie said. 'Would you like some tea?'

As if on cue, Henry appeared with Norma and the best tea service.

'Hello there, Wing Commander!' Henry said jovially.

'Good afternoon, Constable Russell, Mrs Russell.' William was polite as ever. He put down the wrapped parcel, then took off his coat and hat. Norma gave her husband a nudge to encourage him to take them.

'Norma and Henry,' she prompted. 'It's lovely to see you in the village again. And you've finally experienced a real Bramble Heath party!'

'What did you think? Quite a bash, eh?' Henry said with a wink. He took William's things with as much care as if they were spun from cobwebs and headed out into the hall to hang them up.

'I've never seen that village hall so full!' Annie chuckled.

Norma regarded the scene with a smile, then said, 'Henry and I will be back in a little while. We've got a couple of things to finish around the house.' As she retreated through the door, which Annie noticed she was careful to leave open, she was beaming more brightly than ever.

Annie gestured to the sofa, then to the armchair. 'I've no idea who sits where in this sort of situation,' she admitted in a whisper. 'Are we allowed to sit together on the sofa, or do you have to take the armchair?'

'The door's open and we have a chaperone.' Clara chuckled her agreement to William's observation. 'So I think the sofa will be all right, don't you?'

'I'm so sorry, I'm such a novice at this sort of thing.' Annie dropped down onto the sofa, with Clara on her knee, leaving space for William beside her.

'I was a little bit giddy last night,' he admitted, but he seemed very merry about it all the same. 'And I had a fair bit of friendly teasing from the lads this morning, but I don't mind that at all. I'm glad they don't think they have to treat me like a piece of fine bone china!'

Annie was glad to hear it too. They were treating him as one of the boys again, rather than a special case who deserved pity.

'How wonderful!' she said. 'Now, would you mind holding Clara while I pour the tea?'

William took Clara onto his knee, and they sat together drinking tea and eating Norma's home-made biscuits, chatting the time away. As long as there was tea in the pot and they had the December sunlight, they could pretend the war wasn't raging, and that Clara wasn't facing an uncertain future, and that Zofia wasn't afraid to come forward and claim the baby Annie was sure must be hers. They could pretend everything was normal.

'I ought to give you your present,' Annie told him. 'I put it under the tree. Let me go and fetch it!'

She kissed his cheek as she got up from the sofa, and picked out a paper parcel tied with red wool. 'You can open it now. I don't mind if you can't wait until Christmas Day.'

'I never could wait... used to drive Ma and Pa to distraction.' William took the gift and handed Annie the parcel he had arrived with. 'I will open it, if you really don't mind.'

'I don't mind at all!' Annie chuckled. 'In fact, I encourage it!'

William untied the parcel with just the sort of care she would expect from him, his arms still around Clara even as he peeled back the paper. As the blue lambswool gloves Annie had knitted were revealed, his eyes lit up with pleasure.

'Oh, these are perfect!' he beamed, leaning over to kiss her cheek. 'Thank you, darling. I hope you like your gift even half as much!'

'I knitted them myself, although I must admit that Mum had to help me with some of it!' Annie kissed his cheek in return. 'Shall I open mine now?' She was already loosening the paper, eager to know what William had got for her.

'Clara would be disappointed if you didn't!'

He watched as Annie opened the parcel and gasped in surprise.

'It's the mill cottage!' she exclaimed, holding up an exquisite balsa-wood model. 'Does the wheel turn?' She gave it a go, and laughed like a child as the wheel went round. 'Oh, William, you're so clever. This is gorgeous, I love it!'

'It's one of my favourite spots in the village,' he confided. 'I hoped you'd like it. There's something else in there too...'

'There is?' Annie carefully put the model down on the table and delved into the wrapping paper. At the bottom, she found a little framed painting of a long-legged bird. 'How lovely! Wait, I've seen this before, haven't I, on one of your cards at the hospital?'

William nodded. 'There was a chap in the sty for a couple of weeks... Szymon. He'd suffered rather nasty burns to his legs in a wreck. It turned out he knew this part of the world too. He'd been stationed over at Maybridge, and we even had a few friends in common from Brambles. He'd been shipped up to the Midlands a few weeks before I arrived here, and, on his third flight out, poor fellow was shot out of the sky.' He tapped his fingertip against the framed picture. 'Szymon painted this. It's very good luck in Poland, apparently... a *bocian*. I suppose he thought I could do with a change of fortune, eh? And I thought that perhaps you and I could share it together.'

'He's ever so talented,' Annie observed. '*Bocian*? What does that mean in English? Bird?'

Clara gurgled, and Annie glanced at her, then spotted the stork rag doll in her hand. 'No, it's not just any bird – it's a stork, just like Clara's toy! It'd make sense, wouldn't it? Being sent off into the world with a stork for luck!'

William smiled. 'I think it's safe to say you're right, you know. She's definitely a little Polish girl, on her mother's side at least.' He lifted Clara up into the air above him and she gave a squeal of delight, waving her stork in a plump hand. 'Your mummy wanted you to have all the luck in the world, didn't she?'

'Didn't she just?' Annie ran her fingertip across the glass of the frame. In some places she could see the individual brush strokes, and she pictured the young man painting the stork for his friend.

William settled Clara on his lap again, then took a wallet from his tunic. 'He painted this one too. I keep it with me to remind me what we're fighting for.' He opened the wallet and took out a small piece of paper no bigger than a cigarette card. 'The flower of his country,' he explained. 'Isn't it beautiful?'

Annie leaned in to look at it. 'How lovely! Such a vivid red, and look at the white in the middle, just like the...' She froze, then looked at Clara's stork again. There it was, on the wing, such a tiny detail that she hadn't quite made the connection before. An embroidered poppy. Red, with tiny white petals around its centre. 'Oh, heavens! Clara – show Uncle William your stork. Go on!'

The little girl seemed to recognise her name, and smiled as she shook the stork about.

'Look at the wing, William,' Annie urged him. 'There's a poppy embroidered on it, and it looks just like the one in Szymon's picture—' She gasped as a memory came back to her. 'I saw him,' she said. 'I saw Szymon. He was sitting outside the hospital, with paints and brushes and everything. The other men were playing cards, but he was painting a poppy.'

And Szymon knew Bramble Heath and had left just before William's arrival. Surely it couldn't be...

'Most poppies are just red, aren't they?' Her voice trembled with excitement. 'It's very unusual for one to have white in it like that too, but it makes sense, doesn't it? They're the red and white of the Polish flag. And even though the one on the wing is very small, you can see that petal at the front, on the right, sort of drooping down a bit, just like the one in the picture. And see the little notch in the one at the back? The poppies are the same!'

'But... *Szymon?*' Still William was scrutinising the two poppies. 'He was at Maybridge until the new year, then he was posted to the Midlands.' He lifted his gaze to Annie. 'He didn't seem to like talking about those days very much.'

'The new year...' Annie blushed a little. She wasn't normally embarrassed about the birds and the bees, but it wasn't something she'd discussed with a boyfriend before. 'Clara didn't strike me as premature. If her mother carried her for nine months, she was conceived around Christmas time. Just before Szymon was moved. I'm not surprised he didn't like to talk about it – he was taken away from his girl.'

William looked thoughtful as he said, 'We shouldn't jump to conclusions, Annie. Not yet.'

'Could you write to him?' she asked. 'Although I don't know how you'd ask him. You can't just say, "Dear Szymon, please sit down before reading any further. Did you get rather close to a fellow Pole in Bramble Heath? Only we think we've got your daughter here." Poor chap'd pass out.'

'He's working as an interpreter at the Ministry... another grounded pilot. He's in the charming Mr Wyngate's section, poor devil,' William replied. 'I could send a telegram and ask him to get in touch. I think it's best if I talk to him, perhaps sound him out a little bit.' He took Annie's hand in his. 'Don't get your hopes up, darling, but I'll try.'

Annie squeezed his hand. 'At least there's hope. Zofia sees herself as an unwed mother with no one to support her, but if we've found Clara's dad...' She shook her head. She was getting carried away, she knew. 'He might *not* be her dad, of course. And even if he *is*, maybe he and Zofia aren't together because they can't stand each other. It wouldn't be right to force them to get married. I know that's not a popular view, but it's not fair on anyone, including the children.'

'I'll send a telegram as soon as I can, and hopefully Zofia

will get our note tomorrow,' he assured her. 'And I want you to think of me tonight, and keep this picture close.'

He didn't need to say any more than that. Whatever it was he'd been working towards, the thing that had pushed him to the limits of his self-belief, was upon him.

'I'll put it beside my bed,' she told him. 'And every moment, while I'm awake, I'll think of you and the boys.'

'If the siren goes, don't waste a moment.' He lifted her hand and kissed it. 'Get to the shelter. Promise me?'

There was such tenderness in his voice. Annie nodded. 'Don't worry, we'll all go into the shelter right away. Please, William – don't take any risks. I'm so very fond of you, I don't think I could stand it.'

'I'm stuck on the ground. There's nothing I can do now,' he reminded her. 'I'll be there to count them out and back in. All of them.'

Annie hoped they'd all come back safely, because she knew that he would find it incredibly difficult, if not impossible, to forgive himself if they didn't. 'You've done your best. And once they're in the air, it's up to the boys. I'm sure they'll be home for Christmas. I'm certain of it.'

From the kitchen there came the sound of crockery clattering, and Norma announced theatrically, 'Well, Henry, I think we can go and join the girls and their guest now, don't you?'

'Certainly, Norma!' Henry said, his voice echoing loudly in the hallway.

Annie chuckled, the tension momentarily broken. 'I think they think we were kissing!' she whispered. William chanced a very quick peck on her lips.

'They were right,' he said.

Annie's parents came into the room. They admired William's gifts, and Henry and Norma chatted about the mill cottage's history. It was one of those moments when everything seemed so normal that Annie almost forgot there was a war happening. But she was sitting next to a man in uniform. Of course there was a war.

'You're a dab hand with that baby,' Henry observed. 'There's not many men who take to looking after a little 'un like you have.' He smiled at Norma, and Annie knew very well what he was suggesting.

'My parents adopted two babies after me, so I'm *very* used to it.' William smiled. 'She's such a sunny little thing. My youngest sister had a face like thunder until she started crawling, then she created chaos everywhere she went.'

Henry and Norma chuckled.

'Creating chaos?' Henry laughed. 'You should've seen what this one did!' He nodded towards Annie.

'Oh, Dad, no, not the time I drew on the wall...' Annie cringed.

Henry laughed even harder, and Annie knew he was trying to tell the story but couldn't get the words out past his guffaws. The more he laughed, the more William joined in, which just made Henry even jollier. He still hadn't managed to finish his tale when a knock sounded at the door.

'Excuse me,' Norma said, rising to her feet. 'I'll see who that is.'

Annie took a hasty sip of tea. A knock at the door often meant she was about to be summoned. There were a couple of mums-in-waiting in the village, though neither was quite at their time yet. But, as Annie knew from experience, babies would come whenever they felt like it, whether their parents were prepared or not. The least she could do was to be ready when the knock came.

'If it's one of the mums, I'll be along directly,' she told her mother.

Norma nodded, then bustled from the room. A few seconds passed before she reappeared in the doorway with an unexpected figure looming behind her.

'It's a Mr Wyngate,' she said. 'For the wing commander.'

'Adolf's pulled the rug out from under us,' barked Wyngate. Even as he spoke, William was already passing Clara to Annie. 'Come on, man! We need to get to work. Your Polish counterparts are on their way to lend their expertise, along with the brass. If we don't do this tonight, we might never get another chance.'

Annie's heart thudded in her chest. Her words came out in a rush, as she knew she only had seconds in which to say them. 'Do take care, William. And thank you for the presents. Come round again, won't you?'

'Tomorrow,' he assured her, holding her gaze. She could see the hint of fear in his eyes, but something else too: a new determination. It sounded as though everything he had been working for had shifted again. Surely Wyngate wouldn't appear here with such urgency if everything was going to plan. Whatever news he was bringing, it wasn't what William wanted to hear.

William went to turn away, but then seemed to think better of it; instead he caught Annie's hand, drew her to him and kissed her.

She sensed his trepidation in that kiss, but strength too. 'You can do it, William,' she told him. 'I know you can.'

'Nice baby,' Wyngate barked to Norma and Henry as William finally made his way to the door. 'Congratulations, both.' Then he turned and swept along the hallway, leading William away.

THIRTY-SEVEN

Annie had paperwork to do at home that afternoon, but before she got stuck in she told her parents what she and William had discovered about Szymon and the poppies. Norma and Henry were just as excited about the news as Annie had been, but she did her best to temper their enthusiasm; it could just all be a coincidence. But what an enormous coincidence it would be.

Before the winter daylight failed, she went outside to fetch some coal. When she heard the distant thrum of aeroplane engines, she whispered a silent prayer for the pilots' safe return. Then she went back into the house and helped Norma to draw the blackout curtains.

Clara seemed to have noticed Annie's uneasiness and was fretful, whimpering as Norma fed her a bottle. Not long after it got dark, Annie and her parents ate their dinner. At least Annie tried to. Her stomach was in knots, even though William wasn't flying. He was so worried about the mission, and she dreaded to think what it would do to him if it went wrong.

She couldn't imagine what the men from Bramble Heath were involved in that had required such planning, let alone how it could apparently be derailed that very afternoon, but her heart went out to them. And to William most of all.

Just as she got to her feet to help clear the table, the siren sounded and Clara began to cry. Fear lanced through her, but she conquered it. She had to get everyone to safety.

'Mum, Dad, William said we should go straight to the shelter,' she said. She put on her coat, then picked up her medical bag, slipping Szymon's painting inside. Maybe it would bring them luck. Henry reached for the leather wallet in which he kept all the family paperwork and precious photos, while Norma bundled up Clara. They were ready to go.

The sky was clear and the moon bright, and from overhead Annie could hear the throaty sound of innumerable aircraft. There seemed to be more than ever.

'Look,' Norma said, pointing up to the formation of silhouettes passing across the moon. 'They're our boys. I don't think I've seen so many before. But if the sirens are going, their lot are coming over too. Let's get on.'

'Makes your hair stand on end just to see it,' Henry said. 'Shame I'm not on duty tonight.'

'Well, *we're* glad you're safe at home!' Annie said as they trooped to the shelter at the end of the garden.

She opened the door and they went inside. Unlike in the garden shed, she didn't have the impression of innumerable spiders and earwigs scuttling for cover as they entered. It was like having an extra room to the house, with gingham curtains hung up to make it seem as if there were windows, and a rag rug brightening the floor.

They sat on the cheerfully coloured cushions Norma had made for the bench inside and settled down.

'I do hope neither of the expectant mums gets a fright,' Annie commented. 'Their babies might decide to arrive this evening!'

Norma gave a chuckle and snuggled Clara and her stork

down in the little makeshift crib Henry had put together for the shelter. Clara began to calm in her nest of blankets as Norma cooed gently, letting her know that there was nothing to fear.

'We're going to finish our jigsaw tonight, Clara,' she assured the little girl, but Annie caught the wry edge to her mother's voice. The jigsaw of an English country garden was proving more trying than even some of the air raids. It had been summer when they'd started it, but now the shelter was decorated with paper chains and little reminders that Christmas was on the way. Still, at least the lack of progress meant that the raids weren't as frequent as they might have feared. 'Or by the end of this war at least!' she added.

They all laughed. 'I'll make some tea,' Henry said. He'd set up a spirit stove in the shelter after he realised there was no time to make a flask of tea in the kitchen when the sirens went off.

'He was a curt fellow who came to collect Wing Commander Chambers, wasn't he?' Norma sifted through the jigsaw pieces with one hand while stroking Clara's blonde hair with the other. 'No standing on ceremony for that one!'

'And he thought Clara was *our* little 'un!' Henry reminded her. 'Funny chap. Looked important, too, didn't he? Come down from London, I imagine. You met him before, Annie?'

Annie looked up from her copy of *Nursing Times*. 'If I had, I couldn't tell you! Well, maybe I can. He works with William sometimes. He's rather brusque, but it seems his heart's in the right place.'

'Well, if a gent thinks I look young enough to have a nipper Clara's age, I shan't complain,' Norma chuckled. 'Now... about this young William of yours, Annie. Kissing you in front of your mum and dad as though he's in the pictures! He's a dashing lad, isn't he?'

'Very,' Annie admitted. 'I'm sorry, were you terribly shocked by that? Only, he was so very worried about tonight.'

Henry shrugged. 'It was a bit of a surprise, I admit, but

there's a war on, after all. Besides, I'm chuffed to bits to see you happy with a chap.'

'When you've been a midwife for thirty years, not much can shock you,' her mother assured her, glancing up at the ceiling and the sound of another formation rumbling overhead. 'I've seen it all and I know a happy couple when I see one. You've our blessing, Annie; and the way he is with Clara! He's a natural.'

'I'm looking forward to being a grandad,' Henry chuckled. 'Clara's been giving us lots of practice, after all. And Norma's right, you look quite taken with one another.'

Annie smiled at her parents, glad they both approved. 'I like him a great deal. When I didn't know what'd happened to him after the ambulance took him away, I was in pieces. And then when I knew he'd survived – oh, I was just so relieved. So happy.'

'He's a lucky man to have a girl like you,' was Norma's conclusion as she distributed blankets and Henry poured the tea and they snuggled down against the December cold with their jigsaw and magazines and the constant sound of engines overhead. With this many passing over the village, something big had to be on. Blitz or no Blitz, Annie had never heard anything like it.

There was no chance of dozing off. The planes going over were loud enough, but, even though Annie felt cosy and safe with her family, she couldn't help her thoughts from constantly returning to William. She wondered how the mission was going, and how he was coping.

Please let it all go off all right.

As the hours ticked by, she tried to concentrate on her magazine, then on some of the books they had brought into the shelter over the weeks, even on her mother's jigsaw, but she kept thinking of William and the boys from Bramble Heath. Even as her parents dozed and Clara slept peacefully, her rag-doll stork gripped in her little hand, Annie was wakeful. The thud of a bomb slamming into distant ground shook the night, and Norma started awake. She darted her hand to Clara and, finding the baby still sleeping, pulled her own blanket closer.

'Was that a fair way off?' she asked nervously.

'Sounded like it,' Annie replied, although she wasn't sure. But she didn't want to frighten her mother with the thought that the bomb could've landed nearby. 'Get some sleep, Mum. It's all right. We're safe in here.'

As the words left her mouth, there was a frantic tapping at the door. Even that didn't wake Clara, but Norma looked to Henry and whispered, 'If that's a German, tell him he took a wrong turn.'

Henry yawned as he leaned towards the door. 'Who's that?' he called. 'What's happened?'

'It must be one of the mums,' Annie said, collecting up her things. At least she could go and do *something* useful with herself.

'Ewa!' came the urgent reply, then the door opened and Ewa appeared, her thin frame illuminated by the moon. 'You must come to Zofia. I think she is dying!'

Annie gasped. *No, she can't die. Not now!* She grabbed her medical bag and headed for the door. It had to be serious; Ewa wasn't a melodramatic sort, after all. 'Don't worry, I'll come now. What's happened, Ewa?'

Ewa looked heavenwards and murmured something in Polish. Annie didn't know what it was, but she got the distinct impression that Ewa was asking for forgiveness.

For breaking her promise to her friend?

'We have done everything we can for her,' she told Annie, leading the way across the garden deftly, despite the darkness. 'We tried to care for her. We have learned to look after each other, you understand? We had to.'

'I know you have,' Annie said sympathetically. 'But Ewa,

now you have to be honest with me. You have to answer my question without telling a fib, because otherwise I can't help your friend.' She took a lungful of the cold air, and asked, 'Did Zofia give birth a few months back?'

Ewa glanced back at her, then nodded.

'She did,' she said. 'And she lost blood.'

'So you didn't have that woman's complaint you told me about?' Annie said gently. She didn't want to sound accusing. 'You gave the iron pills to Zofia, because you wanted to help her.'

She let them in at the garage's side door. 'We're taking the bike,' she told Ewa, and switched on her muted torch to guide them towards the motorbike. 'It's faster than walking. Just hold on as tight as you can, all right?'

Ewa nodded.

'You must understand, she is from Bydgoszcz,' she said. 'It will mean little to you, but Zofia has lost everyone dear to her. Mateusz and I used my late sister's papers to bring her with us, and she has been like my sister ever since.'

Annie had been rushing about, opening the garage door, prepping the bike. She paused. 'It was very brave of you to do that. I can't imagine what you've all been through – truly awful, awful things. But you and I, we're going to save Zofia, aren't we?' She wheeled the bike outside. 'You came here through an air raid. You wouldn't have done that if Zofia wasn't dear to you. She's not alone in the world.'

She climbed onto the bike, and gestured for Ewa to follow, the medical bag sandwiched safely between them. Then she revved the engine and headed out into the night.

She didn't switch on her headlamps, but instead let the moonlight illuminate the way. No one was around on the roads, save for an RAF staff car she saw turning off to Heath Place, and soon they were at the hamlet.

'Which cottage?' she asked Ewa as they climbed off the bike, leaving it in the lane.

'With old Mr and Mrs Sobczak,' Ewa admitted. Annie would never have expected that; the residents of the hamlet really had come together to look after the young woman who believed she had nobody. 'We women have tried to share our rations, because I gave my book to Clara. But not Mr and Mrs Sobczak; they are old, they should not give up their food.'

'And nor should you,' Annie told her as they headed towards the Sobczaks' cottage. 'You still look half starved, Ewa. I'll bring some food over tomorrow.' She was sure they could spare something. They had to.

Ewa shrugged. 'We all do what we must.'

At the cottage door, she gave a gentle knock, then went inside. Everyone in the hamlet should be safe in their own shelter or, like Natalia and Mateusz, doing their duty for the war, but they weren't. Instead they were caring for Zofia, who had turned to the only people she believed she could trust: those who had lost the homeland they loved.

'We kept it from the men,' Ewa explained as they slipped through the darkness of the cottage. 'But tonight we could not. Mr Sobczak has taken them all into the shelters, but we must stay and look after our friend.' At the foot of the narrow staircase, she turned and laid her hand on Annie's arm. 'Be kind to her.'

THIRTY-EIGHT

Annie looked at the stairs. Zofia was up there, hovering between life and death, and the thought sent a shiver through her. But she was a nurse; she could bring Zofia back from the brink, couldn't she?

She glanced at Ewa. 'Will you come with me? To translate.'

But it wasn't only the language issue. Annie thought she might need someone at her side who had Zofia and Clara's best interests at heart. And that person was Ewa, who looked on Zofia as a sister.

'Of course,' Ewa replied. Then, to Annie's surprise, she reached out and seized her hand. 'You must help her, Annie, please. Please.'

'I'll do my best. That's all I can do,' Annie told her gently. William appeared in her mind at that moment, and she knew that out at the airbase he would be doing his best too. *I just hope it's enough.* 'Let's go and see her.'

She followed Ewa up the stairs. Two doors faced each other on the small landing. One was ajar, and from inside the room Annie heard the sound of fast, shallow breathing.

'That's her?' she whispered.

Ewa nodded. 'I wanted to bring you sooner,' she whispered. 'But Zofia... she wouldn't.'

'I'm here now,' Annie replied, trying to sound confident.

They went into the room. A bedside lamp illuminated it, casting its glow across Zofia, who was lying on a metal bedstead under an eiderdown. Her chest rose and fell quickly, and her face was as pale as the pillow under her head. She opened her eyes for a moment, then closed them again.

Three women were sitting with her. Agata, who Annie had seen in the grocer's once or twice, was dabbing her forehead with a cloth, while Kasia, who she had met sometimes in Ewa's cottage, was mixing something up in a mug. Mrs Sobczak was sitting at the end of the bed, whispering prayers. They all turned to look at Annie, their expressions unreadable. Were they glad she had come, or had they already given up hope?

'Did you tell Zofia I was coming?' Annie asked Ewa. She put her bag on the edge of the bed and took out her stethoscope.

'Yes. This time I would not take *no*.' Ewa said something to the other women that Annie didn't understand, but her tone was softer than she had ever heard it before.

'I'm going to listen to her lungs,' Annie said, although it was obvious Zofia was struggling to breathe. 'Tell me – did she catch the flu?'

'Yes,' Ewa replied. 'She never recovered from the birth of her child. Even when her health seemed to improve, her mood was so sad. But she was coughing two weeks ago, and has been getting worse.'

Flu, followed by pneumonia?

Annie didn't say anything at first. She didn't want to frighten Ewa, but perhaps the other woman already suspected pneumonia too. Maybe that was why this time she had over-ruled Zofia.

Zofia tried to open her eyes again as Annie came to stand beside her. She lifted her hand feebly. Annie wasn't sure if she was trying to push her away, or if she was trying to say that she was glad she was there.

'Ewa, can you tell her to rest, to save her energy?' she said, as she put the ends of the stethoscope in her ears. She lowered the eiderdown and unfastened the first few buttons of Zofia's hand-made nightdress. Ewa sat on the bed and took Zofia's hand, whispering gently to her. It seemed to work, as Zofia sank back into the bedclothes.

Annie tried to warm the stethoscope up a bit first before placing it on Zofia's skin. She couldn't help but notice how prominent Zofia's ribs were as she listened as best she could to the sounds inside the Polish woman's chest.

She took off the stethoscope and slipped a thermometer into Zofia's mouth. Her temperature was very high. 'I'm not a doctor,' she said, 'so I can't diagnose her, but I can assess her. And I think it's pneumonia. She *can* recover, Ewa. Will you tell her that? Make sure she understands?'

Ewa stroked Zofia's hair back from her sweat-slicked forehead and gently explained what Annie had said. The three other women in the room listened intently too, then Ewa asked, 'What does she need? To make her well?'

'First of all, let's get her sitting up. We need lots of pillows and cushions,' Annie directed. She knew the community in the hamlet had the bare minimum, but they had to find some more from somewhere. 'We need to make sure she keeps drinking water. Little sips are fine, she's not strong enough at the moment to drink more than that, but make sure she has enough. We'll get milk, and some soup – nothing with solids in it, and nothing too thick. That'll help her take in more energy and get stronger. I'll give her some medication now to make her more comfortable.'

Ewa spoke to the women again and they left the room, clearly having been charged with finding what Annie needed.

'We need to give her hope,' Annie told Ewa. 'Because if we give her that, she'll have something to live for.'

By the time Annie was ready to leave, all of Zofia's physical wants had been taken care of. The women had fetched pillows and cushions from their own cottages to prop her up, and Kasia was helping her to sip from a cup of milk. Annie could smell the scent of food cooking rising from downstairs, and it was clear that Zofia's friends – her new family – were doing all they could for her.

Mrs Sobczak settled in a chair beside the heavily shuttered window, her hands knitted in her lap. Annie had tended those same hands every week, manipulating the elderly lady's arthritic fingers, gently massaging her bone-white knuckles to keep the blood flowing. All that time Zofia had been sleeping upstairs, and Annie had never known.

As the other women tended to Zofia, Mrs Sobczak began to sing in a soft, lilting voice. It sounded like a lullaby to Annie, but there was something haunting about it here in the sickroom, with the planes flying overhead in front of that bomber's moon.

Just as Annie was putting her things away, she remembered Szymon's painting in her bag. William had given it to her for good luck. Surely he wouldn't mind her passing some of that luck on to Zofia?

'Zofia...' she whispered. 'William, the wing commander, wanted me to have this painting. Szymon made it for him. They're friends, Zofia.' Annie trusted William's judgement, that Szymon was a good egg. 'He knows where Szymon is. Will you hold on? Will you fight this illness? For all your friends here, and for your baby, and, if you love him, for Szymon?'

She stood the picture on the bedside table, and Zofia slowly turned her head to look at it from under heavy eyelids. She was so ill, though, that Annie couldn't tell how she felt about it, or about Szymon. Had she done the wrong thing?

'I'll come over and see her tomorrow morning,' she told Ewa. 'I'll speak to Dr Parry. There's a treatment for pneumonia now, an injection. He might have a stock of it, and that will help. Now take care, all of you.'

Ewa murmured something to Zofia, who acquiesced to her words with a gentle, exhausted nod. Ewa returned the nod, and told Annie, 'She has given me her permission to confirm that Clara is her child. And Szymon's too.'

'Thank you, Zofia. Thank you for trusting me with the truth,' Annie whispered. 'It must've been a very difficult decision.' Bringing her secret out into the open – a secret that many would think was nothing but shameful.

'Szymon did not know,' Ewa explained. 'He was sent away with the squadron, but he would write and Zofia wrote to him. When she suspected she was with child, I took her to a doctor in town, where nobody would know us. The doctor told us...' She took a deep breath, and Annie saw anger and hurt flare in her eyes. 'He told us that it did not do to come to this country and behave so *loosely*, that this was not what real refugees would do. We are good women, but he spoke to us as though we were not even human.'

Annie gasped in disgust. 'That's dreadful – what an awful thing for you to have to hear. I'm so sorry. No wonder Zofia decided she wouldn't trust doctors. And once she knew she was going to have a baby, she didn't write to Szymon to tell him?'

Or did the doctor make her feel too ashamed to even tell her child's father?

'No.' Ewa shook her head. 'The doctor told her that it was not fair to Szymon to have his child. That men in wartime seek comfort and that it was wrong to make him give up his life and future for a...' she set her mouth into a hard line before whispering, 'a bastard.'

'*What?*' Annie exclaimed. 'You will give me this dreadful man's name, won't you? I'm going to report him. And thanks to this monster in a white coat, Zofia decided she couldn't carry on with Szymon? Because this doctor decided to speak for a man he'd never met? Ewa – you knew Szymon. Do you think he would've turned away from his own child, and from Zofia?'

'But he did,' Ewa said flatly, 'in the end.'

'He did?' Annie glanced at the painting. *I shouldn't have shown it to her.* But surely William wouldn't have become friends with the sort of man who'd abandon his girlfriend and leave her with a baby? 'Why, what happened?'

'Zofia never told him. She wrote a letter and asked Szymon not to contact her again. He did, of course, but Zofia would not change her mind.' Ewa squeezed her friend's hand gently, then gave her a soft smile. 'I had promised her that I would not tell him about the child but, when she could no longer go out for fear of being seen, I broke my promise. I wrote to Szymon, and Zofia was so angry and so upset, I thought she would leave Bramble Heath. That is why I will never break a promise to her again, unless her life depends on it.' She murmured to Zofia in Polish, her voice soothing. Then she told Annie, 'Szymon never replied to my letter. We never heard from him again.'

Just as Annie was about to apologise for bringing the picture, a thought occurred to her.

Maybe, just maybe...

'Did you hear what happened to Szymon once he was up in the Midlands?' she asked. Ewa frowned and shook her head, then darted a glance towards Zofia. Perhaps she thought it was going to be yet more bad news.

'He was shot down,' Annie told them. 'He survived,' she added quickly, 'but he was in the hospital with William for a spell. Do you think, perhaps, that he simply never received your letter?'

Ewa's eyes opened wide and she gasped, 'Hospital?' She looked to Zofia again, her words more urgent when she spoke. 'It was months since Zofia had written to ask him to stay away. I wrote to the base they had moved him to and heard nothing. But it... Is he well?'

Annie decided to spare them the details. 'He's got a desk job now,' she told them. 'William knows where he is – he said he could send a telegram to him. Would you like him to?'

Ewa translated what Annie had said, the words tumbling out as she told Zofia about everything they hadn't known until now. Annie held her breath. Might Clara yet be reunited with her parents after all?

Zofia's eyes grew wider, and a spark appeared in them that illness and misfortune had robbed her of. She did her best to speak through her short, shallow breaths, and once she had finished she closed her eyes again, apparently exhausted from the effort.

'She says he must send it,' Ewa told Annie as the sky above suddenly filled with the sound of a wave of aircraft. Whose, they couldn't guess. 'Szymon must know he has a daughter.'

'That's wonderful!' Annie said, even though the passing planes had unsettled her. 'I'll speak to William tomorrow. I'm so pleased, I can't tell you how much.'

'I hope Mateusz is safe tonight.' Ewa's gaze flicked up to the ceiling, following the sounds until she seemed to gather herself and remember the women in the room. 'I shall tell the ladies to go to the shelter. I will stay with Zofia.'

'Of course,' Annie said. She knew there was no point in insisting Ewa go to the shelter too – she wasn't about to abandon her sister.

Annie fussed about with the bedside table, something she always did just before leaving a patient, as she could never bring herself to go. As she moved the lamp, she accidentally knocked a book onto the floor. When she bent down to pick it up, a bright red pressed flower fell out.

She lifted it carefully, such a fragile thing, the petals as thin as butterfly wings.

As she looked at it in the palm of her hand, she realised it was a poppy. And she knew at once that it was Zofia's.

'Here,' she said, and propped the pressed flower up against the picture.

Zofia smiled. 'Szymon...'

Annie wondered how long she had kept it, a secret symbol of her lost love.

'Will you go to the shelter with the women?' Ewa asked Annie. 'You should not try to go ho—'

Before she could finish, there came an almighty crash, one so great it seemed to shake the walls themselves.

THIRTY-NINE

Ewa's hand flew out to seize Zofia's, and even the usually stoic Mrs Sobczak gave a cry of alarm. Agata and Kasia spoke rapidly to each other in Polish. Annie couldn't imagine what horrors that sound, like the sky falling in, must bring back to them.

'Is everyone all right?' she asked, trying to swallow her fear. 'That sounded close, didn't it? I think... gosh, I think a bomb's fallen on the village.'

She forced herself to picture a bomb crashed into an otherwise empty field on the edge of the village, because the very real possibility that it had fallen on a house was too awful to contemplate.

What if someone's been hurt? Or even killed?

For a moment everything was silent. Then another sound could be heard. It was the blast of a fireball.

What if it's the airfield? What about William?

Ewa began issuing orders to her friends, pointing to the door to reinforce her instructions, but, even if Annie couldn't speak their language, she knew what the women were saying in reply. They wouldn't go. Even with bombs raining down, they wouldn't leave their friend, not when she needed them most of all.

Zofia's gaze was fixed on the picture Szymon had painted: a stork, to bring good luck.

'I'm going to go to the airfield,' Annie told them. 'Your friend needs you here, but I rather think *my* friend could need me.'

To Annie's surprise, Ewa put her arms around her and hugged her for a brief, uncharacteristic second. Then she gave one of her typical nods and said, 'Go safely, Annie. We will not forget what you have done.'

Annie didn't stop to listen to the voice in her head telling her she was foolhardy. She should be in a shelter, but she couldn't hide away, not when lives were at stake. Planes were still passing overhead, and her heart was racing.

It was even colder outside now, and the moonlight glittered silver on the frost-rimed village. The only slash of colour breaking through the monochrome was that of the vivid orange flames flickering ahead.

As she carefully navigated the lanes on her motorbike, every second felt like an hour, and when she reached the village, she realised where the flames were coming from.

Just as she had feared, it was the airbase that had been hit.

When she arrived at Heath Place, she took the route past the house, straight to the base. Figures rushed about in the unearthly silver light, and voices shouted commands. She parked up, then glanced around, trying to work out what exactly was on fire. The offices and the command centre? The tower, or one of the hangars?

Firefighters rushed past unrolling their hoses, and she realised they were running towards a far corner of the airfield.

Nobody seemed to notice her at first. Above the roar of the flames and the shouts of the firefighters, she heard the mournful sound of the all-clear as it began to wail across the airbase and the village beyond. Her parents and Clara would be emerging sleepily into the night to make their way to bed, while Zofia and the women who had tended her could finally breathe again, safe for another night. The only planes overhead now must be those that had defended Britain again, returning home once more.

In the moonlight, the door of the command centre opened and a lone figure emerged. She recognised William at once, despite the distance that lay between them. He paused to look up at the sky, pulling on the gloves Annie had knitted as he watched a squadron of Hurricanes pass overhead. All her fear seemed to evaporate as she watched him, because there was something in his behaviour that told her he had triumphed. What it was, she couldn't say, but this wasn't the doubting, anxious man who had been so sure he could only let his friends down. Whatever mission had been balanced on a knife edge when Wyngate appeared at her parents' door that afternoon, it had been accomplished.

She hadn't realised until William had appeared that she'd been holding her breath. Happiness washed through her as she ran towards him. 'William!' she called.

At the sound of her voice, he turned and ran to meet her. 'What're you doing here? This isn't your shelter!'

She wrapped her arms around him, pressing her face against his shoulder. 'I was so worried – I heard the bomb drop and I had to come and see if anyone needed help. But everything's all right, isn't it?'

'Everything's all right,' he assured her. 'They played right into our hands... All we've lost is a little bit of mud at the end of the airfield.' He drew Annie to him and held her. 'But Adolf's going to have a heck of a repair bill on his desk tomorrow thanks to our boys.'

'Oh, what splendid news!' Annie squeezed him tighter. She wasn't going to demand the details – she knew he couldn't tell her. 'I knew you could do it, and so did Wyngate!'

Planes were landing on the airstrip behind them now, bringing home the boys of Bramble Heath, but Annie barely noticed. Instead, she and William clung to one another as though there was nobody else around at all.

'I couldn't have done this without you.' He kissed her tenderly. 'You believed I could, even when I was ready to run away.'

'I never doubted you for a moment,' Annie told him. 'And I wasn't about to let you dash off and hide. I'm so, so proud of you, darling.'

'How was that?' That was Mateusz, his voice raised in excitement as he leapt down onto the runway. A cheer went up from the ground crew and the airmen who had already landed, their celebrations louder than even the all-clear. 'Where's our wing commander? Where's the man who planned this crazy damned raid?'

Annie giggled as she looked up at William. 'Go on, go and see them!'

She released him from her embrace, but kept a tight hold of his hand. Together they made their way towards the men, who cheered to see their skipper. Even though William had shied away from Nicola's offer of applause at the dance, tonight he accepted the congratulations of his boys, at the same time assuring them that they had taken all the risks while he had done nothing more hazardous than sit in an office. But Annie knew none of them would agree with that; everyone had done their bit tonight.

'We gave 'em what for, eh?' said a young pilot sporting an impressive moustache. 'Couldn't've done it without you, Wing Commander!'

The door of the command centre opened and Wyngate emerged, swathed in his greatcoat, his face shadowed by the fedora he never seemed to remove. He leaned one shoulder against the wall and watched the scene, the red glow of a cigarette illuminating his features; then, to Annie's surprise, he joined in with the applause. In his wake, a group of men filed out of the office building, some dressed in the uniform of the RAF, others in that of the Polish Air Force. From their age and the medal ribbons they boasted, Annie surmised that these must be the top brass Wyngate had referred to, who had raced from London to Bramble Heath just a few hours ago. There were others too, younger men adorned in fewer decorations but who were obviously no less overjoyed at what had occurred tonight. One of them, a tall, handsome man with blond hair, exchanged nods with some of the Bramble Heath boys, who called out delighted greetings to him.

'Darling,' William whispered against Annie's ear, 'The chap over by Wyngate... it's Szymon. He's on the translation team.'

FORTY

Wyngate's car purred through the lanes from the airbase, heading towards the hamlet. To a cottage where a woman lay ill in her bed. An ambulance from Heath Place followed behind, carrying Dr Parry to his patient. Annie glanced at Szymon, his face unearthly pale in the silver moonlight. It seemed like a miracle. Less than an hour ago Zofia had thought Szymon had abandoned her, but now he was on his way to see her.

'Zofia hasn't been very well,' she explained. She looked over at William, who was travelling with them. 'But she *will* get better. And what a tonic it'll be for her to see *you.*'

Szymon nodded, then chewed at his thumbnail as he watched the darkened world glide past. How they came to be in Wyngate's car in the first place Annie wasn't too sure, but perhaps there was more to him than the mirthless barks suggested. Or perhaps he was just happy that the mission had been such a success.

'If I had known...' Szymon murmured, shaking his head. 'I dreaded coming back here today. All I had were sad memories... I didn't know.'

'War's a terrible thing for getting everyone in a muddle,'

Annie said gently. *That's an understatement if ever there was one.* 'She'll be so surprised to see you so soon. She was all for William sending you a telegram, but thankfully the RAF sent *you* here instead!'

The car turned off the lane into the hamlet, and Annie pointed out the cottage to the driver. Everything was so quiet and still, as if the entire world was asleep. But she knew that up in Zofia's bedroom, her friends were awake, taking care of her.

The car came to a halt and she hopped out, full of excitement at the reunion, though it was tempered with sadness. Szymon and Zofia would be happy, she was convinced of it, but there was a whole sea of emotion for them to cross first.

'Everything she did, she did out of love,' William told Szymon, who had made no move to leave the car. 'Please don't think otherwise. Giving up Clara damn near killed her.'

Szymon took a deep, shaky breath, and murmured, 'If I ever meet that doctor...' Then he swallowed and peered out of the car at the darkened cottage before settling his gaze on William again. 'Does she know about my injury? The scars on my leg... What if—'

William patted his hand. 'I don't think she's going to care. Good people don't.'

'She knows you were in the hospital, but she's just relieved to hear that you're behind a desk, and that...' Annie swallowed. *And that you didn't abandon her after all.* 'Would you like me to go in first and let them know you're here?'

He nodded. 'I wouldn't want to shock her.'

Dr Parry climbed out of the ambulance and approached Annie. His grave expression was a reminder of what was at stake if Zofia didn't get the care she needed.

'I'll give you a couple of minutes,' he said. 'But then we need to get her to sickbay.'

Annie went over to the cottage and knocked on the door.

She was sure Ewa would have noticed the vehicles pulling up outside.

'Hello?' she whispered. 'You've got a visitor.' Ewa had opened the door before she had even finished speaking, but her eyes were fixed on the point over Annie's shoulder where Szymon and William were climbing out of the car. Her expression was as unreadable as ever, and for a second Annie wondered if she was about to tell him to get back into the vehicle and leave. Then she called out to him in Polish, beckoning him along the path towards them.

'You have worked a miracle,' she told Annie.

Szymon hurried to join the women at the door. 'We will be a family now,' he whispered, accepting Ewa's uncharacteristic hug of welcome. 'We've waited too long.' Ewa spoke to him in Polish, her voice thick with emotion.

As they headed up the cottage stairs, Annie could feel Szymon's excitement, his joy, but also his apprehension. Behind her, she heard William lower his voice and tell Ewa, 'Your husband pulled off quite a few heroics tonight. He's far too modest to tell you, but I wanted you to know.'

When they reached the landing, she slowly opened the bedroom door to find Zofia still propped up on her pillows, her face drawn, her skin pale.

'Someone's here to see you, Zofia,' she said softly, although she needn't have said a thing. Szymon came into the room and the two divided lovers gazed at each other for a moment before he rushed over to the bed and wrapped Zofia tightly in his arms. They murmured to each other in Polish, but even if Annie couldn't understand their words, it was clear that this was the happiest of reunions. Tears began to run down Zofia's pale cheeks, and Szymon delicately brushed them away with his fingertips, as if Zofia was made of the finest porcelain.

Dr Parry appeared in the doorway, his head bowed respectfully. Annie knew that the clock was ticking. Zofia wasn't past the point of help, but she needed to receive it soon. Ewa moved past the doctor and spoke to Zofia in a gentle voice, nodding as she listened to her friend's response. Szymon answered too, and one word jumped out at Annie from both mother and father.

Clara.

'They would like to see their child,' Ewa explained. 'But I have told Zofia that she should go with you, Doctor.'

Taking his cue, Dr Parry nodded. 'If you could translate, Mrs Glinka,' was his polite response. 'I would like to take the young lady to sickbay and start her treatment first, so the little one doesn't catch a dose of pneumonia too. In a few days, though, Clara can certainly come and see her mum.'

With a tender smile, Ewa relayed the message to Clara's mother and father. For a moment they said nothing, then Zofia nodded. There was still hope.

Annie and William were walking back to the Russells' house, having sent the driver back to Heath Place and his bed for what remained of the evening. The night was crisp and clear, but ever so cold. Stars twinkled high in the canopy of the heavens, with not even a whisper of an aircraft to be heard.

Annie leaned her head against William's shoulder. 'At last Clara's nearly home, so long as Zofia pulls through,' she whispered, and dabbed at her tears.

'She will,' he said gently, wrapping his arm around her waist. 'You know... you looked terribly at home snuggling a baby.'

'Goes with the job, being a midwife,' Annie said. But it wasn't the whole truth, and a sob escaped her. 'I love that little girl,' she admitted. 'I really did like being her mum, you know.'

William kissed her hair and observed, 'I think you'd make a dashed smashing mum.'

'Do you really think so?' Annie said, taken by his words.

'And *I* rather think you'd make a fabulous dad. It's funny, I never thought I'd have the chance of being a mum. I've always been so set on being a nurse and looking after everyone else – helping all those other women become mothers, never thinking that one day maybe I could have a baby myself.'

'You know I'll have to have a few more visits to Mr McIndoe as we go along, don't you?' She did, of course. William might be back at Heath Place but, just as she'd told Georgie on that unhappy afternoon in the tea rooms, he was still a work in progress under the surgeon's pioneering care. 'And even after those, I'll never be Cary Grant. But who is?'

'I'm not sure that even Cary Grant is, to be honest!' she chuckled. 'I'm perfectly happy walking out with a dashing and brave wing commander, thank you very much.'

'Well, I'm utterly delighted to be walking out with the finest district nurse there ever was,' William said gently. 'And certainly the only one I'll ever fall in love with.'

He loves me? Oh, he loves me!

They stopped by the gate that led to Annie's home. She smiled up at him, then tenderly danced her fingertips across his face. 'I love you too.' She rose on her tiptoes and pressed a gentle kiss to his lips. She thought of the parachute that had saved his life, which she had carefully kept for a wedding dress. One day, it might be Annie herself wearing it, as William's bride.

FORTY-ONE

Annie was always concerned about her patients, but Zofia's health took over her thoughts. She was on tenterhooks, hoping against hope that she would pull through. Dr Parry assured her that Zofia was in the best place now, in a room of her own at Heath Place. But Annie's anxiety wouldn't let her go.

What if Zofia didn't pull through? What about Szymon and Clara? She couldn't bear it if all was lost at this last hurdle.

She had set to knitting a little cardigan in soft white wool for Clara. She had found some pretty fake pearl buttons on one of her own old tops and was going to sew them on. It'd be a gift – a farewell gift, because soon, hopefully, Clara would be going to her parents.

There was a knock at the door and, for the first time in a long time, her automatic reaction wasn't to wonder if it was Clara's mum. She went to answer it and found William standing there.

'Darling! Is there news?' she asked him nervously.

He took off his cap before he said, 'The best news there could be. Zofia's out of the woods.' He kissed her cheek. 'She'd like to see Clara, so I volunteered to be her official escort.'

To Annie's surprise, at the end of the path she saw Mr Wyngate's sleek Ministry car.

'Of course,' she said. 'Clara's not long woken up from her nap. I'll fetch her.'

She gently lifted Clara from her crib and hugged the little girl. She made sure that Clara was warm, in her knitted pixie hat and a woollen coat, and wrapped her in the blanket she had arrived in when she had first appeared in the Russells' lives.

Henry and Norma watched silently from the kitchen door. They were beaming with happiness for the baby they had cared for and come to love.

Annie smiled at her parents, then turned to William. 'Here she is!'

William greeted Clara with a kiss. 'Time to meet Ma and Pa, Miss Clara.' As they headed down the path towards the waiting car, he glanced at Annie. 'Szymon hasn't left her side, you know. Clara's got two very loving parents who can't wait to see her.'

Annie wondered how William felt, given his own childhood. But the main thing was that Clara would be with parents who loved her, whether by blood or by choice.

She climbed carefully into the car with Clara in her arms. The little girl looked up at her through sleepy eyes, then she cuddled her rag-doll stork closer and returned to her slumber.

'Can you imagine being handed a little bundle like this and knowing she's yours?' William whispered, tucking in the corner of Clara's blanket. 'Clara and her friends won't let this happen again... they'll be far too sensible to go about starting wars.'

As the driver took them through the village and out towards Heath Place, Annie felt she'd burst with joy. She'd wanted this right from the moment she'd opened the lid of the hatbox and found Clara inside. She'd hoped and hoped that she could reunite the baby with her mother – and for her father to be there too? It was perfect.

When the car arrived, Annie and William took Clara into the house. As they walked through the ward, the patients lit up. They knew exactly who the little lady in Annie's arms was, and waved and cooed to Clara.

The little girl gripped her stork, and Annie felt a pang of sadness. She'd loved having Clara at home, taking it in turns to look after her. She'd miss her, and she knew her parents would too. But she knew too that Clara belonged with her own mum and dad.

'Clara's going to miss the Russells,' William told her tenderly. 'Almost as much as you're going to miss her.'

'Is it obvious?' Annie turned to look up at him. 'I'll miss her so much. But she needs her family.'

Dr Parry met them at the end of the ward, outside the door to a private room. He greeted the trio with a nod and said, 'She's still very tired, but she's out of danger.' Then he chucked Clara's rosy cheek. 'In you go!'

Annie slowly opened the door to find Zofia sitting up in the hospital bed, Szymon perched on the edge. Her face was still pale, but there was some colour to her skin now and her hollow, tired eyes had taken on a renewed vitality. Her hands were entwined with Szymon's, and they were whispering together, but as soon she noticed their visitors she gasped.

'Clara!' She smiled, and reached out for her baby.

Clara recognised her name and turned to look at Zofia. At her mother. Then, stretching out her arm, she offered her rag-doll stork to her.

As soon as Annie put Clara into Zofia's arms, a tear trailed down Zofia's cheek. 'Clara,' she whispered. She gazed up at Szymon and whispered something to him, then she turned to Annie and William. 'Thank you,' she said.

'I can't ever repay you for this. You've blessed us,' Szymon told them. He drew Zofia and Clara to him and held them in his embrace, his happy sobs muffled against Zofia's hair.

Annie bit her lip, trying to hold back her own tears. She'd seen scenes like this before in her career, families created with the birth of a first child, but she had never before felt a part of herself attached to them. Clara, the little girl she had found and named, the little girl she had been entrusted with, was now returned to her family.

'As soon as you're ready to leave the sickbay, Clara can come and live with you,' she told them. 'And I'll bring you all her things. So many things. The village really rallied round to help, you know. Everyone in Bramble Heath loves Clara.'

Szymon turned to her, his face glistening with tears.

'She will need good people to be her godparents.' He smiled. 'And I think you are some of the very best we know.'

FORTY-TWO

Annie rode her motorbike carefully through the snowy village. In just a few weeks, the whole country had gone from golden leaves to being covered under a blanket of snow, and it made Bramble Heath look like a Christmas card. The snowplough had been through to clear away the worst of it, and great heaps were piled up against the hedges. The leafless trees wore jackets of white, and the only animals out in the fields were hardy sheep, warm in their own thick fleeces.

The village had rallied round, keen to support the little family in the hamlet, bringing what they could. And although Szymon had needed to head back to London once Zofia was out of danger, the Air Ministry had spared him so that he could spend Christmas with his new family. And for a quiet wedding in the church. On Christmas Day, Annie and her parents had gone with William to the hamlet; there had been so much to celebrate. Although Clara didn't live with the Russells any more, they would all still be a big part of her life, and that made Annie happier than she could say.

As she rode through the hamlet, she saw a tractor with a plough attached to its front. It had thrown snow up on each side to clear its way, and she noticed Nicola hopping down from the seat.

She pulled to a stop and waved. 'Morning, Nicola!' she called.

'Morning, Annie!' Nicola replied. 'Just dropped Jamie off to see our Polish chums with a box of grub the size of my head! What's happened to that lad, eh?'

Annie chuckled. 'He's like a different boy, isn't he? Thank goodness!' She glanced over at Ewa and Mateusz's cottage. Jamie had not only helped to paint out his graffiti, he'd even repainted their window frames. Mateusz was a hero to him now. And it had taken William, who was brave in so many ways, to make the lad see sense.

'Where're you headed to?' Nicola asked. 'Let me know and I'll make sure the roads're clear.'

'It looks like you've already been busy this morning. I'm going up to Heath Place,' Annie told her. 'Off to do my rounds.' *And maybe see William for a minute or two as well.*

'Then you'll have a smooth journey, because I've already been up that way.' Nicola hauled herself back into the cab of the tractor. 'You go careful!'

'You too,' Annie replied. She set off again, making sure to avoid the children who were having a snowball fight in the lane. They waved at her as she passed.

When she arrived at Heath Place, she noticed Wyngate's car parked up.

I wonder what's going on?

But she knew there were secrets she could never be party to. She left her bike under an awning in case it snowed again, and went into the house.

Almost at once, one of the WAAFs appeared. 'Miss Russell, would you come this way, please?'

'Of course.' Annie tried to read her face. Had something

happened to William? Was that why Wyngate was here? What was going on?

The WAAF led her to the corridor of offices and knocked on a door. Annie had been here before; the same room where she had begged William not to resign.

'Miss Russell is here for you,' the WAAF called. Wyngate pulled open the door and met them with a sharp nod that seemed to dismiss the girl without the need for words. Behind him Annie could see William at the window, his hands knitted behind his back as he greeted her with a smile of welcome.

'He has news,' Wyngate told her, jerking his thumb over his shoulder as she stepped into the room. He turned to address William. 'You'll be hearing from us.'

'William?' Annie asked him. Her sense of trepidation ebbed away. He was smiling; that had to be a good thing. 'What's your news?'

As soon as she asked the question, though, she felt a stab of panic. What if he'd been given another posting somewhere else and was leaving Bramble Heath? She did her best to smile, concealing her unease.

Wyngate closed the door as he departed, leaving them alone. Only then did William cross the room to take Annie's hands in his.

'There're going to be some changes here at Heath Place,' he said. 'But I'll be staying.'

'Oh, phew!' Annie gasped, then giggled as she realised she'd given herself away. 'I was worried, I thought you were going to tell me they were sending you to the Hebrides! I'm so glad you're staying, William.'

He kissed her softly, then said, 'I'm not able to say too much about the new section or my place in it, but... well, it's very much a promotion.' He kissed her again. 'And we're going to be taking on some more Polish ground staff in support of the section.'

'A promotion?' Annie beamed at him, then kissed him back. 'Well, I'm not surprised they're promoting you – I'm not the only person who thinks you're splendid! And some more Polish staff? How fabulous!'

'Including translators with air combat experience.' He let the revelation hang between them before adding, 'I think Mr Wyngate may have a hidden sentimental side after all.'

Annie gasped. 'You mean... Szymon's going to be based here? Oh, William, that's wonderful! You're right, Wyngate's not as gruff as he first appears after all. Zofia will be *so* happy, and Clara, too.'

'I think we've still got a long road ahead of us,' William told her. 'But what we do here at Brambles should help to make that road a little bit shorter. And that's what matters, isn't it?'

'It really is.' Annie rested her cheek against William's chest. She listened to his heartbeat and felt safe. 'Brambles looks so pretty in the snow. It's hard to remember there's a war on sometimes. But one day – one day there'll be peace, won't there?'

'There will,' he promised. 'And we'll see it in together.'

A LETTER FROM ELLIE CURZON

Dear Reader,

We want to say a huge thank you for choosing to read *The Ration Book Baby*. If you enjoyed it, and want to keep up to date with all our latest releases, just sign up at the following link. Your email address will never be shared and you can unsubscribe at any time.

www.bookouture.com/ellie-curzon

You may not know that Ellie Curzon is actually two people – and we both hope that you loved *The Ration Book Baby* as much as we do. We also hope you enjoyed getting to see inside Sir Archibald McIndoe's remarkable medical ward, which gave so many casualties of the war a second chance; today, the surgeries he pioneered continue to transform lives.

We would be very grateful if you could write a review. We'd love to hear what you think, and it makes such a difference helping new readers to discover one of our books for the first time.

We love hearing from our readers – you can get in touch on our Facebook page, through Twitter, Goodreads or our website.

Thanks,

Ellie

KEEP IN TOUCH WITH ELLIE CURZON

www.elliecurzon.co.uk

 facebook.com/elliecurzonauthor

twitter.com/MadameGilflurt

goodreads.com/ellie_curzon

ACKNOWLEDGMENTS

Enormous thanks to everyone at Bookouture, especially our editors Rhianna Louise and Natalie Edwards. We're really, really grateful to you for seeing the potential in *The Ration Book Baby* and giving our novel a home! Your insights and enthusiastic feedback have been absolutely invaluable, and the novel wouldn't be what it is without you.

Finally, a heartfelt thanks to all the readers who have joined us on this first trip to Bramble Heath – we hope you enjoyed it!

Made in United States
North Haven, CT
19 September 2023

41734875R00167